PAUL CHARLES
music agent, author and Beatle fan, was born and raised in Northern Ireland but now lives and works in Camden Town. He is currently at work on the fourth Kennedy mystery, *The Ballad of Sean and Wilko*.

Other Detective Inspector Christy Kennedy mysteries, published by The Do-Not Press:

I Love The Sound of Breaking Glass
Last Boat to Camden Town

Fountain of Sorrow

Paul Charles

BLOODLINES

First Published in Great Britain in 1998 by
The Do-Not Press
PO Box 4215
London SE23 2QD

Copyright © 1998 byPaul Charles
The right of Paul Charles to be identified as the Author of this work
has been asserted by him in accordance with the Copyright, Designs
& Patents Act 1988.

Casebound: ISBN 1 899 344 38 1
Paperback: ISBN 1 899344 39 X

British Library Cataloguing in Publication Data. A catalogue
record for this book is available from the British Library.

h g f e d c b a

Printed and bound in Great Britain by The Guernsey Press Co Ltd.

Special thanks to Jackson Browne for giving me permissionto borrow the title of his magic song (from the *Late For The Sky* album). To Jim Driver for continuing to be fiercely independent and to Andrew and Cora for continuining to be my parents.

Prologue

This path, so often her friend, companion and launch pad into her fantasy world, was now the bed of her fear and pain. A couple of trees' worth of leaves could not make the well-trodden path feel any softer as he pumped on and on into her.

She was restrained, hands together above her head by the youngest (she had guessed he was the youngest by the length of time it had taken him to do his ugly business) and legs spread-eagled by the remaining two. She was surprised by how strong they all were in the pursuit of their adolescent urges.

Surprised mostly by the one with cropped black hair, whom she was sure had a couple of sisters, one her own age. She was not surprised at the smell of stale tobacco and beer from their collective breath as each one tried in turn to kiss her – was that meant to be some kind of affection?

She didn't spit at them, she didn't bite at them, neither did she struggle and try to escape her captors. No, she didn't want to be beaten up, she feared for her life and was desperate, to the point of complying, to protect it. At one point during the fumbling of the second and tallest one – thin with badly dyed blond hair, dirty white T-shirt and navy blue jogging trousers with a white stripe down each leg, a white stripe crumpled into six inches as it lay around his ankles, between her legs – she felt for sure they would have to kill her, for she knew them, well at least three of them, while the fourth, the one now restraining her hands above her head, was giving her ample opportunity to note all the imperfections of his spotty face.

She heard the one whose sisters she knew keep telling his partners in crime not to hit her, not to mark her – just restrain her. She also realised that they hadn't torn any of her clothes. In fact they had, again under the direction of their leader, carefully removed her undergarments and raised her skirt to her waist. Hell, they'd even tried to make her wet before penetration.

All such thoughts and observations faded due to the pain; the sharp burning pain. She'd never felt a pain so sharp, it was worse than any toothache she had experienced during her seventeen years. Her brain yelled out, Oh God, why? Why like this for my first time? Where is my father, where is he now I need him to protect me?' Her mouth remained shut for fear of encouraging a tongue.

As the third finished he rose from her, the smirk draining from his acne riddled face, and she stared deep into his brown eyes. She mustered the little energy she had left and her look of disdain screamed at him louder that any voice: 'You can do this my body, but you'll never, ever, have me. You are dirt and I will wipe you from me the way I wipe dog shit from my feet!'

He stood up, tucked his 'Smile' T-shirt into his Levi jeans and zipped up his flies. He then surprised her by not taking over from the fourth, the chubby one currently guarding her left leg, and allowing him to have his turn with her; instead he just walked away. The others stared after him, no one speaking. By the time he had walked forty yards back down the hill, turned right out of Primrose Hill at St Edmund's Terrace and made a quick left down Ormonde Terrace in the direction of the zoo, his friends realised he was not going to return. One by one they liberated her limbs.

The chubby one was about to say, 'What about me?' when the leader nodded in the direction of the zoo, 'It's over. Let's go,' was all he said, and a few seconds later she was by herself. The only sounds she could hear were the noise of her heavy breathing and the flapping of a wind-filled plastic carrier bag trying vainly, to escape the wiry branches above her.

She refused to cry. She refused to lie there feeling sorry for herself. She put on her pants; for some reason she had been gripping them tightly all the time in her left hand. She rose gingerly to her feet, dusted herself down and headed off awkwardly and painfully to the comfort and protection of her parents home, which was no more that 600 yards away.

But for some reason she changed her mind and ventured instead in the opposite direction, towards the foot of Primrose Hill and beyond.

Chapter One

'Let's get this straight,' began Detective Inspector Christy Kennedy, 'All these… these, *people*,' his eyes arched out over Camden Town's crowded Electric Ballroom, '…are gathered here to buy, sell and swap toys?'

'Aye, grown men, and women, still playing with their bleedin' Dinky Toys!' Detective Sergeant James Irvine replied, as stunned as Kennedy at the buzzing sight before them.

'Corgis, actually. The majority of people here today deal in Corgis and Corgi Classics,' came a terse reply from one of the stallholders, a lean red-faced midlander who had been eavesdropping on their conversation.

'Oh, sorry,' said Kennedy, embarrassed. 'We're new to all this, you'll have to forgive us our ignorance.'

Kennedy gripped his DS by the elbow and moved him deeper into the stall-laden dancefloor. 'It's a whole different world,' he offered in complete amazement, surveying the multicoloured, musty-smelling, noisy scene.

Kennedy was surveying the scene, his fingers furiously twitching, with the thought 'What's all this got to do with the dead body?' filling his head.

On this particular occasion the body was that of a middle-aged man, probably late thirties, early forties, discovered by one of the Camden Council bin men – also known and advertised as 'The Dream Team – Working for you!' but preferring the title, 'Refuge Collectors'. The collector in question, who bore more than a passing resemblance to Rod Stewart, was picking up black plastic waste bags from the corner of Gloucester Gate Bridge up at the Regent's Park end of Parkway, when he noticed the body lying face down on a sharp stony bed about ten foot below street level. The body was less than twenty feet away from Camden's most overtly Hollywood styled house.

The occupants of this once elegant residence were shielded from the horrific sight by several bushes and small trees and about twelve years' worth of undergrowth.

The potential future contestant of *Stars in their Eyes* leapt over the bridge to see if he could be of any assistance. Alas, he was ten hours and forty-three minutes too late to be of any help, or hindrance, to this helpless victim. As our adventurer closed in on the body he noticed an incredible amount of blood around the head. The greenness of the spring grass all around the corpse had been stained a very unattractive brown by more blood, dried with the hours but wearing a moist sheen from the dew.

The police had been called and Christy Kennedy had arrived within two minutes and twenty seconds, with his trusted DS in tow. This was the amount of time it took to walk the very short distance from North Bridge House, across the road around very dangerous traffic lights in the general direction of the bridge, the scene of the crime. A set of lights for one direction appeared to be out of sync with its partners, so while two lanes stopped to respect those crossing, the remaining lane spurted its heavy-weight traffic straight at you and the vehicles attempting to cross Parkway, encouraged by the static two lanes. Yes, very dangerous and the scene of many an RTA (Road Traffic Accident) right there on the doorstep of Camden CID.

DS Irvine immediately took charge of the SOC; due to his expertise in the area he was Kennedy's favourite bagman. He made sure no one disturbed valuable evidence, if indeed valuable evidence was there to be found. Four minutes later Dr Bella Forsythe arrived to examine the body. She explained to Kennedy that she would be handling the situation as Dr Leonard Taylor, her boss and one of Kennedy's good friends and trusted team members, was on a week's leave.

Kennedy remembered the earlier scene, as he continued to survey the toy fair, of the gentle and beautiful Dr Forsythe turning over the body to reveal that most of the throat and lower face of the victim appeared to have been ripped away.

'I think you better be on the lookout for a savage dog, Detective Inspector, I don't think I've ever seen anyone so viciously mauled,' said the stand-in doctor. Kennedy was acquainted with her as she had often assisted Dr Taylor on his cases. He knew she was about forty but she looked thirty. Even on an early morning murder case she was sensationally dressed in a stunning, but practical, light grey trouser suit with a blue blouse. No hints of sexuality, just classic appearance, completed by her long blonde hair pulled tightly over her head and tied back in a pony tail. If she wore any make-up it was only hints, but Kennedy found it hard to believe the picture before him was created without help of cosmetics.

Before putting the human remains in a body bag DS Irvine carefully emptied all the victim's pockets, eight in total, two heart and two side in his well worn blue denim jacket and two side and two rear in his darker blue jeans.

The DS's search produced three pound coins, two fifty-pence pieces, four five-pence pieces and six two-pence pieces. The victim had been well flush with paper money, a fiver, three tenners and sixteen twenty-pound notes. The notes were stuffed haphazardly into the various pockets. Further inspection revealed a mini pack (and very handy they are too) of Kleenex, a couple of rubber bands and (neatly folded) a flyer announcing the toy fair proclaiming that it 'specialises in Corgis'. The fair was advertised for that very same day, the first Saturday in April, in the Electric Ballroom, Camden Town.

The flyer had, written in biro in spidery handwriting, 'Harrison – White Metal – Stall B21 – 8.30,' which explained why two and a half hours later Kennedy and Irvine were standing in the middle of the maddest, noisiest and most colourful buzz Kennedy could imagine.

'Different strokes for different folks, sir,' was Irvine's comment.

Kennedy and his DS searched out stall B21; it was right in the middle of the dancefloor. A dancefloor which had once (allegedly) supported eight thousand feet gently tapping to the hypnotic beat of Jim Reeves. B21 differed from all the surrounding stalls in that it offered not a lot of Corgis to the thronging masses eager for a bargains and rare ones at that. In fact it offered not a single Corgi. The proprietor – one 'Geo. Harrison,

Stockport, England,' displayed a sign in large purple and green felt-tip for all to see: 'White Metal Models Only!'

The owner, whom Kennedy presumed was the Harrison from the flyer, was the gent in the space, all one and a half square feet of it to be exact, behind his centrally-positioned stall with everything at arms' length.

Irvine lifted the dearest-marked model, the Rolls-Royce Silver Cloud priced at £320, knowing this was the quickest way to secure the owner's complete and undivided attention.

'Aye, carefully with that one, lad, you won't find many of that one around. I say you won't find many of that one around. I'll tell thee and that's no lie, in fact I'll give you a score if you can find another one of those on this floor today. They only made six of that model. That one, as I'm sure you can see, is in great nick; aye I say that one's in great nick. Mint, yes mint in the true sense of the world.' The owner of the voice had meant world and not word, and he had a twinkle in his eye matched only by a ruby set into his front tooth which gave a sparkle to his otherwise dull and darkening teeth.

As Irvine carefully returned the rare Rolls to its pride-of-place position on the stall he and Kennedy produced their warrant cards.

'Oh, shit, I didn't realise you were cops, although your dress sense... well, the fact that you even have a sense of dress, sets you apart from the collectors. The anoraks around here tend to...' and here the burly northerner paused and thought carefully, '...tend to wear anoraks!' he concluded proudly.

Kennedy wasn't going to wait for the 'I say they tend to wear anoraks,' repeat refrain. He said 'We're investigating... we found a body this morning and he had this flyer in his pocket.' Kennedy produced the flyer which he unfolded and handed to Harrison. 'We're just trying to identify him.'

The colour drained from Geo. Harrison's face till it resembled the greyness of his hair.

'God, it's my handwriting. I gave it to Flute yesterday. To Flute Burton. I was introduced to him yesterday evening in the Spread Eagle by one of the stall owners. Burton wanted some work and I needed someone to help me out here today, I say I needed someone to help me out here. A big day today, lots of Americans in town for some reason. Anyway, my mate Barney, he's over there by the wall.' Harrison pointed behind the two policemen to a stall near the entrance. The stall was easily visible as it was two or three steps higher from the dancefloor they were now on.

'Barney, yeah, he sells display cases. Barney said Burton had worked for him before a couple of times and he was okay, you know, he picked up things fast, he knew his way around the model world. So I hired him, bought him a drink to cement the deal and then he didn't show at eight-thirty this morning, I was really annoyed, I say I was really annoyed and put him down as a waster. Usually my son comes with me but he's just started courting and, well, it's no competition I suppose, but give him a couple of years, a marriage and a few kids and he'll be screaming to get back out with me on the stall, just to get a break and a bit of peace and quiet at the weekends, I say a bit of peace and quiet at the weekends,' Harrison wagered.

'This Flute Burton, did he have dyed blonde hair?' inquired Kennedy, the quietness of his voice not very effective in the present surroundings.

'Yeah, that's him, blonde hair, black eyebrows. I would have thought he was old enough to know better, but I suppose each to their own, I say each –'

At that moment someone tried to push their way past the two detectives. Irvine moved to restrain him but Kennedy nodded negative (firmly) and waited till Geo. Harrison took another step (sixty quid) to catching up with his namesake's fortune.

'Can you tell us anything else about Mr Burton?' Kennedy inquired on completion of the sale.

'No, not really. You know what? I'm not even sure I would recognise him again, apart from the blonde hair and black eyebrows. Barney might know more about him. Was he murdered?'

'We're not really sure if he was murdered or not.' Irvine said simply and honestly.

'Oh I just thought with the police and all that you know.'

'Let's just say that he died in mysterious circumstances and we have to check them out,' Irvine offered

Kennedy helped himself to one of Harrison's business cards which were displayed liberally around the front of the stall.

'Just in case we need to contact you again,' Kennedy told the stall owner. He was tempted to add 'I say, just in case we need to contact you again,' but restricted himself to 'Thanks a million for your time, you've been very helpful.'

Geo. Harrison smiled goodbye to them as his fished around in the deep pockets of his light blue anorak, and with the ease of a magician pulling a rabbit from a hat he produced a large packet of smoky bacon potato crisps. The sombre news was not about to dull his appetite.

Kennedy and Irvine criss-crossed the twenty yards or so to the cabinet maker with great difficulty. The ballroom was now well packed, so packed that Kennedy imagined it was a major fire risk. The smell of the ageing and musty model boxes and packaging – vital to their value – did little to quell his fears.

Barney rubbed his hands with glee as he spied two well dressed gentlemen, one of them looking every inch the country squire, the other in snazzy black well cut suit with crisp white shirt, plain dark green tie and vibrant green waistcoat. The hand-rubbing was abruptly discontinued the moment the two gentlemen produced their warrant cards.

As they were now closer to the entrance the noise was considerably louder and all three had to shout to make themselves heard, but over the din Kennedy and Irvine managed to pick up address (13 Hilldrop Crescent), full name (Neil 'Flute' Burton, unemployed but available for casual labour), and that Burton was not married but living with a woman and child, the father of whom was apparently unknown.

Kennedy and Irvine decided to stop at North Bridge House to drop off some of their recently discovered details of the deceased on their way to visit the girlfriend. This was a task Kennedy would happily have passed on to others, but he always felt more uncomfortable when he did so. So on this beautiful spring morning, when all of Camden and Primrose Hill was showing the first signs of new life, he would be the one to deliver the news of a life just terminated.

Chapter Two

Kennedy was surprised – shocked, indeed – at how well Flute Burton's girlfriend took the news of the death of her live-in lover. Katherine McGuinness showed them into the lounge of her two-bedroom basement flat at the corner of Hilldrop Crescent and Leighton Road, just off Camden Road.

Kate had very fine (unmanageable) natural blonde hair which fell into an ordinary but not unattractive face. She was dressed in red slacks and a yellow shirt which didn't conceal the lines of her underwear. Kate immediately took stock of the situation, and showing no signs of anxiety she picked her three-year-old ginger haired son from the floor and started rocking him on her lap as she sat back on her well worn sofa, which she shared with DS Irvine.

Kennedy sat at right angles to them on a new basketwork chair, low back no sides. The kind of furniture which probably looked great on some student's sketch pad but in the real world was a right royal pain in the neck, or rather, lower back.

'Can I make you some tea, or get you anything?' the senior police officer began, still awaiting signs of a delayed reaction.

'No. No thank you. No, we're okay, aren't we Ken?' Kate McGuinness replied as she continued to rock her son.

'Look, ah, I was wondering…' Kennedy began, but he thought better of asking a direct question.

'Oh, Neil, you poor sod.'

The DI and the DS eyebrowed each other but held their counsel as she continued, 'Look, Detective Inspector, I should tell you that anything that there had been between us, between Neil and myself, was long since gone. He was down on his luck – he was always down on his luck. He didn't have enough money to get his own pad so I let him stay on here, in the spare room of course. When we split up I moved Ken's small bed into the corner of my room; Neil wasn't well pleased, I can tell you; and he moved into the baby room.'

'Do you mind if DS Irvine has a look around in there?'
Kennedy inquired.

She nodded her approval and Irvine left them to see what he
might see.

'Is there anybody you know who would want to do harm to
Mr Burton?'

'Oh, he was always involved in some kind of trouble or
other, nothing serious mind you, he didn't have the brains for
that. Just bits of Arthur Daleying here and there. But I was
always scared it would lead to something serious and he'd end
up in big trouble. That's why we split up. I wanted him to get a
good job. To give up all the shit. The three of us were getting on
good and I thought we might have a chance to make a go of it,
maybe even a sister, or a brother, for Ken.' Kate stopped and
smiled at Ken, wondering if he could understand any of this.
The clean-faced, well dressed child instinctively knew from his
mother's body talk that something was amiss so he clung close
to her, knowing that as in the past his mother would make the
bad things, whatever they might be, go away.

'To be truthful,' she went on, 'he just reminded me of my
step dad and I did not want to go through all that shit again, you
know?' But Kennedy did not know: his mother and father and
always been his mother and father to him and he had never ever
considered the option that they would be anything other than a
couple, a very happily married couple who had the confidence
to sort out each and every problem together as it came along.
'You know,' said Kate, ' ^Oh, God, where is he tonight? Is he
going to come home tonight? Is he going to get caught by the
police? Is he going to get caught by someone else's husband and
get beaten to a pulp? His he going to get hurt? Is he going to get
murdered?'' it was probably so horrible you know. That's probably why I'm…' Kate played with the hair behind her ear to
help the search for lost words.

'I know I'm not yet grieving, although I know I will eventually. I'm… I hope this doesn't sound callous of me, but I do have
to admit that I'm happy in a way that Neil's out of my life. At
last. It's hard, you know, to try and get on with things when
your ex is still in your house and you've got a three-year-old

son… God bless him, though!'

'Can you tell me about the people he was involved with?' said Kennedy, his voice a warm soft breeze encouraging answers.

'Not really – I'd warned him off bringing them around here.' Her eyes wandered around the room they were sitting in. Kennedy followed her gaze.

She had made their home a comfortable one: modest, humble, but clean, Kennedy thought. The lounge was bright for a basement, benefiting from white-painted walls. There were a few pictures on top of the unused fireplace: various shots (colour) of Kate, Ken, Kate and Ken, but none, absolutely none, of Neil 'Flute' Burton. The floor was covered with a hard-wearing but easy to stain wall-to-wall light blue carpet. The three-piece suite, royal blue with cream piping, formed an 'n' around the fireplace and TV. The Sony TV stood on a thick perspex shelving unit which also housed lots of videotapes and a Sony video recorder. Above the fireplace was a print, a winter snow scene with a badly painted human out shooting (and missing) a startled pheasant.

'But I believe they used to drink at the Nag's Head in Camden Town.'

'You're sure there's no one…' Kennedy began.

'No, look, I'm sorry, I was so desperate for him to keep all those people away. I didn't want any of them near Ken, he's so easy to influence at this age. Three years old is when they stop being babies and start asking all their own questions. Of course they still are babies but I mean they stop hanging on to your coattails, they start to explore, they start to think, they start to ask things, they start to want their own little friends. So not only did I not want any of Neil's mates here, I told him if ever I found any of his gear here he would come home to find it and his clothes lying on the street with the locks changed.'

'Gear? Drugs?'

'No. No of course not,' Kate replied passionately, but then continued, seeds of doubt evident, 'Or at least I hope not. No, just videos, CD players, tellys, that kind of stuff. I didn't want this place to become like the Trotter residence in Peckham and believe me Neil seemed every bit as gullible as Del Boy, a lot taller maybe, but equally as daft, if you know what I mean.'

Her son was growing restless and reaching beyond the confines of his mother's protection when Irvine returned. Kennedy used the interruption as an excuse to rise and bid her farewell.

'Is there someone who could come around to be with you later?' Kennedy knew that once the realisation of death had a chance to eat its way into her mind her bravado would fail and then it would be good for mother and child if there was some-one there to provide comfort.

Katherine McGuinness seemed to accept this too, for she replied after a few pensive moments, 'Yes, Ken's nursery mate's mother. She's also a single parent and she lives a few streets away, I'll get her to come around.'

'Good,' said Kennedy, 'Well, that's all for now, although I imagine that we'll probably have to come back as the case develops.' When the look on Kate's face showed she didn't have a clue what he was on about he added, 'Hopefully you'll be able to help us tie up some of the loose ends.'

'So, anything of interest in Burton's room?' Kennedy said as they started their journey back to North Bridge House. As ever, Irvine drove – and it would be forever, because Kennedy was so in love with being a passenger he had vowed that he would never learn to drive. This was probably not a bad idea, for a) Kennedy tended to daydream while travelling, and b) at the age of forty-four he probably would have made a terrible pupil for some poor unsuspecting instructor.

'Well now, let me see,' Irvine began, 'Lots of well worn unfashionable clothes, no button shirts, all T-shirts and from the look of them I'd say he picked them up from the various jobs he worked on, like crew shirts for the Finsbury Park Fleadh – last year's featuring Christy Moore – he's about six of those, and then some Stage Miracles crew shirts. He had a Marks and Sparks carrier bag with about a thousand concert flyers adver-tising the Blue Nile concert at the Royal Albert Hall in June. That item in particular caught my attention as the singer Paul Buchanan happens to be the best singer since Frank Sinatra.'

'Hmmm, I'm sure, Jimmy, it wouldn't have anything to do with the fact that they are from Scotland,' laughed Kennedy and went on, 'No you're probably right, ann rea turned me on to their record, *A Walk Across the Rooftops*, and he's definitely up there with Otis. Anyway why don't you check with the promoter and see what he would have been doing with the leaflets?' And still smiling, he added, 'Anything else of note?'

'No, not really. No personal stuff, just rubbish. A couple of pairs of worn out shoes, dirty underwear, very dirty underwear, and lots of it. It would seem Kate had stopped doing his washing and he was incapable of it himself. He'd a few cassettes, they looked like bootlegs to me, but I've never seen a collection which displayed its owner's terrible taste so quickly.'

'You don't mean he'd Michael Bolton music do you?'

''Fraid so – and several albums.'

'That's the only reason I'd like to win the lottery, you know: so that I could buy up every copy of his recordings and destroy them all so that humans did not have to listen to it again.'

'Ah now, sir, some people must like him, he sells a lot of records.' Irvine tried to offer a voice of reason.

'Yeah, and so did the Wombles in their day; it doesn't mean they were any good, it just means their record company knew how to sell records to a trusting public,' Kennedy replied, but he decided to get off his pet hate or they'd never get any work done on this case. 'Any telephone books or diaries or anything like that in his room?'

'Nothing at all. It's weird. What was he – early forties? And he's feck all to show for his life. No wonder Kate McGuinness wanted to get on to the next chapter of her life.'

'Ah well, let's check with Stage Miracles, The Fleadh and the Blue Nile promoters to see what we can learn from that side.' By this point they were walking up the steps of North Bridge House, and they parted as they passed the front desk, Irvine chirping 'Aye, aye, sir!'

Chapter Three

'Kennedy! What are you doing?' and before he'd a chance to answer the following Monday morning's question, ann rea spat, 'No, never mind. Listen: tune in to GLR.'

'What?'

'Immediately, Kennedy – God I don't believe it. Listen in to Greater London Radio – now!' ann rea pleaded, her voice a few decibels louder that usual.

Kennedy retuned his radio from BBC Radio 4 to GLR, only to hear a faltering in the usual steady voice of the infrequent but popular presenter Johnny Bell.

'Okay, so here we are with this morning's, no sorry, today's guest, Pauley Valentini, and the good news is that we are about to give you an GLR exclusive by playing Pauley's entire new album, yep, that's right, from beginning to end, twelve tracks back to back and no interruptions!'

'Yeah, so what? I didn't realise you were such a big Valentini fan,' said Kennedy.

'I'm not, dummy. Haven't you heard? Hasn't the news reached North Bridge House for heaven's sake? He's just gone and hijacked a radio station. Pauley Valentini has hijacked the radio station. He's bleedin' hijacked GLR with Johnny Bell and he's insisting they play nothing but his music all day long!'

'Wow!' was all Kennedy could say. After they both listened to the first few bars of the first song, 'Here Comes Sad Eyes', he continued with, 'When did all this happen?'

So ann rea retold the tale of how Pauley Valentini, like so many performers before him (but certainly none after him) strolled into GLR with his guitar case and rucksack. He had been directed to studio 2B, the home of Johnny Bell's morning show. He was left by himself to remove his rare Gibson L100 from the battered case. The guitar, approaching its hundredth birthday, sounded like a dream, producing a warm, rich sound not unlike the acoustic guitars at the top of the Beatles' classic, 'Here Comes the Sun'.

Pauley had 'done' Johnny Bell's highly rated and informative show so many times before that no one, including the presenter who shared a studio with him, bothered him. Johnny, however, did think it a bit weird when Pauley removed a large piece of wood, also from the guitar case, and used it to jam the studio door shut from the inside. He then proceeded to take his rucksack and set it up on the table between himself and the presenter. He opened the top zip so that Johnny, and the producer with his engineer both in the control room on the other side of the glass partition, could see the contents of his rucksack. The contents were batteries, wires, and sticks of dynamite: Pauley's very compact but very lethal-looking bomb.

Pauley had then very calmly announced, 'Okay Johnny, at the end of this record,' (which had in fact been Paul Brady's infectious 'Crazy Dreams') 'We are going to go live on air and I'm going to stay live on air for as long as I want. And I'm going to play what I want, and if anyone tries to stop me, or even tries to trick me by not broadcasting to the public then I'm going to blow the lot of us up!'

'Cool, man – whatever you want, whatever you say,' was Johnny Bell's serene response, 'Let's just be cool and get on with it.'

And get on with it they did. As they played music, exclusively Valentini's music, the bomb squad surrounded the building in Marylebone High Street. Traffic was diverted and people like ann rea, who had mates working in the building, scooped the story.

'Are these the lengths artists are now having to go to to secure airplay these days?' Kennedy inquired playfully.

'You don't know the half of it,' was ann rea's instant reply. 'When you get prats making announcements that artists like the Beatles – the group who single-handedly breathed life and soul into pop music – are no longer going to be played on national radio because they are too old, you can guess how big a chance the Pauley Valentini's of the world are going to have.'

'So why did GLR announce this thing about the Beatles? Is

this his gripe?'

'No, not them. It was Radio Wonderful. But GLR is as far as Pauley Valentini is going to get. But then again, maybe now it'll be different for him now he has all of London listening to him. Pretty soon it will be the whole nation and then Europe and then by later this afternoon when they wake up for eggs over easy, America. Everyone loves a story about a nerd taking on the the big boys,' ann rea replied.

'Is this a subtle way of telling me that we are not going to meet this evening?' Kennedy smiled into the phone.

'It depends, Kennedy. Sadly it is a good story and Mary Jones – Remember her? She used to work at Camden Town Records – well she's now the programme director at GLR and she's giving me the inside info as and when it happens. I'll talk with you later in the day; maybe we'll have a chance to grab a bowl of your favourite pasta at Trattoria Lucca at the end of the day. The song's finished. Listen, I've gotta go, talk to you later Kennedy.'

All he could hear was telephonic static in one ear and the next Valentini song beaming out at him from GLR, via his valve radio, in the other.

Chapter Four

DS Irvine, dressed as ever to the nines – Donegal tweed suit, mustard coloured waistcoat, checked shirt, green tie and well worn but even better polished brown leather shoes – walked into Kennedy's office on the third floor of North Bridge House.

The volume from the radio stopped him in his tracks. 'That sounds great, tidy wee song. Who's that?'

Now Kennedy liked music and the music he liked – the Beatles, Otis Redding, Ray Davies, Jackson Browne, the Blue Nile – he liked with a passion, but outside of that he had little or no knowledge of what was going on.

'It's a track from the new, and soon to be very popular, Pauley Valentini album,' Kennedy announced, very matter-of-fact. Irvine was impressed at how effective the crash course ann rea was obviously giving Kennedy in the UK music scene was.

'Colour me impressed, as much with the music as with your knowledge,' he said as he sat down by Kennedy's desk.

'Oh don't be – I mean, do be at the quality of the music but not at my knowledge of it,' Kennedy replied modestly before setting about filling in Irvine on the recent goings on at GLR.

'Holy shit!' was all Irvine could find to say.

'Aye, it might be blessed, but it still smells a bit, or as my mother would say, ^It'll all end in tears." Anyway,' Kennedy swung around in his chair and lowered the volume of his wood-finish radio, 'We'd better address ourselves to our more immediate problems. I'm sure the bomb squad will help Pauley get the hit he so badly needs.'

'Yes, right. Back to the Flute Burton death. I was just coming in to tell you that we've checked with the Mean Fiddler people – they're the promoters of the Finsbury Park Fleadh – and they tell me that they had about six hundred people working for them on the day and of that number thirty would have been the stage crew. Burton was part of the stage crew, he was what they would call a casual humper.'

Kennedy gave Irvine a 'What?' look.

'A humper, sir, someone who humps heavy equipment around the stage. He would have helped unload the artists' equipment from their trucks and move it onto the stage and then at the end of the evening repeat the process in reverse.'

'How much would he have been paid for that?' Kennedy inquired as he tidied his tidy desk.

'About £80 per day,' was Irvine's quick reply. 'After deductions.'

'And how often would he work?'

'Apparently at the moment as often as he wanted: up to seven days a week,' replied Irvine, and went on, 'The people who staged the Blue Nile concert, Asgard Promotions, their offices coincidentally are just directly opposite us at 125 Parkway, their man Steve Cheney says they get all their crew from Stage Miracles. Stage Miracles also supply the Mean Fiddler for the Fleadh and their other shows. Stage Miracles claimed to know not a lot about Burton. He worked for them a bit but apparently would be ^unavailable" for several weeks at a time. Anyway, when they did use him they would collect the money from the promoter, deduct their percentage, NI contribution and tax and pass the balance on to Burton on a weekly basis.'

'Did they give you any indication as to what kind of chap he was? Who he hung out with? That sort of thing?' Kennedy felt that Irvine's investigation had borne little or no fruit.

'Nope, not a lot, they said they didn't know a lot about Burton or what he did outside their work for him.'

'What about the Blue Nile leaflets? What was he doing with them?' Kennedy ticked off another question on his mental note pad.

'Again, casual labour. The promoters pay teams of people to pass out leaflets for their forthcoming concerts to audiences exiting current concerts,' Irvine replied.

Before any further consideration could be given to the death of Neil 'Flute' Burton, someone now arriving at North Bridge House would throw further light on the death. The desk sergeant, Tim Flynn, an Irishman man whose forty-two years in London had not dulled his rich Ballymena tones, buzzed through to Kennedy to inform him that Bella Forysthe had arrived. In the time it would have taken you to walk once around the girth of her boss Dr Taylor, she was in Kennedy's office seated and sharing a cup of tea with the DI and his DS.

'This is rather quick.' began the DI.

'Yes. Normally it would have taken us a little longer but this is quite a straightforward case. Burton was savagely attacked. His main arteries were all severed. As a result of this he bled to death and expired at around eleven-thirty last Friday evening. Basically, the deceased had his throat ripped open by a very large dog or, by a wild animal.'

'Not the Hound of the Baskervilles I hope,' quipped Kennedy, feeling his joke somewhat inappropriate the minute it left his lips. 'Sorry,' he apologised to the shocked forensics woman, 'Please continue.'

Bella Forysthe may not have looked her age of forty-two, but her manner suggested early middle-age. She was dressed very soberly in a royal blue two-piece tight-fitting suit, waisted three-quarter-length jacket and knee-length skirt, with a white blouse featuring an emerald coloured broach in place of the top button. She wore dark shiny tights and classic patent leather shoes in a blue which matched her suit. Although she still wore a simple wedding band Kennedy could tell that there was no Mr Forsythe, not because of any great powers of deduction but because Irvine, who seemed very interested in the subject, had told him so.

She now carefully smoothed her skirt down its full length to her squared knees before continuing. 'There's not much more to tell really, he'd consumed a lot of alcohol just before he died, but he really didn't stand a chance, it was such a savage attack. Hopefully his intoxicated state dulled his senses somewhat during the attack. I'll leave copies of my notes with you, and if you have any further questions you can contact me at the hospital.'

'You're absolutely sure there is no other way this could have happened?' Irvine inquired as Forysthe packed her papers into a smart black leather attaché case.

'Absolutely sure. There's nothing more sinister than a large stray dog, so be careful. Take no chances: this one has tasted blood,' Forysthe replied as she gave Kennedy a copy of her file and Irvine one of her special smiles.

'Well, thank goodness for open-and-shut cases, Jimmy,' Kennedy remarked as soon as she had left.

'What? Sorry, yes, sir. But do you think we should alert people about this dog? I'm just thinking about all the kiddies in the Regent's Park and Primrose Hill play areas,' Irvine replied, recovering from whatever spell the woman had cast over him.

'Yes, lets put out an alert, but let's not make too big a thing about it, we don't want to be causing a panic. Let's have some constables monitoring the play areas. Also have someone go up to the zoo and see if any of their wolves have escaped; maybe they can shed some light on this for us,' Kennedy ordered.

'Okay,' replied Irvine as he finished off the last of Kennedy's excellent brewed tea.

'I suppose,' conjectured Kennedy, 'Burton could have been coming up Parkway last Friday evening four sheets to the wind, met this dog, this large dog, tried to pat it or something and it attacked him.' But he had convinced neither himself nor his sergeant. 'Maybe we should also find out, possibly from Kate McGuinness, if Burton liked dogs.'

'Yes, that might be an idea, sir, but how would he have got from Parkway to the other side of Gloucester Gate Bridge?' Irvine ventured.

'Oh I don't know, maybe when he saw that the dog was not going to be friendly and started growling at him he ran up towards the park and jumped over the bridge for safety's sake.' Kennedy ventured, his mind elsewhere.

Such mental wandering was normal for Kennedy. He had the ability to ponder two or three areas and be distracted by his distractions to the degree that he sometimes threw up a new, and frequently successful, approach to the case in question. But on this occasion his attention was back to the adventures of Pauley Valentini and the hijacking of GLR Radio.

Johnny Bell was now apparently over the initial shock and

was slipping into his professional show-conscious state: he was now considering the entertainment factor of his 'exclusive' show. While Pauley Valentini, as Kennedy turned up the volume on his radio, was being pensive and honest: very honest.

'You know waiting for success has been very hard on my relationships.'

'Yes? How so?' the presenter inquired.

'You know they always say that artists do their best work when they are breaking up with a lover?'

'I've heard that, yes, but do you think it's true?'

'Most definitely yes, it's just that you seem to be more in touch with your creative side when you are feeling that vulnerable. So every time I got around to starting to write the material for the new album I would split with my girlfriend,' Valentini admitted.

'You're not serious?'

'I'm afraid so. And then the sad thing is, if I had been successful around the time of the fourth album I would have liked to have settled down with Carole, I think she was the one. But by the time I realised this I was working on the tenth album and I realised all the songs were turning out to be about Carole and not the girlfriend I had just split up with, so I contacted Carole again.'

'And did you get back together again?' Johnny Bell prodded, hoping for at least some kind of shiny lining to this very dark cloud.

'Nah, she told me to get lost,' Valentine replied. As ever he was honest to a fault, but then wasn't that the reason some songwriters were successful – because they were prepared to make such seemingly embarrassing admissions, immediately striking a chord of sympathy with their audience? Obviously not a chord Valentini had mastered. He continued, apparently happy to talk about his lack of success.

'Where did I go wrong, Johnny?'

'Well what about that stupid bleeding name for starters? Mind you I'm not sure I should be the one to point a finger. Hell, I'm a much bigger failure: at five foot eleven and one half inches tall I couldn't even make it to six foot!'

Both radio presenter and failed artist laughed heartily. Bell, chancing his arm, continued,

'What's the difference between a folk singer and a successful singer-songwriter?'

'You're asking me? I obviously haven't a clue,' Pauley replied innocently.

'Giorgio Armani!' Johnny Bell chuckled, the crack not even close enough to the singer's head for him to realise it was passing.

Chapter Five

That evening Kennedy and ann rea met as (provisionally) planned at the excellent Trattoria Lucca family-run (for forty-five years) Italian restaurant. Kennedy had his usual green salad (minus asparagus) followed by spaghetti with pesto sauce and peas. The detective's favourite was nowhere to be seen on the menu, but since he was a regular the friendly waiters were always happy to encourage the chef to improvise.

ann rea also had her usual vegetarian lasagne, and as usual she failed to finish her meal. However, tonight's reason had little to do with the generous portion served at the restaurant.

'Kennedy, I've got to go away for awhile,' she announced as the bottle of house white was being poured.

'What, you've got an assignment? I thought you'd be working on the Valentini story a bit longer; even the *Evening Standard* had it all over the front page,' Kennedy replied, casually and upbeat. He'd been home, showered, shaved and changed into cream jeans, blue shirt, green waistcoat and black windbreaker jacket. His black hair was combed back over his head, and as the evening progressed it would dry out and fall back down over his ears (just) about a central parting.

'What? Oh, oh no,' ann rea replied almost absent mindedly, 'No, I think I've done my best on that at this stage. Everyone else is on it now, let them get on with it.'

'You're probably right. I've read the *Standard* and I see that Virgin, Our Price and W. H. Smith's have sold out of Mr Valentini's recordings and are trying hard to get more from the distributors to meet the demand. So it looks like Pauley Valentini is going to enjoy the success he craved so much.'

'I wonder if he'll be any happier because of it,' ann rea said as she aimlessly picked around her lasagne with her fork.

'He's going to have to wait until New Scotland Yard are finished with him before he has time to enjoy anything.'

Kennedy paused as he carefully negotiated a forkful of spaghetti, but before fuelling the fire of his hunger he inquired, 'So where is it you're going to, ann rea?'

'Remember I told you about the Elliots?'

'Yes, your landlords when you first moved to London.'

'Mmmm, they were very, very good to me. Treated me more like a daughter, maybe the daughter they never had. Anyway, they retired to their cottage, in Climping, about four years ago. About six months back Lila, who was sixty-seven, caught a kidney infection. She never recovered and passed away two months ago. Daniel wrote and told me.'

'How old would he be now?' Kennedy knew he should have known the answer but he was terrible at remembering people's ages – including his own – his excuse was that this fact changes once a year, although he had noticed that as people grow older their years, when referring to their ages, seem to last at least twenty-four months.

'Seventy-one at his last birthday. Anyway, I've rang him a few times, and he always sounds so down, Christy. I rang him today in fact, just after I had spoken with you, and a neighbour answered the phone. Apparently he's given up. He doesn't even get out of bed any more.' ann rea took another sip of wine.

Kennedy had felt her unease ever since they sat down. He was worried her concern might be about them. Even in her preoccupied state she still looked stunning. She required not a single swipe of make-up to turn the heads she frequently turned. Kennedy sometimes even caught himself stealing glances at his unaware girlfriend. ann rea had wonderful long eyelashes and sharp, full eyebrows. Looking at her eyes Kennedy was convinced that ann rea had some oriental ancestry. His inquiries in that direction had revealed that she was not aware of any, or at least any she would admit to. Her brown hair was cut in a Beatle style (mid-sixties, around the time of Rubber Soul). He loved the way each and every hair fell back into perfect position when she shook her head a few times in a certain way. Indeed such movement reminded him more than a little of the original mop-tops. ann rea unknowingly performed this – one of Kennedy's favourite – gesture as she replaced her wineglass on the table. Other nights he would draw her attention to it and they both would have a laugh, but tonight her Beatle impersonation pleased only one of the couple.

'Is he ill?' were the only words Kennedy could find to say as he regained his breath.

'Nope. The doctor has been around and apparently physically he's fine; he's just lost his desire to live. That's why I want to go and see him. I just have to be with him, Christy.'

Kennedy nodded in agreement and added, 'How long will you be gone, ann rea?'

ann rea liked the way Kennedy would never address her as 'Sweetheart' or 'Baby' or 'Babe' or 'Sugar' or 'Darling' or anything else equally embarrassing. When he wished to talk to her, no matter how intimate the moment, he used her name; wasn't that the purpose of names, for heaven's sake?

'I don't know. I really don't know,' she replied.

'Maybe I could come down at the weekend and be with you?'

ann rea took Kennedy's hand in hers across the table. 'That's kind, Kennedy, but I think I have to do this on my own.' She noticed a flicker of hurt in his clear green eyes and added, 'Don't worry, Christy, this is not about us. I just feel I have to be there for him and it would be...' she searched hard for the correct word, '...inappropriate for me to bring someone with me to help me. Does that make sense to you?'

'Yes,' was Kennedy's simple and honest reply.

They finished their meal and wine in near silence and walked to Kennedy's house where ann rea had parked her car. They said goodnight with a lingering sad kiss on the doorstep. He hugged her five-foot-seven frame, his three-inch advantage allowing him to smell the only artificial scent about her body: the coconut hint from her shampoo.

Kennedy waved ann rea goodbye as she drove off in her maroon Ford Popular saloon, and he returned to his house as dejected as a goalkeeper fetching the ball from the back of the net.

Chapter Six

ann rea felt this overwhelming desire to leave. To go. To get away. She kept hearing the Roches' song, 'I've Got to Get Away From You', in her mind's ear. ann rea wasn't quite sure whom the 'you' of the song was in her case.

Playing the detective, she compiled a list of the likely suspects she wished to get away from as she packed her bag. When she thought about it wasn't even a proper bag she was packing, in the romantic view of packing one's bags to leave someone. It was merely an carpet bag, an overnight bag, a holdall; such was her urgency to get away. 'Hell,' she thought, 'As long as I've got enough clean undies and a few changes of clothes (slacks, blouses) I can buy whatever else I may need when I get there.'

The suspects? Well, there were but three. Three, that is, that she could think of. One, Kennedy. Two, London, and three, herself. She addressed herself to her short list. She knew Kennedy would be happy to have a list so short. She also knew that with his love for the art of detection and his fine team he probably would have her case solved in an afternoon. She wondered, though, would he be happy with the solution?

ann rea couldn't think of anything Kennedy was doing wrong, apart from loving her perhaps.

Why was his love so dammed unconditional and so unreserved? Why was he so fecking sure of his love? He kept saying to her that he had been waiting his entire life to meet the right person and he knew in his soul that it was her.

Where was his soul? Could he open it up for her? Yes – could he open it up for her and show her a sign, there amongst all the blood and blob, which confirmed his belief? ann rea felt bad, very bad, for having such thoughts. Yeah, maybe, just maybe, she did love him. She certainly felt closer to Christy Kennedy than she ever had to anyone else in her life.

Yes even Him, the last Him. Maybe out of respect to

Kennedy that should be the Other Him. But wasn't that further proof that she was right to be doubting her feelings? She'd been convinced the last Him, now know as the Other Him, albeit a long time ago was *the* Him, and that had continued to be the case until he proved himself to be the absolute shit her friends had always been predicting.

But enough had been enough, and when he eventually told her he'd fallen in love with someone else (his child's nanny) she just walked out on him, left all her stuff. It had been eight forty-five on a Wednesday night. ann rea could still see the scene vividly in her mind's eye. But why had he protested so passionately about her leaving when he had just confessed to her that he was in love with someone else?

The line of the Roches' song had progressed to, 'I've got to get away from you, I'll come and visit you in the zoo.' Was the zoo her distorted memories? Soon she headed off in the mini-cab, a blue Ford Siesta, to Victoria Station to catch the seven forty-seven train to Worthing. Once at Worthing she would catch another minicab, possibly another blue Siesta, ann rea would bet money that it would not be as battered as its London counterpart, to take her the additional thirteen miles to Climping in West Sussex.

ann rea wondered if the hour of her departure, early on that spring Tuesday morning, had anything to do with the fact that Kennedy would barely have been out of bed by the time she left her flat. The traffic at Marble Arch, even at this time, was heavy. But she worried not even a little about whether or not she would miss her train. Now ann rea had started on her journey it mattered not a lot when she reached wherever she was going. She was getting her fix – travelling – and it was starting to have an effect. She was feeling better. 'Now explain that,' she thought.

She thought through the other two suspects. London? She supposed in a way London was tied up to some degree with Kennedy; and wasn't he fond of telling her never to underestimate connections between your suspects? Sometimes, he had told ann rea, you can even eliminate a suspect, or even suspects, by working out a connection, if any indeed existed.

'So, lady,' she asked herself, 'How has London, one of the most magical and entertaining cities in the world, wronged you?'

And wronged her to the degree she needed to get out. ann rea was happy she had a ready-made, 'And here's one I prepared earlier' excuse in her need to visit Daniel Elliot. Not that she needed an excuse to return the love and support bestowed on her twenty-five years previously. But her need to get away from you? Damn those lyrics, ann rea thought as they burned their way around her brain leaving skidmarks like Damon Hill's. Her need to get away from you was greater, much greater at this stage at least, than repaying her debt to Daniel Elliot.

Back to suspect number two: London. London, the city which had promised her so much but in actual fact had given her so little, and the little it had given her was anything but pleasant. ann rea liked her job (ish) but she was hopeful that it was exactly that, a job, and not her career. Yes, she had other offers but all from papers where you've got to be careful what you say and even more careful whom you say it about. She didn't want that, she didn't necessarily want to write anything controversial just for the sake of it, but she wanted to write. Well, to write the things she wanted to say, and not necessarily in book form. In fact, definitely not in book form, because the success of what you wanted to say depended on how well your book was promoted. Added to that was the fact it was (at best) a statement you could make (at the most) every other year. No, ann rea would like to have a weekly page to fill in the *Spectator* or any other publication which did not depend on advertising.

Her other dream was a weekly half-hour on Radio 4 where she would have a single guest per week for a discussion; not an interview. She would have a weekly topic of her choice to discuss and the point of her guest would be to give the discussion a balance. Her guest would not have to be someone she liked, as long as she respected them.

She reached Victoria Station and strolled through to her train with three and a half minutes to spare. No whistles blowing, no slamming of doors, no clouds of bountiful white smoke rising up from under the train giving you the impression you were about to make a journey through the heavens. No, none of that. That was all the romance of a long-forgotten time. Now the train merely lurched hesitantly into motion.

But – and here's the big thing – as it did, as the train escaped the grand iron girders of Victoria Station, ann rea felt a release and a relief, a relief she was sure junkies felt with the release of their drug into their system, feeling the warm comforting buzz as it worked its way through the bloodways and byways of the body. Relief, sheer relief. ann rea couldn't believe how good – no, not good but absolutely bloody wonderful – she felt. It was like taking a main drag on a long-lost habit, like smoking, or drinking, or pills, or sugar, or food, or shopping, or whatever evil you helplessly served. All of which brought her neatly to her third suspect: herself.

'And it's yourself is it?' she could hear Kennedy's soft lilting accent say. Oh God, why did he have to have such a pleasing voice and why, Jesus, Mother and Saint Joseph, did he have to have those sad green eyes? Eyes which gloriously drank each and every inch of her body when he thought she didn't know he was looking. How could anyone not help but be drawn into their rich sadness?

But he wasn't a sad man, quite the opposite in fact, at least with her. It was just that maybe he'd been somewhere, seen something which made him think, 'Shit – all this larking around thinking about why, where, who and what comes next and generally contemplating one's navel is all a total waste of time and the only thing which is important is to get on with what little life we have left, and God knows isn't it short enough?"

Poor Daniel Elliot, who had definitely arived at the short end of life, arrived without his true love, now occupied ann rea's mind as the train glided effortlessly through the countryside, green, green like Kennedy's eyes, and past the backyards of people's homes.

Kennedy had been the first one to make ann rea aware of the intrigue of backyard journeys and she was now absolutely enthralled by them. You could build a picture of the inhabitants' lifestyles from their yards, where their guard was always down. The front garden, where they were always on show, gave you the idea of what the owners aspired to; the backyards revealed, warts and all, the reality. That was another of Kennedy's qualities for ann rea; what you saw was exactly what you got. She had to admit that she did like (as in a lot) what she saw. But why then was she having these doubts?

Or were they doubts? Were they not just healthy questions through which she could remove a suspect from her list? 'I've got to get away from you'. Should that perhaps be 'I've got to get away from my doubts'? Now, with the relief ann rea was feeling from leaving London, had she in fact got away from her doubts?

And that morning – as they both dealt with their doubts in different ways – an ever-growing number of miles apart, they were joined by some strange thread. ann rea making her way to Daniel Elliot to offer support and solace, and Kennedy walking over Primrose Hill en route to North Bridge House to find that his day was going to be consumed, not with thoughts of ann rea, but with the beginnings of an investigation.

An investigation into a murder, possibly the most complicated homicide Detective Inspector Christy Kennedy had ever been involved in.

Chapter Seven

'They've found another body up on the bridge, sir,' Irvine announced to Kennedy six seconds after the DI sat down at his American Arts and Craft oak desk and four seconds after the same DI had thought about his first cup of tea of the morning.

'What? The same place where Burton was found? Not that bleedin' dog again?' Kennedy rolled out his questions with the ease of a parent introducing the family.

'No, sir. The other side of the road and just beyond the bridge, you know, just where the fountain is, sir. The one with the bronze statue of a washerwoman on top of it. In fact the body was found in the the little nook underneath the statue.' Irvine then paused for a second before replying to Kennedy's other question.

'And no, sir, not a dog this time either. No, the poor sod looks like he's been bludgeoned to death. Very messy it is too: the scene looks like a butcher's shop.'

The very thought made Kennedy's stomach heave. He was glad that he never, as in ever, took breakfast. Vitamin C drink at home and a cup of tea on reaching the office, followed shortly thereafter by another cup of tea and then another cup of tea, only this time accompanied by Walker's shortbread, at eleven (ish). But no real solid food until lunchtime. This time of the year though – late spring – Kennedy did indulge himself with some fruit, that is, whenever he remembered to stop by Marks and Sparks for it.

Soon, two very smartly dressed policemen (Kennedy: very dark blue three-piece suit, starched white shirt, blue and red old school tie, red socks and well shined classic black leather shoes; Irvine: Donegal three-piece tweed suit, checked shirt, Irvine tartan tie, and brown and cream brogues) were making their way for the second time in two days over Gloucester Gate Bridge to view a dead body.

In a way Kennedy was thankful that Burton had died at the hands, sorry, the teeth, of a dog. Otherwise the media would start to pound out the serial killing stories. Certainly it wouldn't have been true, he thought, but then when did the truth ever get in the way of selling papers?

Irvine had on his earlier visit blocked off the bridge from the Parkway side and blocked the Regent's Park exit at Gloucester Gate. This would mean a lot of pissed-off drivers in and around Camden Town: Parkway was becoming increasingly busy during the rush hours and the forced detours would cause havoc, but there was little to be done about it. Kennedy spied about two dozen officers at the scene of the crime, ranging from the beat bobbies whose main responsibility was to keep the train-spotters at bay to the forensic team who would (literally) scour the scene with a fine tooth-comb. Kennedy had never been able to work out why anyone would want to comb their teeth in the first place. Also visible was a photographer and a pathologist. The pathologist was once again Dr Forsythe and she and Irvine both had smiles for each other.

'Strange,' Kennedy thought, 'Does this mean that the exuberant Staff Nurse Rose Butler is off the scene?' Kennedy would be sad if this were the case because as far as he could see the DS and the SN were made for each other. But then ann rea was always accusing him of being a romantic when he came up with such notions.

Forsythe let the photographer finish work before examining the body. First she sealed the lifeless hands and feet in poly-thene bags, retaining and protecting foreign soils on the shoes (green and white tennis shoes) and skin, or other telltale parti-cles under the nails (dirty and long).

The thin (as in very thin) body was dressed in green slacks and dirty white T-shirt beneath an unbuttoned dark green shirt. The shirt and T-shirt were sprinkled with blood. The once bright red flow of life was now a baked rust which also mingled with his badly-dyed hair.

At the mouth of the washerwoman's 'cave' was a large stone and the body was lain on its side inside, behind this stone. The awkward positioning of the body made the doctor's examination very difficult. The shallow cave also seemed to serve as a bit of a rubbish dump. The forensic team were bagging all the discarded contents, mostly last autumn's leaves, sweet and ice-cream wrappers, and something which immediately caught Kennedy's eye, a half-eaten apple. He carefully picked it up between his forefinger and thumb and sealed it in one of his stash of forensic bags.

'It looks like he was crawling into the cave to take refuge,' Kennedy said very quietly as the surgically gloved fingers of his left hand stretched and contracted by his side, 'But then he'd be on his stomach wouldn't he? No. He was either dumped here or beaten here and the last thump must have knocked him over the stone into the cave. I wonder what the washerwoman could tell us if she hadn't been frozen in bronze by the Drinking Fountain Association on the 3rd day of August 1878.'

Kennedy's last sentence was spoken very slowly as he read the well worn inscription on the fountain's plaque. He looked around, surveying the bridge which separated the SOC team from Camden Town. 'You'd think, though, if he'd been beaten on the bridge someone would have witnessed it and come to his rescue, or at the very least phoned the police.'

'Come to his rescue? In the nineties, sir? I don't think so, sir. I think most people would rather give away their firstborn than interfere in a fight,' Irvine offered.

'You're probably right, but could you check last night's log and just see if any calls were made?' Kennedy seemed distracted by something at the other side of the bridge, or maybe he wanted to escape the glare of the corpse's one visible eye. He always had this weird feeling, when viewing an open-eyed corpse, that they were looking at you from the other side of life, beckoning you into their new, tranquil world. He wandered to the far end of the bridge, on the other side of the road, and hunkered down by a well weathered blue engraving fixed to the parapet, Kennedy guessed, in 1878; the year it was built.

He caught Irvine's eye easily as the DS had been intrigued with Kennedy's distraction. Kennedy motioned to him to cross the road. 'What do you make of this then?'

Irvine was aghast at the sight of the engraving, which depicted a large wild dog, an Irish Wolfhound in fact, attacking a man by leaping, teeth bared, straight for his throat.

'Wow!' was all he could mutter.

'Wow! Just,' Kennedy laughed nervously, 'Let's get this photographed and see what we can find out about the history of this bridge. Tim Flynn will be a good starting point. There's not a lot around the streets of Camden Town that he's not aware of, and I wouldn't be surprised if he was around when the bridge was built,' laughed Kennedy, this time less nervously but still slightly forced.

They returned to see how Dr Forsythe's work was progressing.

Without any prompting, she said 'I'd say he was beaten both by fists and a blunt instrument, possibly, but not definitely, a baseball bat. Positively not an iron bar though, the bruising is too spread out. I can't tell you exactly when it happened, but from the colour of the bruising I would say that late last night would be a good guess. Of course I'll give you a more accurate guesstimate when I've done the autopsy.'

'Would you be able to say if he had more than one assailant?' Kennedy inquired, happy to once more avert his eyes from the corpse.

'Hard to say, unless of course we assume the fist marks are from one attacker and the blunt object another,' Forsythe replied as she turned to face Kennedy, her long ponytail swinging in an arc.

'I'd say two,' Irvine offered.

'Yes, I'd agree. I don't suppose you'd either attack a man with your fists and then start beating him about the head with a chunk of wood, or vice-versa for that matter, beat him with the wood, put the wood down and then beat him with your fists.' Kennedy was trying to recreate some scene in his mind's eye. 'I suppose, though, it is conceivable that our attacker could have started off with the wood, or baseball bat, which he might have dropped in the scuffle, and then had to continue with his fists as he would have been under attack himself at that point. Do you mind?' Kennedy motioned to the doctor that he wanted to examine the body.

'Yes, please go ahead, I'm done until we can get him down to the morgue,' Forsythe replied as she snapped off her rubber gloves.

Kennedy knelt down and over the stone and pulled at the corpse's T-shirt until it came free from the waist of the trousers. He also checked the arms by sliding up the shirt. 'Well, that kinda disproved the dropped baseball bat theory, no markings on the arms, and I just wanted to make sure he hadn't received a good kicking about the body as well.'

As he leaned into the little cave he smelt the smells of dog-do, urine and death, not necessarily in that order. Death has a cold smell – a smell which never changes from corpse to corpse. Kennedy thought it strange how when alive our smell was as individual as our fingerprints, whereas in death we all smell exactly the same. He had the SOC people remove the body from the cave and lay it down on the pavement. The side of the face closest to the ground appeared to be more bruised, but this could have been the blood draining down to that part of the body. The eye on the bruised side was closed tight and it appeared as if the open eye was cocked up at the washer-woman, with her bronze 'wooden' water pail. He looked as though he was beseeching her as to why, in his hour of need, she had not protected him. Kennedy saw that the washerwoman in turn appeared to be staring beyond the corpse, her eyes full of remorse, not daring to look upon that which had happened beneath her at this her fountain of sorrow.

Chapter Eight

Twenty-seven minutes later Irvine walked into Kennedy's office and presented him with a large sealed plastic bag full of smaller sealed plastic bags, all bearing the contents from the pockets of the corpse found under Kennedy's newly named Fountain of Sorrow.

Moneywise the deceased had two £20 notes, four £10 motes, three fivers, three pound coins, a fifty-pence piece, six twenty-pence pieces, a ten-pence piece, three five-pence pieces and four two-pence pieces; a lot of change, all things considered. There was also a small, credit-card size wallet with a Mastercard valid until July the following year. The name and initials on the credit card were J. B. Stone. Also found in the wallet was a BT phone card worth five pounds, seven business cards with the legend, 'John Stone – Estate Agent – Camden Bus Estate Agents – 0171 387 4099', a tube ticket outward from Camden Town (£2.50) and a National Lottery ticket.

Kennedy was bemused at the lottery ticket. When the lottery had started up he had been one of the millions keen to spend a few bob to be in with a chance of the big shout. Then on about the fourth week he was queuing at the Woolworth's lottery desk and he spied, about three places up the queue, a woman and her kids, one barely a month old hanging from her hip, one, dummy-mouthed, hanging on to her leg for dear life, and a third, about four years old, crying and demanding sweets. All four were poorly dressed and dirty and Kennedy thought, 'You know what: you need this chance, I don't,' and he turned on his heels and left Woolworths swearing never to buy another ticket. London Met Police pay, even for a Detective Inspector, wasn't exactly great but Kennedy was a man with simple needs – music, books, clothes, movies and theatre; no cars, no other vices – so he found it easy to get by 'comfortably' as they say, and was happy to do so.

Another sealed plastic bag contained the remains (two

fingers) of one of the three million bars of Kit Kat sold each and every day in Great Britain. But the other contents were by far the most interesting to Kennedy.

Two of the sealed bags contained older, partly soiled plastic bags, these containing what appeared at first sight to be cannabis in one and tabs of E in the other. Kennedy guessed, due to the small quantities of each, that the drugs were for personal use and not for dealing. And that was the entire contents of John B. Stone's pockets – assuming of course, as Kennedy must at this stage, that the cards belonged to, and were not stolen by, the victim.

Kennedy summoned Irvine and WPC Anne Coles into his office.

'Okay, it's not a lot to go on,' he began. 'He's an estate agent, travels by tube – sometimes? frequently? seldom? – from Camden Town, likes Kit Kat, smokes a bit of grass, likes to party and drop some E. He dyes his hair from black to blonde and gets himself beaten to death.'

Kennedy gestured at the plastic bags on his desk in front of him, then clasped his hands and studied this intriguing array of pocket contents. Irvine and Coles followed his gaze, not sure what exactly to look for.

'Let's get on to the credit card company and find out Stone's address, and maybe a copy of his last statement or three so that we can at least build up a picture of his recent shopping trail,' Kennedy ordered Coles, 'And could you, DS Irvine, visit Dr Forysthe and attend the autopsy. I've got a weird feeling about this one. It might just be the memory of Flute Burton yesterday with his throat torn away and then this morning Mr Stone beaten up and left to die on the other side of the road.'

'Not to mention the engraving,' Irvine added and then explained to the WPC about Kennedy's gruesome discovery on the end of the bridge.

Kennedy pondered as he wrote down the telephone number of Camden Bus Estate Agents. He wanted to find out their address, for he intended to visit them himself and begin his inquiry into the death of John B. Stone.

Chapter Nine

They say that in the seconds before you die your entire life flashes before you. But how on this earth would they or anyone know?

Nevertheless, in Brian B. Stone's minds eye he would see the following flash past in the final seconds. Being out in the cold hallway every Sunday afternoon. That was a strange thing: in his memory the hall was always cold, even in the summer. This may have been due to the fact that the hallway was very large – but even this perception could be due to a child-size view – and was unfurnished and uncarpeted, with black and white chess-board tiles.

On those Sunday afternoons his parents made brutish noises in the living room in front of a blaring television, but he could still hear them.

His father being killed in car crash when John was seven years old. Stone saw, vividly, the scene of the police car pulling up outside his house, heard his mother say, 'What have you been up to this time, what trouble have you gotten yourself into? Just you wait till your father comes home!' as she glared straight at him, not at either of his two brothers; why was it always him? He could see a policeman and a policewoman exit the panda car and make their way along the well trodden path across the grass to his house.

John B. heard the knock on the door, saw his mother wipe her hands on the apron, which she then removed and placed behind a cushion on 'daddy's chair', saw her close the living room door behind her and open the front door. He heard mutterings for a few seconds and then he heard this high-pitched, evil-sounding animal whine coming from his mother. He and his sister ran to her but it was too late and she had collapsed into the policeman's arms. He then saw his father's coffin set proudly on mobile wooden legs in his parents' bedroom; surely his mother never slept in the same room as the coffin? But he didn't know for sure because he didn't feel he should ask her that question, perhaps that's what his relations meant when they brought him to their house saying his mother has to spend some time alone with the thoughts of his father. Next the day of the funeral and all the people dressed in black wandering around his house.

He saw his two brothers (whom he cared little about) and his sister (whom he cared a lot about). Stone saw himself practising dancing, and kissing, with his sister. When they were left alone in the house they would seek out their father's precious recordings of the Kinks, the Small Faces, the Who and the Rolling Stones. They were precious only because they were the sole things their mother kept in memory of her husband.

The passionate hate he felt for his maths teacher who now flashed across the screen making little of Stone in front of his classmates and sure he wasn't he only five foot nothing, or knee-high to a packet of Surf as his mother would say, had bad teeth and a poor attempt at a Bobby Charlton haircut. Agreed he knew all about numbers and times tables but was that really anything to write home about? The only image which kept reappearing was one of this black box floating in and out of view mixed up with all the other images. The main difference, apart from the frequency of views was that this image was in black and white while all the others were in living colour.

Also included on this, the final rerun, was John B.'s first concert, Thin Lizzy at the Hammersmith Odeon, the classic 'The Boys are Back in Town' concert in the days when the Odeon was a great gig and not a poxy advert for a Canadian beer, beer definitely with a small 'b'.

Early fumbling with girls (some of them on dates fixed up by his sister) behind the bushes of Primrose Hill. His first full sexual encounter was at a party in his friend's flat over on Camden Square. He got so drunk he remembered little about the sticky, sweaty affair but he ended up marrying the girl five years, and few sexual encounters, later. His first mode of transport was a Vespa 125 scooter and he had a reoccurring image of himself driving around the streets of Primrose Hill and in and out of Regent's Park. His first car was a clapped-out green

Volkswagen and it had, in fact, clapped out completely about a mile from his house on the very night he bought it for two hundred and eighty pounds.

The next scene was a scary one; he saw himself drenched in sweat as he sniffed his first, and last, hit of cocaine. He felt terrible after it, didn't manage to get high on Snow White, the only distortion he managed to experience was a rough, gravelly feeling at the back of his throat. This thankfully disappeared as the cocaine worked its way out of his bloodstream.

Now John B. was the camera and was flying over a football field as he watched himself try unsuccessfully to score a goal. He knew what to do, he knew all the tactics, knew exactly where and how he should hit the ball to effect the desired result; it was just that his feet, particularly his right one, would never ever do as his brain ordered. Was it an important goal he had missed? He didn't know and he didn't care save for his single thought that the only important goals in life always turn out to be the goals you miss.

Again he sees himself sweating, and as the camera pulls back it discloses John B. Stone trying to have sex; he just, barely, accomplishes penetration. So in his book of life it must qualify as his first time but he never considered it to be and, sadly, it was rarely, if ever, better. Then he spies the black box floating past again only this time it's against a blue background. A beautiful blue, like the Williams Racing blue. John B. thought that people take the colour blue too much for granted, but really it's such a beautiful, soulful colour, and now all his vision was taken up with blue. The Black Box had disappeared and now the life-giving blue was dissolving into a wedding scene.

The bride was stunning, in white, and Stone felt proud, but then as the camera pulled back he saw not himself by her side but his brother. This made the scene very painful for him to watch. Now the camera moves on, racing away at such a speed that everything it catches is blurred, but when the picture comes back into focus again it reveals another funeral in progress, this time his mother's and everyone is getting drunk at the wake. His sister-in-law is getting particularly drunk and he sees himself join her, his head swimming in alcohol, and they go off for a walk down the garden, through a hedge – all of this is in very sharp focus – now they are kissing and she is responding passionately to his kiss. Then she realises she's with the wrong brother and so she starts to push him away. In fact she pushes him away with such force that she loses her balance and falls back into the bushes.

Now he's on top of her and she's struggling but she's too drunk for her struggles to secure her freedom. He sees himself, from his vantage camera position, interfere with his sister-in-law's underwear, sees her start to cry but without tears, it looks like she's started to enjoy the encounter because instead of trying to push him off her she is using her hands to hold his shoulders, maybe even tenderly, and she appears to be trying to steady Stone as he uses one hand to undo his fly and release himself. He uses his other hand to play gently with her. No aggression now, just pleasant floating waves and she's on the high of a wave when he removes her underwear and places himself between her legs and as he tries to force himself into her she regains some of her senses and starts to struggle against him again. But it's to no avail, he's inside her, and her struggles just add to his pleasure. Her face dissolves into another face, one he fails to recognise, then it returns to the face of his sister-in-law who has given up the fight and is sobbing.

The camera pulls back again, only slowly, very slowly this time, and he realises that it's today, much earlier today and he can see that he's dressed in his current outfit and he's leaving his house, his lonely house, this morning. He's on a bus and the bus is moving but he feels it shouldn't be moving and it's all very confusing. Then it's later in the day and someone is talking to him, the conversation seems quite friendly, but then a split second later they are out in the dark and he is being beaten up.

Next he sees himself receive a good beating. He's in shock and he's doesn't know why he's being beaten and he can see blood, his own blood, fly everywhere and he hears himself thinking, 'Shit I'm going to get blood on my shirt, who is going to wash this blood out?' On and on the hiding continues and he's surprised by the fact that there is not as much hurt, or as much pain, as he would have thought on receiving such a hammering. With all the blood flying about, and the wet and warm liquid flowing about his head and out of his mouth, nose and ears, he feels he should be dead at this point. He's aware that he's still alive, surprisingly, but feels himself helpless about doing anything to stop this wreckage of his body.

Then he sees and feels himself drop into darkness; is this death, he wonders. But in a few seconds he knows it's not death because he can taste the mixture of liquids from his nose as it flows into his mouth. But the beating has stopped and he finds peace, solitude and rest in this darkness.

Oh, he's so happy for the rest and the fact that the beating has ceased but, now that it has, he feels the aches start to creep all over and through his body. There is not a single part of his body which does not hurt. Every time he tries any movement he feels like someone is drilling into the small of his back with an electric drill. It seems like he is lying in a cave, he feels some kind of happiness in his place of solitude, and he wants to sleep. It's like when he used to be very drunk, too drunk to drink that special pint of milk, or water, before falling asleep. He would be so drunk that he wanted to escape the dizziness and the buzzyness and the fuzziness and he would be happy to find sanctuary in sleep. He always knew that he would pay, in trumps, the following morning when he would wake up with the mother of hangovers, but it just didn't matter, sleep was bliss.

So he sees himself drift way off into the distance through the quietness and into the darkness. Next he hears the cracking again, loud and getting louder, and he realises he is hearing bones being cracked. He regains a little consciousness and then realises it is his own bones which are being cracked. This time, though, the thumps are different, not so forceful, but seemingly more effective. Probably just his imagination but he does wish it would stop. Stop this tirade of thuds. Now he hears them very clearly, thud, thud, thud, like a chef beating a steak to tenderise it. So much violence for such a compassionate act.

The thuds are getting louder and louder and he realises this is because the thuds are getting closer to his ear, the one ear he can still hear with.

He hears just one more thud and the lights go out.

Chapter Ten

Kennedy visited the Camden Bus Estate Agency on Arlington Road opposite the Rat and Parrot. The enterprising owner, instead of paying the usual high local rents for office space bought himself a beautiful 1948 London Transport Routemaster and parked the double-decker behind the Tupelo Honey Cafe. His initiative had supposedly irked the other Parkway estate agents, of which there were many. But the novel approach served him well.

The manager of this successful business, Mr Arnold Cooper, now conducts Kennedy to his office on the top deck. He invites the detective to take a seat in front of the desk. As they both sit down Cooper gives Kennedy the estate agent handshake, firm, quick and you come away with a business card planted so firmly in your palm an imprint of the ink remains on your skin.

'What can I do for you?' Arnold, never Arnie, inquires. He is a pleasant enough chap, dressed in the estate agent's uniform of white shirt (first of two for the day) a lime green tie, thick red braces and a light blue suit. His hair is ginger and wavy and looks like it is permed, though close examination reveals that this is not the case, it's just that he has very think wavy hair which he likes to grow long but dampens it down on his head to retain a semi-presentable look. Kennedy wonders does Cooper's hair fall all about him à la Jerry Lee Lewis when he's partying. His appearance is set off with large blue-framed glasses, the lenses of which are so strong they make his eyes look too big for his little head.

'John B. Stone I believe…' begins Kennedy.

'Oh. I see,' the other cut in. 'You want John Boy. He's a… he's not in yet. Most unusual for him.' Cooper speaks with perfect diction in short clipped sentences.

'No, I'm sorry. I didn't explain,' says Kennedy. He won't be coming in today or. I'm afraid I have to tell you he's dead.' Kennedy notices the colour drain slowly from the office manager's face, so he lets the news settle in for a few moments before continuing, 'We found his body this morning at the other end of Parkway.'

Parkway is the busy street which connects Regent's Park with Camden High Street (the direction of the one-way traffic). It is the heart of Camden Town due to the fact that it is less touristy than the High Street and the businesses and their owners create an informal community atmosphere. The aforementioned owners form one of the best bush telegraph systems in London. News and gossip travels the length and breadth of the street in as short a time as Radio 1 spends considering what good music it will play. So now Kennedy has advised one member of this tightly knit community the rest of Parkway will know about the death of John B. Stone by the time Kennedy walks the short distance back to his office.

'He was beaten quite badly and died as a result of his injuries.'

'Oh my God. I was just drinking with him last evening. We all drink in the Spread Eagle, it's very friendly in there, recently refurbished and there is a younger rock and roll type crowd,' Arnold Cooper announced proudly as if he was trying to sell Kennedy the property.

'What time did he leave?'

'I don't know. I didn't stay very long myself, to be honest. The wife you know. We've got two young children.' Cooper glanced to the photos on the desk. Kennedy followed his gaze and saw in an eleven-by-nine pinewood frame embossed with sea shells, a woman, mid-thirties with a bit of a haircut problem, and two (one of each) very cute children. 'And my wife keeps telling me I've got to concentrate on bonding with them at this stage in their life. So she likes me home for dinner before she puts them to bed,' Cooper said with a shrug of his shoulders, 'No more late nights in the boozer for me I'm afraid.' He smiled an 'I'm not really henpecked' smile which soon disappeared from his face. Kennedy assumed he had remembered the death of his colleague.

'Listen, I'm sorry. What else can I do to help you?' he said solemnly.

'Well, for starters, what can you tell me about him?'

'Now let me see. He is… sorry I meant he *was* good at his job. He was one of our best agents. In fact I believe he was our second best in last year's figures.'

When Kennedy failed to ask the obvious question Cooper continued unabashed.

'I, actually, was the best last year. It was a tricky year for our business, you know. Although the property slump was over punters were cautious as we came to the end of the last government. I think everyone knew the Tories were going to be beaten but people felt the need just to sit tight and see what happened. But we got by and this year is much better. In fact John Boy is having a tremendous start to the year and if I don't watch myself he'll bea… oh shit I've done it again. It's hard to comprehend the fact that he no longer going to be around and part of our life and business.' Cooper's voice trailed off at the end of the sentence.

Kennedy merely coughed to fill the silence. Cooper shook his head and continued.

'John Boy. We called him John Boy here because he looked so young. He's about forty-one or forty-two I think, but you'd swear he wasn't a day over twenty-four. I swear it should be illegal for a forty-year-old man to look so young,' Cooper said as he patted down his bushy hair.

'How long has he worked for you?' Kennedy inquired.

'He's been here about three years now. He'd had a few jobs in his life. He came here with a great set of references. But he always seemed to want to be on the move. I think this might have been his first job in North London. He told me he grew up around here somewhere but he'd spent his recent years around Wimbledon and Raynes Park.'

'What about relationships?'

'Well I'm sure some of the others in the office, who socialised with him more, would know about all of that better than me. In fact Jane and William were still with him last evening in the Spread Eagle when I left. But really, from what I can gather, he didn't seem to have much luck with the ladies.'

Once again Cooper looked at the photograph of his family, 'I think he really could have benefited from settling down with a good woman. A good woman, you know, makes all the difference. Both of John Boy's parents are dead and he has some brothers, two I think, and a sister. I never listen to office gossip you understand, but I did hear something about the family not getting on too well, something weird happening at his mother's funeral. All this chatter was going on on the lower deck and I couldn't hear properly. I could never exactly find out what had happened.'

Kennedy tried a different line. 'Would he have made any enemies in this business?'

'You're kidding of course. Don't you realise we're the most loved people in the community?' Cooper smiled briefly at his own attempt of humour, and Kennedy shared his smile, if briefly. 'Well, we do get a bit of flack from time to time, as I'm sure you'll know. A perspective buyer will make an offer, the offer is rejected. Guess who is to blame? Your friendly estate agent. A seller won't get the million he was told his property is worth at a dinner party. Who is to blame?'

Kennedy nodded at carrot top, who replied with a smile, 'You got it! Or, a deal falls through at the last minute and we get blamed by both parties. No, I reckon we're as popular with the general public as Yoko Ono is with Beatle fans.'

The detective, a Beatle fan himself, thought Cooper was being a bit hard – on estate agents, that is.

'So taking all this into consideration, are you aware of any clients who might have had a grudge, a big enough grudge against John B. Stone to beat him up, and maybe just overdo it?' All this talking without a cup of tea was making Kennedy's seat very uncomfortable.

'No. Not to my knowledge.'

'Was there ever a big deal of Stone's which went sour?' the dry-mouthed detective pressed.

'No. Nothing like that. He had quite a few of his own clients. Property developers in the area. He'd be on the lookout all the time for 'his people' and they'd take care of each other, if you know what I mean,' Cooper replied vaguely.

'Not exactly.' Kennedy longed for a cup of tea, if only to say

'I'd a cup of tea on the top of a double decker bus today.' That would certainly be a good opening line to ann rea. He wondered when he would speak to her next. She hadn't left a contact number and Kennedy hadn't pushed her on it.

'Look,' said Cooper, 'here's the thing. We estate agents and developers are both in a similar business. We sell properties and they work with us at both ends of the transaction. They will sometimes take derelict properties off our hands spend a lot of money redeveloping them into flats, shop units, commercial units or houses. They then come back to us to sell their properties when they've completed the work.'

Either Copper Cooper was a mind reader, or all this talking was also making him thirsty, so before continuing with his tale he inquired if the Copper Kennedy would like a cup of tea. Kennedy felt like replying 'Does a bear defecate in the woods?' but he felt his, 'Yes, please, that would be excellent. White with two sugars,' was somewhat more appropriate.

The order (definitely an order and not a request) was made on the intercom and Cooper continued, 'So anyway, as I was saying, we look after them and they look after us. Occasionally, if they make a good sale, or even a great sale, then they will show their gratitude in the time-honoured fashion.'

'What? You mean a bung?' Kennedy wanted to make sure he got this right, he didn't want to be thinking one thing when perhaps the estate agent might have merely meant they exchanged Christmas cards. Pigs might fly but if they did Kennedy wanted to make sure Cooper had a strong umbrella, a very strong umbrella.

'Hmm, yes,' Cooper replied hesitantly as he smoothed out his unwrinkled braces with his right thumb.

'Are we talking tens? Hundreds? Thousands?' Kennedy added the third zero after the first two failed to produce a reaction.

'Yes, sometimes.'

'Yes? Sometimes thousands?'

'Yes, sometimes,' Cooper replied meekly. He wasn't as on with his answers as he was at straightening his Ferrari-red braces. 'You've got to realise on some of these deals these people are making, say, a hundred grand, or maybe even as much as half a mil. So what's a couple of grand to them out of that?'

'Are we talking cash-cash, here?' Kennedy smiled, with a smile as genuine as a contestant on *Blind Date*, but he hoped it would encourage Cooper to loosen up a bit with his answers.

Sometimes in the course of an investigation Kennedy was privy to information which would be very helpful to others, such as the Inland Revenue for instance. But feck them, thought Kennedy, they could certainly do their own dirty work (The Inland Revenue, he reflected, could rival Yoko Ono in the unpopularity stakes; but on second thoughts, perhaps not). If people like Cooper could be made to feel their information was merely that, information, information to help Kennedy on his pursuit into the mystery of the death of John B. Stone, then hopefully would talk more freely.

'Well, I can only talk for myself. On the large ones, of course they go through my books. But, er, some of the smaller ones, you know what it's like, it ends up being beer money,' Cooper replied as the tea arrived. He then threw another tangent at Kennedy. 'Do you have any idea what food costs today? The wife, when she goes to Marks and Spencer, and she goes there twice a week, she rarely comes back with any change out of a hundred pounds... So anyway,' Cooper disclosed, 'A hundred pounds here and there soon disappears.

Kennedy had to agree. 'Yes, it sure does.' And he paused as he supped his (perfect) cup of tea. Then he went on: 'Could you possibly give me the details of Stone's regular clients?' He could see resistance in Cooper's enlarged brown eyes. If he was ever to play poker Cooper could find it profitable to invest in a pair of contact lenses. 'Of course, he added, 'I will treat the information you have just given me with the strictest confidence.'

'Yes, well I assume nothing less, Detective Inspector. Yes, I'll put something together for you. But I can tell you here and now that his main client, is National Properties. They work out of Islington. Their main claim to fame, and I can assure you that it is only a claim, is that they did work on the, then, future Prime Minster's house. Apparently, and again allegedly, it's the sister-in-law who makes all the artistic decisions.'

Cooper's Rolodex was a cramped as Saturday nights at the Camden Palace and he fuddled through the cards to extract the one bearing the details of National Properties. He gave Kennedy the number, the address and the name of Mr Kevin Burroughs.

'Tell you what,' Kennedy took some more tea and watched as Cooper struggled to replace the card in the Rolodex, having the same trouble someone trying to enter the toilet at Camden Palace on a Saturday night, 'I'd like to have a chat with the rest of your staff, particularly...' Kennedy checked his notes, '...William and Jane, the couple Stone was having a drink with last.'

'They are not a couple,' Cooper replied, just a touch too forcefully.

'What?'

'Jane and William, they are not a couple, they were just in the pub last evening at the same time. No big deal. They are... well, colleagues you know, not a couple that's all.'

'Oh, I see,' Kennedy replied as his mind's voice went, 'Funny!'

'Look, why don't you see them up here and I'll make myself scarce and have Helen my secretary do you up that list,' Cooper suggested.

'Great, yes thanks, that would be great.'

'Shall I send them up together?'

'No. Let's see Jane first, please.'

'Okay, She'll be straight up. Oh – would you like a refill?' Cooper nodded in the direction of Kennedy's empty white china cup in its clean saucer. Kennedy didn't believe in wasting a good cup of tea by spilling half of it in the saucer. The saucer was a supporter of the teacup, not an overflow. Although Kennedy could remember his grandmother, teeth missing, pour her tea from the cup to the saucer so that it would cool quicker before she could drink it. Sadly, this meant that she was never able to participate in one of Kennedy's favourite pastimes; dunking.

'Yes, yes please, and could you please tell whomever made

the tea that it was truly wonderful,' Kennedy beamed.

Cooper made his way down the narrow winding stairway at the rear of the deck. Kennedy could hear him say to the office in general and Helen in particular, 'Here, Helen, I say, if you ever leave us you've got a promise for your next job.'

'Oh yeah? And wot's that then?' Helen replied, rising to the bait with her high-pitched cockney accent wafting its way up the winding stairs to Kennedy's ears.

'Make tea for the force up in the Camden nick.'

Kennedy could hear a lot of forced laughter, then a bit a talking, and then footsteps (female) making their way up the stairs.

Chapter Eleven

Kennedy wasn't sure this was going to be the best way to start off an interview; he heard Arnold Cooper prompt Jane as she hit the stairs, 'He wants to talk to your about John Boy, he was found dead this morning.'

Subtle? Or what?

Jane made her way towards Kennedy, who by this time was seated in Cooper's chair behind the black synthetic wood desk, small but with enough space for a Rolodex, a notepad (foolscap), a telephone, and the regulation estate agent's 'don't leave home without one' Filofax.

'Detective Inspector Christy Kennedy,' Kennedy announced as he stood up behind the desk and flashed his warrant card with his left hand and offered his right. She and shook his hand very firmly.

Jane was wearing the shortest of black mini skirts, proudly showing off her magnificent muscular legs, and a red shirt (man's) which was pulled up and puffed out from her shiny black leatherette belt. If you looked closely at her well filled blood-red shirt, and Kennedy did, you could see an AIDS ribbon. Her curly brown shaggy hair spilled over her shoulders and down the back of her shirt. She was heavily made up, with bright red lipstick and eyebrows which were like two tadpoles swimming towards each other in an elaborate synchronised routine.

'Jane Oddie,' she announced, giving away no trace of an accent as she shook his hand. Miss Oddie carefully manoeuvred herself into the seat. Should Kennedy have looked, and he certainly didn't, he would have seen that she expertly revealed no more of her legs than she did when she was standing. She smelt of perfume, a natural perfume but a perfume nonetheless. Kennedy detected a hint of heather. Jane Oddie kept fidgeting with and looking at her small blue purse-cum-handbag which hung from her shoulder on a leather strap no thicker than a shoelace.

'I can't believe it. Is it true? You know? What he said, like, what Mr Cooper told me?' she gushed, slipping now into her broad Manchester accent, an accent now popular in London the way the Liverpool accent was hip in the sixties. Kennedy thought there was hope still for the natives of Birmingham if they were prepared to wait a century or two.

'Yes, I'm afraid it is.' Kennedy replied wishing he'd remembered to instruct Cooper to tell his staff nothing about the death of John B. Stone. But the Camden bush telegraph was now effectively (very effectively) at work.

'Ohmigod. I can't believe it. We were all together last night. Well, Mr Cooper, William, John Boy and myself, that is. We were up in the Spread Eagle,' she replied as she nervously stole another glance at her bag, swapping it from one hand to the other without removing the strap from her right shoulder.

'Listen. Do you want to have a ciggy?' Kennedy smiled.

'Do you think it would be okay? I'd love one. I mean… Mr Cooper, well… let's just say he doesn't encourage us to smoke in the office.'

'Yes, I'm sure it'll be fine. I did notice large amounts of butts on the pavement outside,' Kennedy replied. Unable to find an ashtray, he took Cooper's dark green metallic waste paper basket from behind the desk and put it over beside her. As he did so he couldn't help but steal a glance at Miss Oddie's perfect legs. To his eyes she wore neither stockings nor tights, just a beautiful, naturally tanned skin (little did he know the disguise techniques of nineties girls). Kennedy blushed slightly but Jane Oddie didn't notice: doubtless she was too desperate to light up her ciggy to notice a middle-aged policeman drool over her legs, besides, it probably happened all the time.

Kennedy could never understand why otherwise intelligent men would do anything to catch a glimpse of ladies' underwear. Was it because it was forbidden? Was it a private view only for their partner? But then this was hard to accept with such recent public views of titilating underwear. But why are men turned so on by it? Yes, he stole glances of ann rea in various stages of dress and undress but wasn't that, for them, all part of the bigger, sensual picture? Kennedy had spied men in cafes peeping out from under their newspapers as they slid further down in their seats. He had spied them staring blatantly at reflections in street windows, the same in mirrors in theatres, cinemas, hotel lobbies and so on to the degree where he wondered if he got as big a fix out of catching men waiting for the big flash as they did out of the big flash itself. He had seen men fight for the right to follow a short-skirted woman up the stairs of a double-becker such as the one he was now on. He could never suss out why men did so. He was more than happy to view legs, legs as beautiful as Jane Oddie's where he knew the legs on view were as much as he was allowed to view.

She fumbled in her bag and produced a ten pack of Silk Cut and a cheap green lighter. Drawing heavily on her first hit she relaxed visibly as she exhaled the smoke, away from Kennedy towards the open window, helping it on its way by fanning it with her hand. Then and only then did she replace the lighter and packet of Silk Cut into her minuscule hand bag and sink deeper into the seat as she took her second drag.

'Oh, thanks Luv, that's much better, do you know what I mean?' she said, then, 'What happened?'

'It's still very early in our investigation; we found the body a few hours ago. What time did you leave the Spread Eagle last evening?'

'It must have been about ten-thirty. Yes about ten-thirty. I live up in Kentish Town, Just the other side of the Tally Ho, and I caught a bus down by the tube station, outside RockOn Records. I was home by eleven and I had to wait awhile for my bus so I must have left the pub about ten-thirty.'

'Was John Stone still there?'

'Yes.' Jane seemed a little confused. 'It's just odd hearing you call him John Stone, know what I mean? He was always referred to here as John Boy.'

Jane Oddie uncrossed and crossed her legs, and took another large drag on her ciggy. Kennedy was shocked to notice that she had nearly finished it with just four drags. She exhaled slowly, enjoying the release, and once again fanned the smoke towards the open window. When she had completed the ritual she continued, Kennedy by now becoming accustomed to the swagger and roll of her Manchester tones.

'Yes. He was still there, he was talking to William and a friend of William's when I left. They were drinking quite a bit. They liked their drink, particularly John Boy. But they were always pleasant on it, good company, know what I mean, never trying to paw you or grope you.' She glanced quickly at the Cooper family photograph before adding, 'They were good fun to be out with, know what I mean?'

'Do you know any of his other friends?'

'No. That's a funny thing, really. He seemed to be a bit of a loner. Yeah, he'd hang out with us but he never seemed to want to do the usual laddish things –'

Kennedy cut off a potential 'know what I mean?' with a quick 'Like?'

'Like trying to pull birds all the time. Like football. Like clubbing. But William will be able to fill you in more on that side of things, they were mates or friends or whatever, I think they confided in each other. You know, you come into their company and they'd be rabbitting away nine to the dozen, then they'd see you and they'd stop talking. A bit too secretive if you ask me. But then that's boys for you isn't it, they think with their... well I'm sure you know what I mean. Oh gosh, I didn't mean that you...'

'It's okay. I think I know what you mean.' Kennedy smiled and continued, 'Is there anyone, anyone at all whom you know would want to do harm to John Stone?'

'No. Not really. It's not really that kind of world, is it? I was just about to say that sort of thing only happens in the movies but then it's just happened to John Boy. I just can't believe that he's dead,' Miss Oddie sighed.

Kennedy reckoned he had got all (not a lot) that he was going to get, and said, 'Well that's all for now – I may need to speak to you later.' Kennedy rose from his chair, Jane Oddie quickly stubbed out the remains of her ciggy on the inside edge of the green waste paper basket, ensuring it was totally dead, before dumping it in the bottom. She rose from her chair carefully swinging the bag on to her hip.

Could you send William Boatend up please?' Kennedy requested.

Chapter Twelve

A pair of crimson braces was the first thing Kennedy noticed breaking the floorline of the top deck. The braces were followed very quickly by the estate agent's snazzy outfit. The trousers of a dark blue suit, but instead of the traditional tie he proudly displayed a red-and-white polka-dot bowtie set well against a Michael Parkinson blue shirt grounded, if you could call it that, by a pair of green canvas shoes.

'Hi,' a North London voice announced, 'I'm William Boatend,' and he extended his well manicured thirty-year-old hand in Kennedy's general direction. He had brown hair styled by a razor-sharp parting. Boatend had a habit, which would very soon become evident to Kennedy, of taking the hair out of his eyes and flicking it back over his crown but always retaining the razor-sharp parting.

Kennedy motioned him to the seat still warm from Jane Oddie.

'So, how'd you get on then with Mr Cooper's pet, our Jane?'

William began as he winked at the detective.

Weird start, thought Kennedy, but at least here was a witness who was not going to be backward at coming forward.

'I found her to be polite, very pleasant,' he replied, not wishing to dwell on this particular line of conversation.

'Nah, don't believe any of that – she's got a tongue which could clip a hedge,' Boatend laughed.

Kennedy did not join in. 'So, I guess you've heard about John Stone?'

'Yes. Wow, that's heavy man, isn't it? I can't believe it. Or can I?' William Boatend's mood seemed to darken somewhat, at last.

'It would seem you were the last person we know of to have seen him. Yesterday evening, ten-thirty in the Spread Eagle?'

'Oh, we were there till chucking out time. John Boy was flush. He had come in to a bit of money, as in cash, and he was really knocking them back. He was a bit of a magician, you know.'

Kennedy looked at Boatend, puzzled to his toes.

'Yes he could turn beer into water quicker than the charity boxes come out in cinemas at Christmas time.'

The detective sat silent, he didn't wish to encourage Boatend in his gaiety. The estate agent eventually continued, 'Yeah, a mate of mine, Alan Hodge, joined us around ten-fifteen. Then when John Boy was getting the last round in I saw him speak to some older bloke at the bar. John Boy came back with the drinks, supped his and informed us he was going back to see the older bloke, he thought there might be a bit of business to be done but he was very cagey about it. Obviously didn't want me to get a whiff of what was going down.'

'This older chap, you didn't know him by any chance?'

'Nah, never clapped eyes on him before.'

'Would you recognise him again if you saw him?' Kennedy quizzed.

'Probably not, Guv, we only saw part of him and that was from behind. But he was thinning a bit on top, quite solidly built, dressed in smart threads though, very smart for an older geezer.'

Death hits different people in different ways. Kennedy thought that if one of his own friends or colleagues had just died, or worse still if they had been murdered, he wouldn't be anywhere as near as chirpy as Mr William Boatend, but that's estate agents for you: the sale must go on, along with the show.

'Did John Stone have any close friends?'

'Strangely enough, Guv, none to speak of. I mean, we hung out quite a bit together, and we'd occasionally run into people, people he'd known, and he'd be friendly enough to them, but not really any close friends, to be honest,' Boatend replied haltingly.

'Girlfriends? Partners?' Kennedy pushed.

'Well, let's get the second point out of the way first, shall we? He definitely wasn't gay but at the same time he didn't seem that interested in women. Sure we'd go out sometimes and pull and he'd definitely do the wild thing, or at least say he did.

Boatend hesitated, before continuing, 'There was apparently something weird which went down with his sister-in-law. Some big hoo-ha which went on at his mother's funeral. He'd talk about it a bit when he'd had a few, but he'd never entirely spill the beans. It must have been pretty serious though because the entire family, well, all that was left of it, his dad died in a car crash when he was very young and his mum, that was her funeral I was just talking about, that happened about two years ago – but his two brothers and sisters anyway, well, they haven't talked to John Boy since the funeral.'

'What about Christmas and things?'

'He's not really into them, neither am I for that matter, last year we just partied at his flat from Christmas Eve through to New Year's Day.'

'Where does he live?'

'He's got a flat in this block overlooking Primrose Hill and Regent's Park, quite close to the zoo actually. I suppose you're going to want to take a look. Yeah well actually I can help you there, I've got a spare set of keys.'

'Great. Excellent,' Kennedy said. This chap was turning out to be useful, very useful indeed.

'He must have been doing okay to own one of those flats.

They'd set you back a few bob, wouldn't you say?'

'Well, if *we* can't get a good deal on a property, who can? Answer me that one then?' Boatend boasted.

'Which brings me neatly to my next question. Were you aware of any of the deals John Stone was doing with National Properties?'

'Ah. I see your connection. No, not really. I mean I knew they were clients of John Boy's and he was always telling me they were keeping him sweet but I wouldn't know any of the details. Old tight ass – oh, sorry, wash out my mouth with soapy water, I mean our leader Mr Arnold Cooper – would have all the figures on the official side of things but there would have been only two people who knew the exact deals, and one of them is dead. I'm not sure that you're going to find that the sole survivor is going to be, shall we say, forthcoming.'

'Anybody else you know who might have wanted to do John Stone some harm?'

'I've been thinking about that since I heard the news downstairs and you know what, Guv, I can't think of a single person. I mean I'm being dead honest with you and I'm probably thinking along the same lines you are. You know; one of his deals screwed up big time, lost someone a load of money and people who have got loads of money, although they can usually afford to lose loads, they do not take kindly to anyone they feel is depriving them of their lifeblood. It's like that Bob Dylan line, 'Money doesn't talk, it swears,' and so when John Boy couldn't make good the funds they topped him. But I'm sure even if he was under that kind of pressure and he hadn't told me about it I would have noticed him being a bit on edge. And I can honestly say that recently he was his usual carefree self.'

Boatend stopped and thought for some time, then leaned over the desk which separated him from the detective and said, 'And that other thing, the family feud over his sister-in-law which happened at the funeral, was that serious enough to warrant…' He left the sentence unfinished and continued, 'I don't know about the ins and outs of that either, but I'd definitely look into that can of worms if I were you.'

Kennedy returned to North Bridge House with a few

addresses, a set of keys (for Stone's flat) and a little (not a lot) of background information on the deceased. He was eager to see what the others had discovered in his absence.

He wondered whether it was an advantage to have two suspects this early in the case. As he walked back to the police station he also noted how much illegal parking there was on the streets of Camden Town and wondered, with amusement, whether it had anything to do with the traffic wardens who had recently been arrested in a drugs swoop.

Chapter Thirteen

On reaching the top of Parkway, Kennedy, acting on impulse, continued past North Bridge House, took the first right along Prince Albert Road and headed across Primrose Hill to Ormonde Terrace, home of the recently deceased Mr John B. Stone.

Kennedy had felt an overwhelming urge to view the place this strange man had called home. He was strange because he didn't appear to have many, if any, friends. He didn't have any family connections and didn't seem to have any desire to start his own family. And then, for one who seemed to have led such a scattered social life, he had been picked out to be murdered.

This was a subject Kennedy pondered a lot on. How, and why, do you decide you are going to murder someone? Yes, in a fit of rage most of us will say, 'I'll kill him/her', but 999 times out of a thousand it is a cry of anger and not a threat. But that one time in a thousand, when the cry is uttered under a seething breath, what triggers that? Is it physical? Is it mental? Is it a combination of both? Is it merely a God-complex: 'Death to this scum!'?

Yes, Kennedy was aware that from time to time their were murders of passion where a jealous lover goes out of control and regrets it for the rest of their life. Or a row spills over into a fight and the victim gets knocked down, hits their head on a stone, sharp object or whatever and ends up dying, the sort of thing that usually qualified as manslaughter. Kennedy put a few of these down to the apparently current lack of respect for life. Was this due to TV? Or was it due to the removal of the death penalty?

He could remember when he was growing up how a murder, even as far away as London, would still cause ripples in Portrush, whereas one down in Belfast could send a tidal wave across the entire province. Nowadays murder victims seldom made the news unless there was a 'sexy' angle.

He was intrigued by the way that 'sexy' in media circles now meant 'instantly sellable'. So was this loss of respect for life due to the passing of time, the lack of deterrents, or the fault of media eager to fill their slots with anything 'sexy'?

Are murderers capable of only killing certain people, or can the wrong person simply be in the wrong place at the wrong time? Kennedy had yet to meet a murderer who wasn't an ordinary person, at least on the surface. That was why they were so hard to catch. They were, mostly, ordinary people living and working amongst fellow ordinary people; the perfect hiding place. That is why Kennedy was intrigued to see what he could feel and pick up from a visit to the home of Stone.

On the game of just-supposing you could just suppose that 'John Boy' had met this geezer in the Spread Eagle. He had left to do some business with him. What business exactly? Perhaps they'd gotten into a fight because they couldn't conclude the deal; the beating had gone just a bit too far and John Stone had died as a result. Such thoughts filled Kennedy's head as he took the lift to the seventh floor and arrived at flat 7D with its brightly painted green door. Kennedy let himself in with two keys (Yale and Chubb) and closed the door quietly behind him, careful not to disturb the silence and solace within.

He did a quick recce before a more detailed room-by-room search. The first thing which hit him was the smell. The place smelt like a hotel room: there were no distinct personal odours, just disinfectant from the bathroom and television dust.

To the left of the front door was another door (pine) which

led to a three-foot-square boxroom obviously used as a dump.
Every home has one, but it was unusual to find it so close to the
front door. It contained shoes, several pairs obviously no longer
in favour with their owner. And there were jackets, lots of them,
some hung properly on a hook rack to the left of the door and
some just dumped over cardboard boxes.

The boxes had once contained a TV, a video player, a stereo
midi system and a Dualit toaster. There was also a stack of
newspapers, mostly *Evening Standards*, *Time Outs* and *Camden
News Journals*. In the corner there was a left-over (blue) carpet
rolled up and looking like a psychedelic Swiss roll, and there
was obviously more junk concealed under all this.

The next room to the left was a small bedroom, obviously
spare since the bed was striped while the walls were adorned
only by a nine-gear racing bicycle leaning against the long wall,
a large yellow-and-black scarf draped carelessly over the
handlebars. Beside the bed was a reading light on top of a white
cube which also served as a magazine rack. The rack was empty
so required no further examination. The next door, the last on
this wall, led into a large master bedroom. The entire flat was
floored with bare, sprung pine, which with the combined effect
of white walls everywhere made the space look a lot bigger than
it actually was.

Kennedy felt quite weird wandering about the dead man's
home by himself. This was the home to which he had failed to
return last night. Kennedy wondered if Stone imagined yesterday morning when he was leaving for work that the next person
through the door would be a policeman. Kennedy kept having
this strange feeling that he was going to find someone in the flat.
He kept hearing noises, floor boards breathing, the wind
against the windows, the water pipes creaking into action as
someone somewhere else in the building activated their taps,
dogs barking on the distant Primrose Hill. There were always
dogs on Primrose Hill. But most of the sounds were from within
these walls; perhaps they were just groans from the flat, upset at
trespasser intruding on its luxurious, human-free time.

About five paces from the master bedroom door was a very
large bed. It was low to the floor and covered in light blue

bedclothes, and had white bedside tables on either side, each with identical reading lights. Beyond the bed was a window which spanned the entire length of the room. The curtains, light blue to match the bedclothes, were closed, and should Kennedy have pulled them open, which he didn't, he would have had a magical view of the zoo in the foreground with Regent's Park behind.

Opposite the main window and adjacent to the bedroom door was another similar door leading to the ensuite bathroom. Very simple: everything tiled white, floor, walls and ceiling. The toothpaste, toothbrush, soap, shampoo, facecloth, towels (white) all awaited (in vain) their owner's return. A large mirror covered the wall behind the sink and a small magnifying shaving mirror had been set into it at head height, lower than Kennedy's, the curve of its lens giving him a distorted view of himself. The bathroom, like the two bedrooms thus far visited, was reasonably neat and looked more like the hotel suite that Kennedy initially sensed than part of a permanent residence.

Back out into the rectangular hallway and the next door directly opposite the front door led to another bathroom, similar but smaller than the ensuite one. Then directly opposite the master bedroom door was that which led to the main lounge-cum-living area, a large, grand room which had a kitchen off to the right (as you entered) and a doorway leading to a reasonably sized balcony directly in front of you.

This was definitely the funkier room. Three large brown sofas made an 'n' shape in front of the fireplace, which was to the left and directly opposite the dinning area. On either side of the fireplace were Ikea shelving units arranged symmetrically to accomodate CDs, books (mainly paperbacks), the midi system, the TV, the video recorder and two units fronted by doors.

Above the marble mantelpiece was a large, twenty-by-sixteen photograph and it looked as if it could possibly be John Stone and his sister and two brothers from the distinct family resemblance. The boys had done okay on the deal, but to have those looks as a girl was somewhat less desirable. The were all smiling and joking. Someone, probably an amateur judging by the way the shot was composed, had obviously managed to catch a magic moment so Kennedy guessed the photo to be more than two years old. But he felt a distinct spookiness at John B. Stone smiling down at him from above the mantlepiece. A chill ran up his spine and he had a growing urge to get out of the building immediately.

Kennedy was not particularly superstitious, nor did he believe in ghosts, but there were thoughts filling his head which he couldn't expel and he could see himself trying to explain them to ann rea later, with both of them having trouble believing his words. But at that moment he was there facing the picture of a smiling man who had just died an ugly death, and the spirit of this man seemed to still be in the home and willing Kennedy to find his assassin.

Kennedy froze, and as the hairs on the back of his neck stood at attention he could feel himself breaking into a gentle sweat. He wanted to break away from the smiling faces in the photo, leave the room and get out of both flat and the building as soon as he could. But that wasn't logical, was it? He could feel the fingers of his right had flexing furiously and he started to concentrate on that, and by doing so broke away from the picture and, against his better judgement, continued his search.

Although the lounge was the main living area and clearly the most used it still looked like a hotel room after a weekend's occupancy. He turned to the kitchen: again clean, functional and mostly white, it had the general vibe of a man unable or unwilling to put any of himself into his home.

However, this lack of clutter – apart from the dump room, threw up one major advantage for Kennedy. He did not have a difficult search, everything was on view and the two Ikea units with doors beneath the TV and the midi system produced all of John B. Stone's correspondence, files and note books, not to mention a couple of naughty videos.

Kennedy retrieved the midi system's box from the dump room, placed all the files and paperwork therein and set it on top of the large marble-topped coffeetable situated in the centre of the fort created by sofas and fireplace.

He quickly glanced through the books and CDs. Stone had

been the proud owner of each and every one of Dick Francis' forty-odd books. He'd also quite a few of the Penguin Classics. But the books were by and large airport paperbacks. On the music side Stone shared his taste with Essex Man: Tina Turner, Dire Straits, Simply Red, Phil Collins and even Michael Bolton! On the positive side he had a copy of Nick Lowe's classic *Fourteen All Time Lowes*, an album which contained one of Kennedy's favourite singles, 'I Love The Sound of Breaking Glass'.

He quietly let himself out of the flat, easily bearing the weight of his spoils. He added an inch to his step as he quietly hummed Lowe's perfect pop single. All things considered, this case was developing quite well.

And pigs might fly!

Kennedy should have know that the only time pigs fly is when rashers are thrown into the frying pan.

Chapter Fourteen

'Our friend Stone has been flexing the plastic a lot recently. And guess what he been buying?' WPC Coles inquired of Kennedy and Irvine in Kennedy's office mid-Tuesday afternoon. Irvine and Coles liked being in Kennedy's very personalised office. The DI had spent a great deal of time, and a little money, making his office very comfortable and more conducive to thinking. He still couldn't work out how some of his real-life colleagues and the majority of TV cops could do any work at all considering the tips they worked in. They were mostly ugly, untidy, uncomfortable and dirty, and one could rarely find a pencil in the disorder, let alone a clue to a major crime. No, not for Kennedy. He preferred a tidier, more comfortable space in which to address the puzzles before him.

To Kennedy, that was exactly what the art of crime detection was: solving a puzzle. That was also what he loved about it: pitting your wits against the criminal. Sometimes you had the pressure of time also tapping not so gently on your shoulder. The colder the trail the less likely you were to pick up the scent. Sometimes you were also fighting the fear that the murderer may strike again and it could be all down to you to save a life by apprehending the criminal before they had a chance to strike again.

'Yes. Now let me see,' Kennedy replied. He was about to show the fun side to the art of detection. 'I would say a Panasonic remote control 21-inch colour TV set, a Sony Stereo Nicam Video Recorder and, let's see, don't tell me,' he went on, milking the joke somewhat, 'a Sony midi stereo system and a shiny Dualit toaster. It's not as great as it looks – the toast doesn't pop up when it's done.'

'Shit! You're absolutely correct, they're all here,' the WPC replied. 'How on earth did you know that?'

'Easy,' Kennedy laughed, his green eyes twinkling. 'I saw their empty boxes up at his flat.'

'That's cheating. I was beginning to think you'd some weird mind-reading qualities.'

'No, not really. Cheating that is. How you gather your information is not important, it's only important that you gather it in the first place. Then you need to know what to do with it once you have it. So what other information did you gather from the credit card statements?'

'He seemed to run up monthly bills on an average of £850. That was until two months ago. The last two have shot up to £1670 and, the most recent, £2150.45.'

'Did he pay promptly?' Irvine, as a member of a nation not noted for prompt payment, inquired.

'Yes, there are no penalty payments of interest on the last twenty-four statements,' WPC Coles answered as she consulted her notes. 'Lots of off-licence bills, lots of eating out, some clothes, not a lot and never very expensive, and some W. H. Smith's, which would be either books or CDs.'

'I'd say you're correct. His CD collection definitely came from Smith's, cut in Kennedy. 'Anything else in there which may be of use to us?'

'Nope. Don't think so.' Coles replied confidently, evidently enjoying being on another case with Kennedy and Irvine.

'Well, it's my turn I suppose,' Irvine began. 'I attended the autopsy with Dr Forysthe and, between the three of us, I don't think I'll be having any tea this evening. She reckons he took a series of blows around the head, anyone of which could have killed him. But she thinks that because of the state of the bleeding it was one of the later ones which finally did it. The bleeding stops when the heart stops pumping.'

Irvine added this last bit as way of explanation, since Forysthe had taken the elaborate trouble to explain to him. A little less vividly would have sufficed and perhaps encouraged his teatime appetite. But another memory prompted the next part of his report.

'She seemed very upset, Bel – Dr Forysthe that is, at the state of the body. I would have thought she'd been used to seeing battered bodies by now. Perhaps it was just the barbaric attack which upset her. He was drunk as well, too drunk to drive,' Irvine added.

'I don't think he did drive. No credit card bills for petrol or car kinds of things,' the WPC interrupted.

'Death would have occurred at midnight-thirty, give or take a few minutes either way. Our Mr Stone was thin, very thin, but he was in the best of health,' Irvine concluded.

'Did Dr Forysthe have any ideas on the instrument of death?' Kennedy asked.

'She reckoned fists and a blunt object like a piece of wood or...'

'A cricket bat or a baseball bat?' Kennedy offered.

'We talked about that and she said that baseball bats were becoming very popular instruments of crime. She agreed that a baseball bat could possibly, but not definitely, have been used. However, on the good news front the forensic department were on the phone a few minutes ago claiming the half-eaten apple is a bit of a find. They say they are going to be able to get a perfect mould of a set of molars from it.'

'Excellent,' Kennedy declared. 'But we first need to find a suspect before the apple's going to be of any use to us. Once we find him we can positively put him at the scene of the crime.'

'Are we assuming, at this stage, that the murderer is a man?' Coles inquired.

'Aye. I'd say so,' offered Irvine. 'I doubt if a woman would do that much damage to another human. Mentally yes, physically no.'

Coles mildly raised her perfectly shaped dark eyebrows but kept her own counsel.

'Well, that seems to be all we have to be going on at the minute,' said Kennedy. 'I think it's about time we moved the inquiry out a bit. What I'd like to do is have some of our people go down to the Spread Eagle and interview the bar staff and some of the regulars and see if we can't discover the identity of our mystery man. The chap who was talking to Stone at the bar at closing time. Also we need to find out what happened to Stone between 11.00 p.m. and 12.30 a.m. Someone must have seen him. Most of the Parkway businesses are closed by then, but lets do a check and find out who was on the street last evening and what they might have seen. Could you organise that, DS Irvine?'

Irvine nodded and left to get the team on to it.

'Now, that leaves you and I to track down and interview the sister and two brothers,' said Kennedy to Coles. 'That's certainly going to be very interesting if we can get them to talk. I'm intrigued by this funeral incident. It's sure to be thirsty work all this talking, isn't it? Let's treat ourselves to a good cup of tea first.' And he rose from his desk and made his way to the kettle, rubbing his hands in glee.

Chapter Fifteen

Irvine was pleasantly surprised that his trip to the Spread Eagle bore fruit. Two of the bar staff and three of the regulars all came up with the same name for the mystery man seen talking to John B. Stone the previous evening. The name produced from the lips of the five witnesses? Mr Hugh Anderson.

DS Irvine was aware (well aware) of Hugh Anderson; he was a regular (criminal) of the parishes of Camden and Islington. In point of fact Irvine was sure that Anderson had been in court no less that three weeks previously on GBH charges. The charges had been dropped. This was not unusual with GBHs; witnesses, on the rare occasion there are any who can still speak, always seemed to suffer from memory deficiency. In view of the recent development, Irvine returned to North Bridge House and put out an all ports bulletin on the same Mr Hugh Anderson.

In the meantime, WPC Coles traced the address and telephone number of Stone's younger brother Brian. She rang the house and spoke to Brian's wife, who informed her that Brian was at work and happily supplied his work telephone number. Mrs Stone also supplied the names and numbers of the rest of the family, namely Stephen, the eldest, and Helen.

Coles and Kennedy would also (eventually) learn that Helen not only separated the brothers Stephen and John B. age-wise but that she was the main person to pull them apart at the famous wedding incident.

Kennedy was keen to start interviewing immediately and as Brian was the only one Coles had been able to track down he was automatically at the top of the chat list. This decision had been made all the more easy when Kennedy learned that Brian Stone worked for Camden Town Records who were located, as luck would have it, in the blue-framed, glass-fronted building directly opposite North Bridge House on Regent's Park Road.

But it was Kennedy and not the youngest of the Stones who was in for the first shock.

Brian Stone looked like he was in his late twenties and seemed to be just the type to work for a Camden Town music business. He had the geeky appearance which seemed to have become popular, if not standard, in such places. He had a stud in his nose, another through his lip and yet a third through his eyebrow.

Kennedy knew that certain companies went to extreme financial inconvenience to advertise substances which, if taken regularly and in vast quantities, would remove pimples, zits, other facial imperfections and (sometimes) even moles from about one's face. In view of this, Kennedy could not work out why the younger generation covered themselves in metallic zits. Perhaps these pet carbuncles were the equivalent of the 'freak flags', the long hair styles of the sixties. It wasn't something which really bothered Kennedy: it certainly didn't give him sleepless nights in the way ann rea was now doing. No, it was just puzzling the way some people apparently went out of their way to ensure they looked less attractive.

Brian Stone, who turned out to be an assistant in the International Department of Camden Town Records, greeted Kennedy and Coles in the busy reception area. He was wearing dirty (formerly white) pumps, wrinkled tartan trousers (greenish) and an Oasis (very hip and not to mention successful pop band whom many thought were the best to come along in many a year, maybe even since the Beatles, upon whom they seemingly based their entire career – and was there a better band to base your career upon? Kennedy thought not) T-shirt.

'Can we go somewhere private?' asked Kennedy after the identifications and introductions.

'Yeah, sure, we can use the tea room, there's no one in there at present. What's this all about anyway?' Brian Stone's reply was a lot more pleasant and well spoken than his appearance would imply.

'I'd prefer to wait, if you don't mind,' said Kennedy as he ran his hand through his hair as a diversion, a stalling tactic or maybe even both.

They made their way through the buzzing, open-plan office which was packed to bursting. If you could hear your way through the noisy maze of people, there was also music hitting you from three different directions at once. One was a radio, probably even a pirate, Kennedy deduced from the unbearable level of distortion. The second audio attack was from behind them and from behind a closed door, but still so loud Kennedy could not make out what Stone was saying to him as they made their way through the heavily peopled office. Kennedy assumed, from the way Stone's unkempt and longish ginger hair kept bobbing about, that the information he wished to impart was important.

The third attack of music, which seemed to be the magnet to which they were being helplessly drawn, he recognised as the Beatles' 'Ticket to Ride'. But the closer they moved towards it, the more he realised that it wasn't the Beatles' version but a new one by the aforementioned Oasis. This was by no means better than the original classic, but served to show that the performers were a cracking good band.

They arrived at the tea room and for the first time since their brief chat in reception Kennedy could hear was Stone was saying: 'I love that version, far superior to the original if you ask me. Hey, did you see that prat Valentini hijacked GLR yesterday?'

The two officers nodded to the positive but Kennedy had forgotten all about it.

'Yeah, anyway he's created such a demand that all the record stores have now sold out of his music and everyone in town is offering him a record deal. Shit, even the people upstairs are trying to sign him.'

Kennedy looked around as he closed the glass door to the tea room behind them. He couldn't for the life of him see any evidence of an upstairs.

Coles went over to the tape machine, and when she couldn't work out how to turn it off she simply removed the mains plug. She and Kennedy both breathed a major sigh of relief as the room fell (relatively) quiet.

'I have to tell you that your brother John was found dead this morning, and – '

'Greeeaat! Great! Someone gave the... the...' and Brian stared at the WPC before carefully choosing a word, '...bastard... gave the bastard exactly what he deserved!'

Kennedy and Coles were, to say the least, somewhat taken aback by this response.

'Look, I should tell you this now,' said Brian Stone, ''cause you're going to find it out anyway. Our Steve and Helen and me, we couldn't stand the... the...' He once again looked at Coles and even then in his deepest anger he still managed to curtail his manners, '...the waster, as far as the three of us were concerned – he just didn't exist and I'm afraid you won't find any of us shedding a tear. We just – I mean I certainly do not care. In fact if you want to know the truth I'm just annoyed that I'll have to spend some of today dealing with this... dealing with him.'

'Why do you all hate him so much? What on earth did he do to you?' WPC Coles asked automatically.

'Well...' Again he paused, then said 'Listen, you'd better ask Steve about that one. It's his business and I'm certainly not going to go blurting it out to strangers. And look, if you've nothing more to ask me I'd prefer to get back to my work. I've got a lot to do today and I'm certainly not going to let my work suffer because of that bastard.'

'Mmmm.' Kennedy stared suspiciously at Stone, but seeing betraying reaction, said 'I suppose we can leave it there, for now, but I may need to talk to you again, so stay available.'

He watched Stone jump up from his seat and dart for the door. 'One final question Mr Stone: what were you doing last evening between the hours of eleven-thirty and one o'clock?' It was a question Kennedy felt compelled to ask in view of the blatant bad blood.

Stone froze in his tracks, turned nonchalantly and replied, 'Well I was out with a few mates. We were in the Dublin Castle till chucking out time. We'd been there to see one of our new bands, a waste of space if you ask me, a girl band whose backing tape kept breaking down, they couldn't even sing let alone sing in tune, but since the Spice Girls everyone wants a girl group. I tell you, this one couldn't even pass an audition for *Stars in Their*

Eyes, but as I say the people upstairs wanted a girl group. They probably signed them before they'd even heard them sing a note. Now the rest of us have to do the work on them.'

'And after chucking out time?' Coles asked, interrupting the lecture on corporate record company procedure.

'I, ah, I went and got a takeaway down on the High Street and walked home.'

'At what time did you arrive home?'

'This last question of yours, Detective Inspector,' Stone smiled a natural smile at Kennedy, 'Has as many parts as an A-level exam question.'

'At what time did you return home, sir?' Kennedy repeated firmly.

'Ah, about twelve o'clock, I think, not much later. I'm afraid I really must go now,' the man pleaded.

Kennedy nodded consent. He closed the door after Stone and said to Coles, 'Do you still have his home telephone number?' He could smell her perfume as he did so.

Coles checked her notes and confirmed that she had.

'Good, I'll delay him and you ring his wife immediately and check with her what time he really got home.' Kennedy had opened the door before he finished the request and called loudly after Stone, 'Sir! Excuse me, sir!' But Stone ignored him. Kennedy called again this time at the top of his voice, 'Brian Stone! A word please!'

This time one of Stone's colleagues caught his attention and pointed in the direction of Kennedy. Stone walked back towards them with all the pretence of a football player sent off for a bad foul but still protesting his innocence. WPC Coles meanwhile went back over the road to North Bridge House to make use of Sgt Flynn's desk telephone.

'Yes? What is it now?' Stone barked at Kennedy.

'Sorry, it was just out of interest, really. I was wondering what happened to that chap, you know Pauley Valentini and GLR?'

'Really? I would have thought if anyone had the inside track on that it would have been the police,' Stone replied in apparent disbelief.

'I'm afraid I've been busy on this inquiry all day and haven't had a chance to check with the officers working on the case.'

'He's still there,' said Stone, 'He's still on air. Johnny Bell has taken a few hours of snooze but Pauley is still up and going strong.'

'How's he managing that?' Kennedy said, pushing his luck as far as he possibly might.

Brain Stone merely looked at Kennedy, smiled a smile of 'silly question' and attempted to turn away from Kennedy, who persisted with 'So do you think you'll be successful in signing him to Camden Town Records?'

Brian Stone sighed, stretching the first word of his reply to what seemed like an eternity, 'We-ell, I know they want to. They've been faxing him at GLR. Apparently they want to record a few voice and guitar versions of some of his new songs with Johnny Bell producing. They've even offered Johnny a great deal to help put it all together. They want him to get it over to us this afternoon so that we can get a CD out before all this fuss dies down.

Kennedy grasped at another straw. 'What's the quickest you could get it in the shops by?'

'Ah I suppose if we pulled out all the stops we could have it out in twenty-one days. Well, at least a limited supply of it by that time. He's not Lady Di after all. That would have us taking everything down to the wire, but if this is going to be a nine-day wonder then I suppose we're going to have to be...' Stone paused for a few seconds and Kennedy could see from the smile creeping across his mouth that another joke was due, '...twelve days too late.'

Kennedy laughed, and Stone went on, 'Personally I feel we'd be twenty days too late. This guy Valentini used to be a tour de force, but now he's forced to tour. He's had his crack at it, you know. The majority of acts, they get one stab at it, one big album, one big single and that's it and they've got to make sure they maximise their profile during the period of their success to ensure them a career. There's only a handful of artists, people like the Beatles, Dylan, Van Morrison, Ray Davies and possibly Paul Simon, who consistently write great songs.'

Kennedy was happy that he'd pressed the right button and Stone was off on automatic, he smiled to himself, thinking that he would have added Jackson Browne to the list and maybe a few others, but he decided to hold his own council and let Stone continue, 'But apart from that it's one big hit, and why on earth would they expect any more? So now Valentini is pissed off that Radio Wonderful won't play him. Hey, join the queue mate. Besides, have you heard his recent stuff? I mean please, what's that all about? Come on Pauley, I think you need to get out of the house a bit more. Before this hijack he was someone with only one career move left: to die.'

Kennedy felt compelled to cut in at this point, 'A little harsh perhaps?'

'Perhaps, but only a little. Anyway with all the European and American interest we'd maybe even have to add a week to that twenty-one days. Now, if you have no more real questions I should be getting back to my work.'

'No, no more,' Kennedy replied, with a 'for now' under his breath as he slowly left the building whistling the Beatles' 'Hello Goodbye', which the Fabs recorded late October 1967, completed mixing on the 15th of November, had it in the shops on the 24th November, and had a number one single in Britain and around Europe by the 29th November. It stayed in the top 30 for the following three months. The Beatle fan detective wondered what the record company executives upstairs would do with such a group today.

Chapter Sixteen

By the time Kennedy had reached the final bars of 'Hello Goodbye' he was entering North Bridge House to find WPC Coles catching many the eye as she passed the time waiting for his arrival chatting with Sgt Flynn.

She hurried across the well worn wooden floor to meet him. 'Guess what, sir?'

'Well, I'd say judging by the lightness of your step that either Tim Flynn here has at last got some new jokes, or Mrs Brian Stone didn't exactly collaborate Mr Brian Stone's alibi.'

'Correct on both accounts, sir. His wife told me that Stone returned home about ten past one. She says the reason she's so sure of it is because, to quote her, 'He'd had a skinfull', and apparently made a bit of a fuss getting into bed, so much so that he woke her up, she checked the clock and it was one-ten. So there.'

'Aha, interesting. All our suspects seem to be falling into our lap in a heartbeat. The Dublin Castle is just across the road from the Spread Eagle; the brothers Stone would have been leaving their respective drinking houses around the same time; maybe they even met at the top of Parkway. You know, both a bit the worse for wear on drink. They spotted each other, the old family feud sprung up again, they had a go at each other and John B. came off the worse. Possibly, but I don't remember seeing any marks about the hands or face of Brian, so either it was a one way scrap or…'

'Or,' Coles took up the theme, 'Or Brian spied his brother coming out of the Spread Eagle, followed him and got a bit of wood or a baseball bat and whacked him a few times?'

'Two problems with your theory. One, neither of their journeys would have taken them up and over Gloucester Gate Bridge. Two, he couldn't have very easily strolled into a shop at that time of the night and ordered a baseball bat, could he?' Kennedy surmised as he led the WPC through the pass door to the inner office and up to his own on the first floor. As the pair of them made their way in silence up the stairway they met DS Irvine coming down.

'I heard you were back in the building, sir. Bit of good news on our side of things, sir. We've found the mystery man – you remember, the chap who was drinking with John B. Stone last evening in the Spread Eagle – and guess who he is, sir?' Irvine gushed.

'Ah now, let me see…'

'I'm sorry, sir. Of course you couldn't guess. It's just…' Irvine cut in, trying to save his soul.

'No. No, please don't tell me. Just concentrate, Sergeant. I'll get it. It's coming to me. Just a minute, I've got it. It's OJ Simpson!'

'Yeah, okay, silly question I know,' Irvine managed to get out through Coles' hearty and sensual laughter. 'It's Hugh Anderson!'

'Hugh Anderson?' said Kennedy, somewhat taken back.

'Yes, Hugh Anderson.'

'God, the suspects are dropping out of the trees like flies on this case. First the property developer, Kevin Burroughs. Then the younger brother Brian Stone, who has in turn implicated the older brother Stephen, and now a professional criminal, Hugh Anderson.'

'Who's Hugh Anderson?' asked Coles.

'One of the old school. He's been on the manor a long time. Used to be a member of the O'Griffiths firm over in Islington in the fifties and sixties. They were mighty powerful then, probably second only to the Krays, but they were clever enough to keep out of all the other firms' way. However, in the late sixties when the drug thing was starting up they made a mistake and went to war with a south London outfit called the Cheneys, and the police just stood back and watched them literally blow each other out of the water. A couple of members on either side, including Hugh Anderson, went to ground and resurfaced a couple of years later when the dust had settled.'

'Didn't he go to Spain, sir, until it all died down?' Irvine suggested.

'Didn't they all, though. No, seriously, that was one of the stories floating around, but there was another one which had credence which had him going to Dublin. I think I'm more likely to believe that one. Someone was over there in the early seventies helping them get the drug thing started up. I also heard he had to leave there in a hurry, something to do with getting involved in politics.'

By now they'd all arrived at his office and he opened the door and led them in.

'But I'd have to say I'd be surprised, very surprised, if he was involved in this. Not his style. No, he's been keeping himself clean for a good while now. Hasn't been in any trouble since he took up with that Scottish singer Ginger Buchanan.'

'Except, that is, for the GBH thing a few weeks ago,' Irvine reminded the DI.

'True, but the charges were dropped on that one and you would have thought that even if he were involved, the skirmish with the courts would have been enough to remind him the next time he goes down he needn't bring a suitcase. Let's get him in for a chat, shall we?' Kennedy rubbed his hands.

'He's already in, sir. I put out an all ports on him, word got around we were looking for him and he walked in to the station himself bold as brass and as sharp as sixpence about five minutes ago. Of course he was with his brief, sir.'

Kennedy smiled. 'Okay. I'll have a chat with him. But do me a favour first, have someone put a bowl of fruit, you know, a few apples, bananas, oranges, in the interview room. And then while I'm talking to our man you and the WPC can go along and interview Kevin Burroughs at National Properties. It will be very interesting to see what kind of story he has to tell. Make sure he's aware that we know all about his kickbacks to John B. Stone.'

As Kennedy left Irvine and Coles to their chores he was thinking about how easy some cases seemed to fall into place for you. This John B. Stone definitely had the knack of troubling the waters of his life. Kennedy also realised that his day was nearing an end and he hadn't up till now given a thought to ann rea. He found it somewhat ironic that the first time he thought about her was because he had found himself not thinking of her.

Chapter Seventeen

Meanwhile, down in West Sussex, ann rea was in fact sparing the occasional thought for Christy Kennedy, even though most of her time was being spent with her friend and former landlord Daniel Elliot.

ann rea pondered a considerable amount of her time on the difference between the magnificent man she had met on the door of his home in Belsize Avenue all those years ago and this poor specimen lying on the bed fading away before her very eyes.

Could this be the same man who had first met his wife in an orphanage when he was sixteen and she fifteen? He had left her, and the orphanage, promising to return, and walked from Antrim in Northern Ireland to Dublin in order to join the Irish Guards. By the time he reached Dublin he looked desolate, his feet were bleeding, his clothes were torn and he was in bad need of a bath. Daniel Elliot, as he himself had fondly recalled on many occasion, was about to be turned away by the barracks guards, who had listened to his story and informed him he was not what the Irish Guards were looking for.

Fortunately for Daniel, a sergeant major had been passing the gate at that time and had interceded on his behalf, saying that this poor specimen had exactly the kind of spirit the Irish Guards sought. Even though the SM didn't believe Elliot's claim to being seventeen years young he enrolled him immediately. Daniel Elliot did the sergeant major proud and impressed everybody with his honestly, natural ability and enthusiasm for hard work.

Three years and many letters later, Daniel Elliot returned to the orphanage in Antrim to claim young Lila as his wife. They lived happily in Dublin from 1942 to 1967 when Elliot was decommissioned. He moved to London, too young to die and too old to change. He became a commissionaire at various buildings around London until 1979, when he retired for the first of many times.

At the end of the seventies the Elliots had a comfortable little nest egg and their own (unmortgaged) London house. This was the house ann rea rented a room in when she first came to London in 1981. The Elliots also had a small cottage in Climping. Climping, as ann rea was now discovering, was on a small undeveloped part of the south coast between vibrant Brighton and vulgar Bognor Regis. Their cottage, number 3 Ryelane Cottages, was a two-minute walk from the stony beach. The very beach ann rea was walking on last evening at near enough the same time John B. Stone was being battered to death in Camden Town.

She was still high from the relief of escaping London, this relief was somewhat tempered by how poorly Elliot was looking. This saddened ann rea immensely, not least because Daniel Elliot and Lila had always treated her, she thought, like the daughter they never had and she had grown genuinely attached to them.

'You know,' Daniel said weakly the previous evening, 'You think it's going to last forever, all of this, don't you? You don't think it's ever going to end. Yes, you can see your body fail you, and how the paunch is coming and the hair is going. But inside my mind I'm still having conversations with myself the way I did when I was eleven years old.'

'Of course you're going to be around for ever, you old warhorse, you're going to outlast all of us,' ann rea had enthused.

'You're so kind, you've always been good to Lila and me. Why couldn't she have been as good to us as you were? I hope that policeman is taking good care of you, he'd better had or he'll answer to me. He's a Northerner isn't he?'

'Yes, he's from Portrush.'

'Ah, you'll be okay then, he's a good Derryman, they'll never let you down.'

'I don't know, Daniel,' ann rea cut in. She wasn't sure she was happy to go along with the thing of Kennedy taking good care of her, about anyone taking good care of her come to that. Hadn't she been taking great care of herself all these years? She certainly wasn't going to creep under some man's wing. 'I mean I know he won't let me down,' she went on, 'I know he's a good man and all that but I'm not sure he's the… I'm not sure I want him not to let me down. You know, if he let me down I'd have an excuse not to feel bad about how I'm feeling.'

'Why? How are you feeling?' the old man inquired, seemingly happily to withdraw himself from the spotlight.

They were in his bedroom. A bedroom littered lovingly with the memories of his wife and their rich life together. Daniel now looked tiny in the bed he had once dominated. ann rea felt quite heartened that Daniel had been happy to leave the bedroom styled as it had been by the femine touch of Lila. As she leaned him forward to puff up the pillows behind him she thought, here I am down here to comfort him and now he's turning the tables on me and he's comforting me. Guilty though she felt about it, she wanted to talk to him about this. She desperately needed to talk to someone about all these bad feelings and for sure there was no one excepting Daniel whom she felt comfortable talking to about all this stuff.

'Well,' she continued as she sat in the easy (very) chair beside his bed. ann rea was sipping red wine and Daniel was enjoying a pint (ann rea had fetched one from the Black Horse pub next door as she returned from her walk on the beach), 'It's just that it feels like a trap. Like there we are together and I want to know am I doing it because I love this kind considerate man, or am I doing it because I don't want to end up alone and if I don't take him now someone else will take him from me for sure, or am I being hesitant because I think, 'No this isn't love – there is someone out there waiting for me whom I will love and will love me,' you know? And I don't want any Tom, Dick or Hari Krishna and it might even be Kennedy, it's just that I don't know and if I don't know is that some kind of sign for me?'

'Well, lass, all easy questions, but sadly you are the only one who will have the real answers. I only know that I can tell you that I knew Lila was for me the first time I set eyes on her and we had to wait for four and a half years to be together. A couple of kisses and lots of letters and that was it, no hanky panky till we were married.'

'Yes, Daniel. Things were different then,' ann rea replied feeling tears starting to rise from somewhere deep within her.

'Yes, darned right they were different then. And have you ever thought that this just might be part of the problem today. Look: two things. None of us had se... were intimate – I believe that's how you refer to it these days – with each other until we were married. And we found out if we liked each other during our courting days. The courting time was long, sometimes years, and always painful, particularly for the man when he had to walk home after a date. So by the time we were wed and tasted the ultimate pleasure we were sure, for we had to be sure. Do you know why we had to be sure?'

ann rea knew it was a rhetorical question so she didn't upset his flow.

'I'll tell you why we had to be sure. We had to be sure because marriage was marriage and a commitment for life. Separating was never an option, never a consideration. We had to deal with each other. If it's not broke don't fix it, which is exactly what you appear to be doing at the minute. Equally if it is broke then fix it. There's always a way to fix it. Oh, I'd loved to have been a carpenter; carpenters can fix absolutely everything.'

'But it's not as simple as that, Daniel,' ann rea complained, not altogether sure about her friend's new tangent.

'Oh but there's where you're wrong. Of course it's as simple as that. Be sure, and once you are sure, know that you can take on anything together. I mean for heaven's sake I hear stories and read in the papers about everybody, including royalty, sleeping around and sleeping together, sometimes even on the first date. What on earth do you know about each other on the first date. I mean a man and a woman seeing each other's naked body for the first time, that's such a beautiful spiritual thing and shouldn't be wasted on a flippant encounter. I knew I wanted to be with Lila from the first minute I saw her. Now perhaps that could be described as infatuation, because I didn't know her at all when I first saw her. But I got to know her and I did like her as a person and as a friend and I loved her and that was it, we were set for life.' Daniel paused for another sip of beer using his grey moustache as a filter, leaving some of the white foam stuck there, froth he would lick off after he had swallowed, creating a sweet aftertaste to compliment the bitterness of the beer.

ann rea was about to say something, anything, to take the conversation away from herself and Kennedy, when Elliot swallowed, licked his lips, smiled and continued:

'Now lass, my fear is this; you might, with your doubts, take a bit of the romance out of your relationship. When you feel you know what's happening it's so much more enjoyable. But now you are having doubts, even though your doubts may eventually turn out to be unfounded or ungrounded, but you will still have done some damage to the relationship. Mind you that's not a major problem. If the relationship is solid you will make your way through these troubled waters. But just questioning something, someone, yourself, just for the sake of it, is unhealthy and certainly unwise.'

'That's certainly told me off, then,' ann rea smiled, wanting desperately to let the subject drop. 'You said earlier when we were talking, you said, ^Why couldn't she have been as good as you?'' I'm confused, surely you didn't mean Lila?'

'No. Of course not for heaven's sake, she never had a bad thought in her body. I meant Anna, our daughter Anna, you know her don't you?'

'What?' ann rea said in disbelief, 'Daughter? What daughter? Daniel, I never knew you and Lila had a daughter, come on, we've never ever discussed it before.'

'Oh, sorry, yes. Lila was so embarrassed she didn't like people to know about her, felt we'd failed her, failed her so bad. I just thought you would have known because you lived with us; I thought Lila might have discussed her with you,' Elliot replied.

'No, never, Daniel. What on earth happened? I can't believe you had a daughter. What happened to her? Where's she at? What did you mean when you said you failed her?' ann rea hoped she wasn't gushing too much. This was definitely a bombshell. She thought it was like a movie script, only if it were, the old man would die at this point before he could tell her any more.

'Well,' began the old man, taking in a large breath, 'She was raped when she was young and I think Lila felt we let her down then, felt that Anna never forgave us.'

Elliot started to gaze off into the distance, just above the flowery red-and-white curtains around the small window which proudly showed a cornfield taking seed several months shy of the harvester.

ann rea followed his stare and drank greedily the rich Sussex scene and a little of her wine. The next thing she was aware of was Elliot's gentle snoring. She took his half-empty beer glass and placed it quietly on the bedside cabinet, removed his glasses, stroked back his long grey hair and stared at the man, this man she thought she knew, and wondered what other secrets he might have.

Chapter Eighteen

By the time Kennedy entered the interview room those in attendance were PC Gaul, Hugh Anderson with his brief, the nattily dressed Leslie Russell, and the bowl of fruit placed on the table in front of Anderson and Russell. Kennedy removed his jacket and placed it over the back of his chair opposite them. They were like two teams squaring up on a pitch not over a football but a couple of ripe green Granny Smiths, a banana and a few excuses for oranges.

Kennedy switched on the tape recorder and announced all present and the date and time.

'I would like to put on record at this point,' Leslie Russell began in his usual friendly manner, 'that my client Mr Hugh Anderson came in to the police station of his own accord and is happy to help the police with their inquiries. He will try to answer any and all questions.'

'Noted,' was Kennedy's reply.

Kennedy could not help but admire this specimen of the old school criminal. Crime was their business. Indeed, that had been their motto and when people who got in their way were upset over their not so gentle methods of persuasion, the firm would state 'It's not personal, it's business.' Equally there was the legendary honour amongst their own; everyone on the firm was taken care of, including the relatives of the unfortunates sent down. They behaved and dressed like regular business-men; the only difference was that their business was crime in general and thieving in particular.

Hugh Anderson was solidly built, built like a roadhouse in fact. The trouser creases of his black pinstripe suit were keen enough to sharpen your pencil on. His black shoes, Kennedy could tell, were spit-and-polished every day to the extent that you could see the reflection of the interview room lights in them.

Anderson rose from his seat and he too removed his jacket, revealing a pink shirt, and placed the jacket carefully on the back of his chair. Beneath his arms the shirt was a darker and damper pink. He sat down on the chair, which was taxed to the limit of its support. He smoothed out the ice-blue tie, magnifi-cently done up in a Windsor knot, down the front of his shirt with large, but gentle and unmarked hands.

The criminal's thinning, greying hair was parted with a line so straight you could have lined up the Queen's Guards to it. His brown and challenging eyes were protected by bushy grey brows. His clean-shaven face proudly displayed a nose obvi-ously well versed in the Glasgow handshake, and his celebrated scars testified to long forgotten but frequently discussed skir-mishes. He fixed Kennedy with a stare, his head tilted slightly to the right, and willed the detective to ask his questions.

'Well, Hugh, long time no see.'

Hugh Anderson moved restlessly in his chair, not taking his eyes off Kennedy's. 'You know me, Guv. The firm's gone legit, there's never much need for me to be in the cop shop. Not unless it's like this of course – a respectable member of the community happy to help the police with their inquiries.'

'You're looking really sharp. Very fit,' remarked Kennedy.

'Look, I'm sure we all have other things we could be doing, Inspector, could you please be a chap and get on with the questions?' Russell fidgeted with his clean notebook, pen hovering at the ready to jot down any and all infringements. Anderson, however, was proud of his looks and happy to continue with this line. 'Thanks, yeah, I guess it's the new diet. You eat nothing but fruit before midday, no coffee, no fags, lots of green, a little steak, no fried food. Hey, I've got to look after myself at this stage in my life, I've got a new lady, you see, and I want to stay around for a bit to enjoy her. Know what I mean, Guv?'

At that point Kennedy helped himself to a banana. Anderson averted his gaze from Kennedy and glanced down at the fruit bowl. He reached to it, displaying an expensive-looking gold watch and a simple gold cufflink about the size of a five pence piece with the letters HA engraved on it. As Kennedy concluded his banana peeling exercise – he hated bananas and hoped he wouldn't be forced to eat one – Anderson helped himself to the largest of the apples, slowly polished it on the leg of his trousers and pushed it into his mouth. A third of the apple disappeared behind a fine set of snow white molars untainted by the years.

'Ah, look, you've spilled some apple juice on the cuff of your shirt,' Kennedy said as he rose and handed Anderson a Kleenex (one he'd prepared earlier) from his waistcoat pocket.

'Thank you.' Anderson placed the apple on the table and started to wipe the nonexistent stain under Kennedy's direction.

'No, there, yes there, just by the cufflink.' Kennedy leaned further over the table, 'carelessly' knocking the third-eaten apple to the floor. 'Oh shit. Sorry. I am sorry,' he said with all the sincerity of a hotel receptionist taking a complaint. He went round to Anderson's side of the table, retrieved the apple and carefully placed it in the waste paper basket. 'Listen, help yourself to another one,' he suggested, returning to his seat a contented man.

'No, Guv, it's okay. Look, you've got some questions for me and you know briefs aren't cheap these days.' Anderson smiled in the at his ever ready solicitor. 'Perhaps we should get on with the questions.'

'Yes, certainly,' replied Kennedy, happy to have avoided the banana now also resting in the waste paper basket guarding the precious apple. 'You were in the Spread Eagle around closing time yesterday evening?'

'Yes, as it happens, I was actually.'

'And you were talking to an estate agent, Mr John B. Stone?'

'Was that the little geezer with the funny hair at the bar?'

'Yes.'

'Yeah, I did as it happens, I did talk to him a bit.'

'Well he was murdered last evening. About an hour after you were seen talking to him he was beaten to death.'

'Dead! Beaten to death? Surely not. Are you sure he's dead?'

'Yes, quite sure,' Kennedy quickly replied.

'Excuse me Inspector Kennedy,' said Russell, 'but is there any way my client is a suspect in this murder case? I'd like to go on record and remind you that Mr Anderson came in here of his own free will to help you with your inquiries but certainly not to incriminate himself.' The page in his notebook had its virginity.

'No, it's okay Mr Russell,' said Anderson, 'I've got nothing to hide. He, the geezer in the bar with the funny hair – '

'John B. Stone,' Kennedy interjected.

'If you say so, Guv. Anyway this geezer Stone had heard I was looking for a property to invest some money in. I'm into those kind of deals these days.'

Kennedy shifted in his seat, nodded and said nothing.

'Anyway, he had this little garage the other side of 125 Parkway, and it was in bad nick and he reckoned I could pick it up for about eighty G. He thought if I put another thirty or so into it doing it up I could sell it for about two hundred G. Apparently the property on the other side, the York and Albany pub, had been bought up by a theme restaurant group and when they do it up the garage will be a prime site.'

Anderson and Kennedy continue to stare one another out during this exchange.

'I told him I'd have my people check it out and I'd get back to him. He worked down the other end of Parkway in the Camden Bus Estate Agents. That was it basically: I bought him a drink, a white wine, poofs drink if you ask me, Guv, and we went our separate ways.'

'Did you leave the pub together, or separately?' Kennedy inquired matter-of-fact.

Anderson hesitated for the shortest of beats, which would not have been noticeable had they not been eyeballing each other.

'As it happens, I believe we did leave the pub together. He went up Parkway and I went down.'

'Where did you go after that?'

'I went to a card game up in Islington and then on home from there. I was home around 2.30, I think. I couldn't swear though, it could have been ten minutes either side.'

Kennedy decided to leave it there for now. There was no point in continuing until he had something more to go on. He announced the termination of the interview, said his goodbyes and hung around the interview room until PC Gaul had shown Anderson and his solicitor out of the station.

He then carefully retrieved the apple from the wastepaper basket. Already the exposed fruit was turning brown as the air contaminated it. That was in a matter of minutes; what must the same atmosphere be doing to our bodies in a day, not to mention a lifetime? Kennedy gingerly carried the apple between thumb and forefinger out to Sgt Flynn and asked him to send the evidence to forensic with specific instructions to see if the teeth prints matched those found in the apple discovered at the Fountain of Sorrow, the final resting place of John B. Stone.

Chapter Nineteen

'You're looking like you lost a fiver and found a tenner,' Coles, at the wheel, announced to Irvine as they drove the short distance to the offices of National Properties at the Old School House on Regent's Park Road just across from the (pedestrianised) bridge over the railway at Primrose Hill station.

'Is it that obvious?' Irvine, evidently well pleased with himself, replied.

'Frankly, yes. No need to ask who's got the spilt milk. But should I be asking to whom does the spilt milk belong?'

'Well, it's Bella Forsythe's actually, if you really want to know,' says Irvine, no great deal of prising required.

'Really? What about... I thought you and Rose Butler were stepping out,' said Coles, risking another question into no man's land. She and Irvine usually didn't get into this kind of conversation, but he'd opened it up by volunteering Forsythe's name.

'As eloquent a turn a phrase as my mother would have used,' Irvine replied, 'But sadly, no.' He volunteered no more, and Coles refrained from pushing any further.

She would have liked to pry but she thought better about it. Rose Butler was a true bright burning flame, she believed in true love, Christian values, cannabis (a little), sex (a lot) and Ferrari red lipstick, lots of lipstick. If Irvine had been prepared to offer more, or indeed if Coles had been prepared to pry just a little bit deeper, she would have discovered that James Irvine and Rose Butler had reached the point where they either had to discharge their bowels or arise from the chamber.

They had agreed (reluctantly) to the latter, at least on a trial basis. It had been Irvine's sad experience that when you reach the 'Let's take a break from each other for awhile' point you usually mean 'Let's end this as painlessly as possible.' And so they had, and so they did.

Irvine thought as they drove towards Primrose Hill that he would have relished the opportunity to discuss his romantic situation. He had recently been considering it a hell of a lot himself in private and he had come to the conclusion that he had a character flaw. The flaw was no matter how much he liked his (romantic) partner he always reached the stage where he found himself looking for the hit of the excitement of a new playmate. He hated himself for it and he had so far avoided cheating on his lover. But eventually his eye would wander, and then it would be great: the whole chase ritual, the romancing, the wining and dining, the lovemaking and then, as sure as New Year's Day follows Big Ben's chimes, the distraction.

'So is this the first date?'

'No, the second,' sighed Irvine as he was drawn away from his reflections and regrets.

'God, two already. You kept that quiet.' Coles smiled, happy that Irvine was for the first time opening up to her.

'Well, me ma said never kiss on the first date, so I always start with the second,' Irvine laughed, avoiding further revelations as they were pulling into a gift of a parking space opposite the Boys' School on Regent's Park Road in Primrose Hill Village. Within two and a half minutes they were sitting in the extremely modern offices of Mr National Properties himself, Kevin Burroughs, drinking coffee. Irvine, white with one sugar, and Coles, black no sugar, watched in amusement as the wagons began to circle before their very eyes.

Burroughs was not what either had been expecting. He was friendly, very friendly in fact. He dressed well: designer denim jeans, mustard Doc Marten boots with protected toecaps (Irvine guessed) and a denim shirt, all buttons opened revealing a blinding white T-shirt. He had long (ish) blonde (ish) hair parted unevenly in the middle, the beginning of the receding hairline visible through the drape-like arrangement of hair behind the ears. Burroughs had a weatherbeaten but plain face distinguished only by his dark eyebrows.

The office had plans of his various current development projects covering the walls. The only distraction was a twenty by thirty (inch) poster of the waif-like Kate Moss. Behind his door hung two yellow hard hats.

'We understand you did some business with Mr John B. Stone of the Camden Bus Estate Agency?' Coles opened the bidding with a single club.

'Yes, love. I've heard from some of my mates that he went and got himself topped,' Kevin Burroughs replied with a hint of Brum drawl.

'When did you last see him?' Irvine offered two spades. A bit of digging was going to be necessary.

'Let's see. Yesterday I guess. The days pass so quick, don't they? Sometimes it's hard to place people to the days. Yes, it was yesterday. He dropped in here after lunch time. Yeah that's it, he was in the area, he had a bunch of people at the Queens and he came around to see me afterwards.' Burroughs spoke in fits and starts like a car with its choke out too long trying to get up to speed.

'What time would that have been?' asked Coles.

'About two-thirty, give or take.'

'How did he seem?' Coles continued.

'Fine, I mean fine, same as usual. There wasn't much to him, little chap, but he seemed fine to me.'

'He didn't seem worried or anything?' Coles again.

'I mean he didn't seem unduly concerned.' Burroughs shrugged his shoulders. 'But it's like you don't exactly pay that much attention. I mean if I had known it was going to be the last time I saw him I would obviously have looked at him differently. To be perfectly honest I wasn't particularly interested in how he felt, or looked for that matter.' The Birmingham drone was less concealed now.

'Oh?' nudged Irvine.

'Yeah, well he was bringing me some bad news,' Burroughs replied, rationing his words.

'Which was?' Coles uncrossed and crossed her legs.

'We'd done a deal? Like on a property?' His accent had a habit of making some statements sound like questions, American-style. 'The large one out the back, actually. Part of it used to be the local mission house, probably a toilet or something, and some of the local tossers got together and tried to block planning permission. Well, they won first time around, then we appealed and got it by the council, and then they appealed and he'd come to tell me that he'd heard we were going to lose the appeal. He was tipping me to put the property on the market quickly, before judgement was announced.'

'Were you annoyed at him over this?' Irvine raised the bid to a three diamonds.

'For heaven's sake, no.' Burroughs laughed nervously. 'What? Do you mean did I top him? Top him just because a deal went pearshaped? No, not at all. I blame the local authorities. Look, if I lived around here, I mean it's beautiful around here isn't it? Well I wouldn't want any major development going on in my backyard. But you get the feeling the council don't give a toss about the people around here, if anything they even resent the residents, so they don't go out of their way to discourage people like myself. And so, you know, if there's a few bob to be made I might as well be making it as someone else.'

The developer let his eyes wander to the plans on the wall to his right and maybe even allowed himself to think, just for a few moments, on the money he was losing. He continued to address the two police officers.

'No, I think all our lives would be easier, much easier, if the councils would do what they are meant to do and protect the interests of, and listen to, the locals. Instead they seem to spend most of their time battling with each other.' And Kevin stopped talking. Maybe he'd had a revolutionary thought or revelation or maybe he'd said all he needed to say on the matter and was awaiting the next question.

Neither Irvine nor Coles had the next question lined up and each left it to the other, resulting in a silence which Burroughs felt compelled to fill.

'No, of course I didn't feel bad about John Boy and top him just because of one bad deal. I mean on our slate he's still very high in the black, his standing here is good, or should I say was good. And you know, on the place out the back, who knows how it's going to turn out? I can afford to sit on it and see what happens. Maybe even let it get run down a bit over the next few years until it becomes an eyesore and then cop a few bob from the council or English Heritage to restore it to its former glory and sell it on. No, don't worry about me, a deal's never over until the fat lady stops sinking in the cement.'

Irvine saw fat ladies sinking to the bottom of cement foundations and wondered if that was the metaphor this property developer wanted to leave the local police with.

'Besides which, we had a couple of other sweet deals about to go down,' Burroughs added as an afterthought.

'And what will happen to those?' Irvine inquired.

'Oh, I imagine Billy Boatend will finalise them for me now. Billy Boatend, what a name for an estate agent!' Burroughs laughed.

'Do you know of anyone who would wish to harm John B. Stone, sir?' Coles asked, deciding it was time to shift direction.

'No, not really. I mean in the area he's in, it sometimes borders on… well, you don't really know who you're dealing with, do you? Maybe he pissed somebody off. I don't know. He was a bit of a loner really, wasn't he?'

'Apparently,' was all Irvine would offer in reply.

'Did you ever mix with him socially?' the WPC asked, feeling they were about to run into a wall. She also knew that there was more information to pick up. Kennedy was always telling them that the information is always out there waiting for you to find it, all you had to know was where to look and what questions to ask.

'A couple of times yeah, but not a lot. Look, my vice is the grape, I'm not into the chemical stuff, if you know what I mean, and well, our two cultures didn't really mix well.'

'I see,' the WPC replied, hoping that she did see. She shrugged at Irvine while Burroughs' eyes were elsewhere. Irvine nodded and said, 'Well that seems to be it for now, sir. We may need to question you further but before we leave could you tell us what you were doing last night between the hours of eleven-thirty and one-thirty?' It was a four clubs bid but Irvine wasn't really sure it was strong enough bid to win the hand.

'What? You still think that I could -'

'No, we just have to eliminate you from our inquiries, and if we know for definite you were elsewhere yesterday evening we do not have to consider you further.' It was time to see Burroughs' hand.

'Well, you see that's the thing, isn't it? I don't really have an alibi for last night. I was here till about ten o'clock by myself costing a new project. By the time I finished that, I was so cream crackered I went straight home, made myself some tea and toast, watched TV for about ten minutes and then went to bed.'

The WPC replaced a few wisps which were threatening to escape the clips which restrained her beautiful natural blonde hair, giving her more of the main mam look which she liked to cultivate for the force rather than the wild child she could just as easily have played. She was thinking, Wow he's a decent enough looking chap, dresses well, takes care of himself, in good shape, obviously well off, and he's going to bed at ten-thirty by himself with tea and toast and a bit of telly. Why do all these people work so hard if that's all the life their money is going to give them? Or is he saving for his retirement when he'll have no energy, and even less inclination, to spending money and partying?

'What exactly was on TV last night, that you saw?' Irvine asked.

'Oh, nothing really. I did a bit of channel surfing; there was some music, an American movie, some political debate, a wildlife thing, two football matches and Channel 5 was crap.'

'Just your average night on TV then, eh?' Irvine smiled as he and the WPC placed their empty cups on Burroughs' desk. They then said their goodbyes and departed the office.

'We'll see he's entered in the competition, then?' Coles smiled as they got in the car.

'What competition is that then?' Irvine replied.

'The one to see who can be richest corpse in the graveyard,' was Coles' reply as they headed back to North Bridge House.

Chapter Twenty

Late in the day Kennedy noticed amongst his messages one which said 'area rang'. For a split second he wondered which area had rung him and who from that area. But when he spotted the space between the 'a' and the 'r' he realised ann rea had rung him and left no number.

Kennedy knew she was happy to use the trip to see Daniel Elliot to put a bit of space between them. He didn't know why he felt things were going 'okay' between them. But then perhaps 'okay' was a bad, if not terrible, word to describe a relationship between two people. He really was becoming fed up with all this 'in between' period which seemed to be continuously going on with them. For heaven's sake, he had realised the moment he had set eyes on ann rea, at Heathrow, that he wanted to be with her for the rest of his life. Scary, perhaps, but then sometimes the truth is.

But perhaps that last statement is a bit naive. Kennedy certainly knew that he wanted to be with her above all else and to enjoy each other's company in a commitment to each other. The commitment being (for his part) 'I want us to be together,' the commitment being, 'You can count on me,' the commitment being, 'I care for you and I will not, knowingly, hurt you.'

Now to Kennedy all of the above seemed easy. He knew and could express his feelings. He was confident enough to trust them. But equally he knew that ann rea was forever in this (in his opinion) self-made turmoil of 'Is he the right one?' or 'Do I really love him?' not to mention 'What if I'm wrong?' So because of all this baggage their relationship was ultimately suffering. Kennedy wondered if ann rea had already decided that it was over but because she liked him so much, she didn't want to hurt him. Her quandary, to Kennedy's mind, made her steal numerous glares at Kennedy to see how he was really doing. When he caught her doing this it was so infuriating – and she was as successful at hiding it as someone trying to retrieve wind passed in a socially embarrassing situation. Her thoughts were her own, they were honest, he hoped, but they certainly weren't bad.

Come on, he was a grown man, it wasn't his first romance. Yes, perhaps he had hoped it was going to be his last, but if it was going to end it was going to end and the healthy thing to do was to admit it was over, get over it and get on with life.

Having said that, he couldn't really see life without ann rea; they now had become a couple in the true sense of the word. Perhaps that's what she was reacting against; maybe she didn't really want to be part of a couple. If she were to go what would he do? Kennedy certainly hoped he wouldn't mope around after her thinking of all the good times they had had together, but come to think of it there certainly weren't many, if any, bad times to dwell on.

Kennedy now asked himself, as he walked home over his much loved Primrose Hill, what he would do if they were no longer a couple. Would he try and date someone else immediately to get over ann rea? He thought not. The last time he'd dated (before ann rea) was five years ago and, as with ann rea, it wasn't like he'd scored on a night out on the pull with a bunch of blokes behaving laddishly. Kennedy had never been 'out on the pull' in his life; he just wouldn't know what to do.

Instead of turning right at Magpie Corner and heading towards the Queens and his house he continued to the top of Primrose Hill. Magpie Corner was the name Kennedy gave to the fork, just by Andy 'Cat' Collins' (dog lover and friend of the people of Primrose Hill, 1946-1996) chair, the morning he spied thirteen magpies hovering around. He knew the nursery rhyme up to 'six for a wish' and when he couldn't go any further he doubled it up to twelve for two kisses but then found himself left with a balance of 'one for sorrow.' He wasn't yet ready to go home. If he were to be alone tonight then he wanted to spend some of the time wandering around Primrose Hill, a ramble he never tired of. As he walked up the hill the sun was going down, nearly gone and it looked quite spooky. There was an orange haze backlighting the hill and it picked up the silhouettes of fifteen or so people wandering aimlessly around the crown. It caught the trees in a similiar manner and made the hill look more like a scene from a Hitchcock movie than sunset on London's most beautiful park.

He considered whom he could ask out now he was (mentally) single and enjoying his newfound freedom. Let's see... there was Anne Coles. Kennedy found her incredibly attractive and very sharp, intelligent and funny, in her own way. He'd only once seen her with her hair down and in civvies and she had looked stunning; there was no other word for it. Kennedy quickly, perhaps sadly, dismissed the WPC for professional reasons. The next, and final, one on his shortlist was Bella Forysthe. Still a bit of a professional dilemma, but less so than Coles because although they occasionally (more recently) worked together they were in different departments.

Dr Forysthe was totally different to the WPC. Darker in both looks and mood, and probably a lot more difficult to get to know. But then again wasn't Irvine getting ready to beat a path to her door? As he reached the crown of the hill and became a silhouette, Kennedy's mind wandered to his last girlfriend, the one before ann rea. She was a photographer called Georgie Conway. They'd had a good time, a great time, but they weren't in love, neither with either, so by the time of the inevitable parting, although it was very painful, they had committed to staying friends. This they duly did following a period of cooling down.

Kennedy completed the triangle from Magpie Corner by walking down the hill and exiting through the gate at the corner of Regent's Park Road and Primrose Hill Road. He crossed the road and turned into Rothwell Street, where he lived behind a deep blue front door at number 16. As he let himself in he found himself thinking about James Irvine and Rose Butler. He didn't know Irvine well enough to ask him what happened, but it had been his considered opinion that James and Rose were made for each other. But then perhaps people had been thinking the same thing about himself and ann rea.

'God, why is it so hard?' he said out loud as he climbed the stairs. No one was there to hear him and no one did, except maybe the ghosts of his 105 year-old house. As he reached the first landing the telephone rang and he jumped the remaining stairs in two's, nipped sharpish into his study and wrestled the handset from its day-long slumber.

'Hi.'

'Hi, Kennedy!'

'ann rea, hey it's you. How are you doing?'

'Fine, listen I tried to get you earlier.'

'I know. I got the message.' He hoped he was sounding friendly and his mood would not be obvious.

'Hey, I'm missing you.' ann rea's voice sounded somewhat feeble. That's encouraging, he thought as he said, 'I'm missing you too.'

'I think they're on a Wembley soon,' she replied, using Kennedy's once-amusing line.

'What? Oh yes, of course.' He was happy to see it was still *Life with the Lyons* as usual. 'How's Mr Elliot?'

'Oh. Bad really.'

'Aha,' was all he could mutter.

'It's sad really. It's not so much his poor health, it's just that he seems to have lost the will to live.'

By this point Kennedy had his coat off and was sitting in his favourite chair to the side of and facing away from his American Arts and Crafts desk. He was leaning back in his chair drinking in her voice. Even though it was now sad he still loved the sound of her voice.

'It must be really terrible to have your love taken from you and be forced to live the rest of your life without them,' she said.

Kennedy could see this, see it big time in fact, but decided it might be just a little bit too selfish to get into it at this point, so he held his counsel.

'It's so sad, Christy. Sad to see this once great man literally waiting to die.'

'Have you been able to give him much comfort?'

'We've been talking a lot. Sometimes he just rambles but... Oh yes, you'll never guess what? Remember I used to think Daniel and Lila treated me so well because I was the daughter they never had?'

'Yes.'

'Well, they had one.'

'What?'

'Yes, they had a daughter. He started talking about her earlier, just before he dozed off. He was going on about how she never treated them properly and how maybe it had been their own fault because they hadn't taken proper care of her after she was raped.'

'Sorry?'

'Yes, apparently they had a daughter, she was raped, she left them shortly thereafter and totally disowned them.'

'Incredible!' Kennedy breathed into his mouthpiece.

'I couldn't find out any more about it because he fell asleep at that point. God, I can't believe how sad and hard a life Daniel has had.'

'You're not kidding,' Kennedy sympathised.

'How are you doing, Kennedy? Oh, and what's been happening to Pauley Valentini?'

'Fine, and he's doing good too. People are offering him record deals left right and centre. I'm not sure if they're going to be much good or if he's going to be able to enjoy the money. I'm convinced he is going to spend the rest of his life playing to a captive audience, as it were, maybe even performing for them.'

'Gross, Kennedy. But I'm sure the record companies will not be worrying too much about his welfare. They'll be more concerned about their own coffers. Listen, Christy, I don't want to run up his phone bill too much, I'd better be going soon,' ann rea sighed.

'Yeah, I suppose so. I miss you, though.'

'Kennedy, it's only been a day since I left.'

'Yes, I know, but it's been three since we last…'

'Oh, Kennedy,' ann rea laughed, 'I can't believe you, why don't you go to sleep and have a Lloyds?'

Now it was Kennedy's turn to laugh. 'Don't you mean have a Lloyds and then go to sleep?'

Either way, Kennedy concluded the teleconversation a little more contented than he started it.

Chapter Twenty-One

As one romance appeared to be ending, another was showing signs of a promising beginning. Kennedy could very well be wrong if he felt his relationship with ann rea was over. Equally, James Irvine could be wrong in supposing that he and Bella Forysthe had a future. Irvine recalled Kennedy telling various members of his teams, on the odd occasion he had overheard them 'wishing' for something to turn up on a case: 'Wish in one hand, pee in the other and see which one fills first.'

Mind you, with the way the woman looked the minute she walked into the Engineer, Irvine would have given up any wishes for a long-term future for the guarantee of a short-term one, even as short-term as in one night. She was simply sensational. This was the first time Irvine had seen her with her hair down: tonight it flowed. She was also wearing more make-up than she did at work. She was dressed in figure-hugging black slacks, waist-length black leather jacket and an orange shirt. Irvine found it hard to accept that this stunning woman would want to spend her time fiddling about in dead bodies.

Irvine doubted if the Engineer, in its many and varied incarnations, had ever witnessed a vision as engaging as this. He didn't know whether to shake her hand, or what. She went for 'or what' by gently squeezing his elbow and kissing the air beside his cheek, rather than smudge it with her rich orange lipstick. As she did so he caught her scent. It was hypnotic.

Irvine didn't exactly consider himself to be a ladies' man, neither did he think himself a failure at that particular sport. But he was certain that in this case he was out of his depth. The Scots, like the Irish, have a good way of hiding this: they give you a big warm smile and say, 'What's your poison?'

'Oh, I'll have whatever you are having,' Bella smiled.

They found a quiet corner and sat down with two Glenfiddichs. She had already lit up a long menthol ciggy and offered Irvine one.

'No thanks. Never touch them, although I do dream about someday in my old age smoking a pipe, like my dad did.'

'You don't mind if I do?'

'Heavens, no!' Irvine replied. The 'heavens' was pure Sean Connery, and he added, again in his best Connery, 'Anyway, bottoms up.'

They touched glasses, and whereas Irvine then sipped about a quarter of his ration, Bella knocked hers back in one swig.

'Mmm, I needed that. Okay, my round. That was nice, what was it?' she said, admiring her empty glass.

In precisely sixty-five seconds she had returned bearing for him a gift of a double. She rescued the remainder of her cough stick from the ashtray, flicked off the dead ash and took an incredibly long drag. 'It's great here, very buzzy. I've never been here before.'

'Yeah, I like it. DI Kennedy and his lady ann rea come here a lot. They also do great food. Maybe we should see if we can get a table,' Irvine suggested, thinking that they were going to need some solids to soak up the Glenfiddich.

'Perhaps,' she replied, taking one last, long, drag and stubbing out the cigarette. 'Let's see how we feel after a while. So, you're from Scotland. How long have you been in London?'

'About eight years. When I made DS I asked for a transfer, I felt the promotional prospects would be better. And yourself, where are you from, I can't quite place the accent.'

'I'm actually from around here originally,' she laughed, 'But I worked in the midlands for several years until about nine months ago. I needed a break and I left London after college and travelled around a bit. Spent quite a time in Bristol, I liked it down there, the people are really nice. Anyway, my work took me to the midlands, and when I'd picked up some more qualifications I came back to London to work with Dr Taylor. Hopefully I'll get his job when he retires.'

'If he ever does. Taylor's as strong as a fox, an elephant or whatever doctors are as strong as.'

'Penicillin?' said the doctor, and they both laughed.

'So what is it like working for DI Kennedy?' she said. 'He

seems a bit of a dark horse.'

'He's great, really. He just loves the art of detection and spends a lot of his time teaching us about it. He can go off on these amazing tangents, but has an incredible ability to back-track, pick up new information, drop what he doesn't need and head off in a completely different direction. He's inspiring to work with. He encourages us to get stuck into a case and gives us our head when we come up with a promising lead. And he always gives us credit when credit is due.'

'How are you getting on with the John Stone case?' Bella inquired as she helped herself to another large swig of the malt.

'We've had a couple of lucky breaks. I don't think we're going to be too long putting this one to bed.'

'Yes, it seems pretty straightforward, doesn't it? Some thug beat him to death and left loads of clues – they're not the clever-est of people, are they? He's probably just waiting around for you to pick him up. I say 'he' – by the marks on the body it's unlikely any member of the gentler sex could have attacked someone with such force.' Irvine was convinced she flashed her long dark eyelashes as she concluded this sentence.

'Yes, probably,' he said, 'though I'm not sure I'd like to have a run-in with the Fatima Whitbreads of this world, if you know what I mean. But you're probably spot on. Actually I'm more puzzled by the other one.'

'What other one?'

'You know, the one you examined yesterday, Neil Burton.'

'Oh, that one. There's nothing mysterious about that one. Just a case of mad dog attack. Simple: arteries severed by extremely sharp and very strong teeth.'

'Yes, I know it appears that way,' mulled Irvine, 'but there's some funny business going on.'

'Like what?'

'Well, for instance, do you realise what's engraved on the plaque at the end of that bridge?' he posed, happy her attention to the Glenfiddich had been temporarily diverted.

'No, what?' she asked as she disappointed him by finishing off her drink.

'A dog! A very large dog! And guess what the dog is doing?'

'I'll buy it,' she said. 'What is this very large dog doing?'

'Attacking somebody, looks like a tramp, a dosser, and it looks like the dog is going straight for the throat. Now don't you find that to be just a wee bit too much of a coincidence?'

'No, not at all. Amusing though, don't you think?' She laughed and rolled the empty glass around in a semi-circle using her thumb and forefinger.

'Same again?' Irvine felt compelled to ask.

Chapter Twenty-Two

DS James Irvine, Superintendent Thomas Castle and DI Christy Kennedy all appeared to be wandering around North Bridge House aimlessly at just after eight o'clock on this the third day (excluding Sunday) of the third tale. Appearances could be, and in this case were, deceptive. The Super was looking for Kennedy for an update on the body found beneath the fountain. He still had not got his brain around the case title, Fountain of Sorrow, unlike everyone else in the police station.

Kennedy's mind was not, surprise surprise, on ann rea, although he had suffered quite a sleepless night. The only conclusion he had reached was, 'whatever will be, will be.' No, his mind was on the mystery surrounding the life of John B. Stone. He was seeking out Irvine to see what he and Coles had learned from their interview with Kevin Burroughs.

Irvine's mission was to get as much black coffee down his throat as possible before the nine o'clock brief. Bella Forysthe had been a revelation to him. They had got on well, very well. Perhaps that should be qualified with, as well as one could get on with someone slipping, falling rather, into the abyss of a drunken stupor. Unlike most people Irvine knew, the more Bella Forsythe drunk, the more she drank. And the more she drank the more energy and vitality she seemed to gain.

At first, thinking he might be on a bit of a promise, he had matched her drink for drink, but by about ten-thirty, after much of whisky and no possibility of food, he switched, first to lager and finally to mineral water when he eventually realised that a) this woman was not going to be in a state for physical activity of any kind, at least any kind that she would remember, and taking advantage was not his style or desire; and b) as midnight fast approached he began to worry that this cloud of fuzz forming rapidly in and around his head like an afro hairstyle à la Jimi Hendrix, would not evaporate within twenty-four hours let alone the seven and a half which remained before he had to show up at North Bridge House with a clear head and a sharp brain.

After encountering Kennedy by the front desk, the Superintendent invited himself to the DI's nine o'clock brief.

'No point of you going through all this stuff twice, old son,' said Castle. 'I'll sit at the back and you won't even notice I'm there.' And he left Kennedy and Flynn together as the Desk Sergeant tried to track Irvine down.

'He's by the coffee machine, apparently,' Flynn advised Kennedy in his soft southern (Irish) tones. 'It appears he's trying to find a way of lying under its tap and swimming upstream. Apparently he's been quoting Oscar Wilde to anyone who'll listen.'

'Really?' Despite his urgency Kennedy afforded himself a wry smile.

'Yes, well he does that a bit, you know, after a night of… recreation.' Flynn brushed his hand back over his head, straightening the memory of some hair, once brown and thick, now white and thinning.

'Aha.'

'I believe one of his favourites is ^Love is about deceit: we start off deceiving ourselves and we end up deceiving our lovers."'

Kennedy smiled, not one of been-there-done-that, for he hadn't. A glass or three of wine was his maximum and even then it might be only every other week or maybe once a week at a push. He craved the state of clear-headedness and he couldn't (ever) work out why people wanted to blemish this mood. 'Poor

Irvine,' he said quietly to no one in particular.

Poor Irvine had his wits about him enough to give Kennedy a concise recall of the Kevin Burroughs conversation. Forty minutes – and three more cups of coffee for Irvine, two cups of tea and four fingers of shortbread for Kennedy – later, they all arrived in the conference room.

The conference room, unlike the rest of the building, was a sanctuary of a space polluted by neither posters, newsletters, want-ads, union reports, dirty tea cups, ashtrays, files, boxes, desks, various sizes and colours of chairs, noise, nor natural light; it was in fact the mirror image of the canteen, only at the northern end of the basement. A simple brown carpet covered the floor. The walls and ceiling were painted white and Castle, unable to raise a budget for one large central table, had placed together ten eight foot by four metal tables. He had the adjoining legs fixed together firmly using the plastic restrainers now used sometimes instead of handcuffs. Around this creation were placed twenty-four matching armless chairs. On the wall towards the natural (northern) head of the table was a painting of a well remembered Camden Police Chief, Commander P. R. Fenn.

'Okay, let's see exactly where we are on this one,' shouted Kennedy above the hum created by those present, who included Superintendent Castle, DS Irvine, WPC Coles, Dr Forsythe (looking as fresh as a daisy and as alert as a Camden Market trader), PC Allaway, PC Gaul, WPC Franklin, PC Tony Essex and a few other DSs and PCs. There was no real need for Forsythe to be present, but Kennedy traditionally invited Dr Taylor to these briefings, so he was happy for the man's stand-in to be present. There was always the chance of a useful lead from this source.

'It seems to me that what we know is that two nights ago John B. Stone spent several hours drinking in the Spread Eagle.' At the word 'drinking' Irvine and Forsythe stole a glance at each other and exchanged smiles.

'Arnold Cooper, his boss; June Oddie and William Boatend, his work colleagues, were with him and left him, apparently in that order. He then met up with Hugh Anderson.' Kennedy's delivery was interrupted at this point by a grunt from Castle at the opposite end of the table, a grunt which implied, 'Oh him, if he's involved that's the case solved then, I can leave the tidying up to the team.' Kennedy and Castle's eyes met and Castle shrugged an apology.

'The last time Stone was seen he was drinking at the bar of the Spread Eagle with Anderson. Anderson claims Stone was making a property pitch to him. He further claims that as they left the Spread Eagle he went down Parkway while Stone went up it towards Regent's Park.' Kennedy paused to check his notes.

'Now Stone apparently didn't make it very far because he was met by person or persons unknown who gave him a serious beating, and as a result of injuries caused by this beating John B. Stone died around about thirty minutes past midnight. For a case so new there is no shortage of suspects.'

'What?' said Castle, 'You mean as well as that thug Anderson? I always said we should have locked him away in the sixties and thrown away the key. We tried, I'll tell you we tried. Bloody do-gooding meddlers with all their ^He's no longer a menace to society, he's paid the price for his crime,'' blah, blah, bleeding blah.' Castle's heated commentary raised smiles from several quarters.

Kennedy waited until he was sure Castle had completed his diatribe. 'Yes, sir. As well as Hugh Anderson we have, let's see:

'One, William Boatend, business colleague who stood to gain Stone's cash business in his absence.

'Two, Kevin Burroughs, from Northern Properties. We still have to find out more about the Primrose Hill deal that went pearshaped.

'Three, Stone's younger brother Brian. There is mega bad blood in the family. None of them, the two brothers and a sister, were talking to John B. at the time of his death but most of the hate would seem to lie between John B. and the older brother. However, we'll come to that shortly. Brian Stone seemed totally unperturbed at the loss of his brother and he gave a false alibi for the time of death. Which brings us to

'Four, the older brother, Stephen, whom I'm going to see

after we finish here. Apparently he was away somewhere yesterday but is due in his office this morning. From what we can gather there was a bit of competition between John B. and Stephen for the woman who eventually became Stephen's wife. Then there was this incident, people keep talking about it, at their mother's funeral. And finally,

'Five: person or persons unknown.'

'And Hugh Anderson,' added Castle.

'And Hugh Anderson.'

'But surely if Anderson is involved it would be on behalf of someone else, wouldn't it?' WPC Coles asked carefully.

'Good point!' Irvine said, testing his voice.

Kennedy took up Coles' theme and developed it. 'In which case he would be acting on behalf of any one of the people on our suspect list. Which means the motive is going to be extremely important. A true professional criminal is not going to give up a name to us, is he?'

'Listen, another question I have for you.' Castle took a pencil from his top pocket and twiddled it around as he spoke. 'This Neil Burton chap who was found the previous night on the other side of the bridge from John B. Stone – have you thought about the possibility of that being murder as well?'

'Not possible,' said Forsythe. 'Mr Burton definitely died as a result of his arteries being severed by the teeth of a dog.' She was sitting on the same side of the table as Irvine, something both of them were happy about.

'Yes, yes,' said Castle, 'I know about that, but what if our madman, Hugh Anderson, our one man bleeding Camden Town crime wave, what if he had a rotweiler, or whatever, and he set the animal on Burton? That could be the connection between Burton and Stone. I think that's a line of investigation I'd like to see you follow.' So much for the Super's 'you won't even know that I'm there' promise.

'Yep, good point,' a bemused Kennedy replied, because it was indeed, and furthermore it was one Kennedy hadn't even considered.

The flow of conversation was interrupted with a knock on the door and Sergeant Flynn let himself into the conference room, announcing his arrival with a polite, 'This just came through, sir.' He made his way across the room to Kennedy, 'And Forensic said you should be given the information as soon as possible.'

Kennedy unfolded the crisp piece of white paper, the sound was not unlike wind rustling through leaves – very loudly in Irvine's ears.

The former native of Portrush smiled as he read aloud: 'The teeth marks in the apple found close to the body of John B. Stone have been positively identified as the teeth marks of one Mr Hugh Anderson.

A certain Superintendent beamed from ear to ear.

Before dismissing everyone Kennedy gave instructions as to the activities he wanted his team to undertake during the next few hours. He wanted more information on the property deals Camden Bus Estate Agents were involved in, particularly the ones worked on by John B. Stone on behalf of Northern Properties. He required more information on Northern Properties. And a check through the files to see exactly what Hugh Anderson had been up to for the past ten years. He also wanted more background information on John B. Stone.

'And check if Anderson has a dog,' Castle ordered.

'Yes, sir,' Kennedy agreed.

'If he does have a dog, do you think the new pathologist – what's her name?' Castle inquired after the briefing had broken up and he and Kennedy were walking back to their offices.

'Bella Forsythe, sir.'

'Yes, Forsythe – do you think she could match Anderson's dog to the marks made on Burton's body?'

'If he has a dog, sir. No, I doubt it; the body was in too bad a shape. I'm convinced no such identification could be made,' Kennedy replied firmly.

'Shame.'

'But perhaps something can be done with DNA testing. They might be able to get a match there,' Kennedy offered.

'Good, let's hope so, shall we? Still, I've got to tell you Kennedy, I thoroughly enjoyed this morning. Great fun, much more invigorating than this thing with five traffic wardens lifted on a drugs raid. What's that all about, Kennedy? And then this GLR Radio hijack. What's happening out there, old son?'

Before Kennedy could reply, Castle had reached his office, and quicker than you could say 'Pauley Valentini' he was inside, leaving Kennedy saying 'I don't know' to a closed door.

Chapter Twenty-Three

Stephen Stone was waiting for Kennedy as Kennedy knew he would. No doubt the surviving Stone brothers would have spoken the previous evening. Would they have compared notes? Would there, in fact, have been notes to compare? Would they, could they, have been guilty of fratricide? Brian's alibi was at best shaky and as Kennedy and Coles entered the elder brother's office, a travel agency above a toy shop halfway up the west side of busy Kentish Town Road, Kennedy speculated on the alibi he was undoubtedly about to hear.

Total Travel, the brass plaque on the door proudly proclaimed. Kennedy and Coles were buzzed through and made their way up the narrow staircase to the first floor and through to a large open plan office. The walls were covered with posters of French skiing holidays, weeks in Barbados, fun in the sun in Belfast, no rain in Spain, weekends in Dublin and a month in the Highlands. Bikini clad (barely) nymphs were seen enticing blotchy pink-skinned males into joining them in deep blue swimming pools to sample the sun, water, drinks and maybe even more. But as 90 per cent of family holidays were surely booked by the female partner, these enticing worlds would probably be avoided in favour of religious trips to Palestine and tours of Cornish tin mines.

'Mr Stone is waiting for you in his office, one more floor up,' said one of the staff, a young girl beautiful enough to be prancing around one of the poster beaches.

'Good morning. I am Stephen Stone and I've been expecting

you.' The owner of a very firm handshake greeted them on their arrival on the next floor.

'Good morning,' Kennedy replied, 'I'm Detective Inspector Christy Kennedy and this is WPC Anne Coles, and we'd like to talk to you about your brother John B., who I'm sure you've –'

'Yes, Brian reached me yesterday evening with the sad news.' The elder Stone seemed polite and was well spoken like Brian, but unlike the latter he was betraying some (apparent) grief at the loss of a brother. He led them through to his cluttered office where more posters adorned the walls, this time all of Italy.

The desk was littered with various brochures, a notepad containing neat handwriting, two telephones, a clock and a photo of his wife, who was also a partner in the travel business. Kennedy had gained this information by reading one of the Total Travel's letterheads on the noticeboard downstairs. Stephen looked like he was in his mid-forties. He had short, well kept brown hair and an equally well kept short beard. He wore a bottle green shirt with a red tie (knot and top button of shirt undone), tan Chinos and brown moccasins (obviously bought on one of his many free trips abroad). He sported lightweight, silver-framed glasses.

'Look, we keep hearing that you and your brother weren't exactly the best of friends, and…' Kennedy began.

'That's an understatement if ever I heard one.' Stephen Stone laughed. 'Let me ask you a question, Inspector. How would you feel about a man who raped your wife?'

Kennedy and Coles both looked (and were) stunned. In this game of poker faces the golden rule was to give nothing away, a rule they had just broken.

Before either of them could comment, Stone continued, 'And before you answer me let me further ask you how you would feel if you brother raped your wife at your mother's funeral.'

So that's what happened, Kennedy thought, no wonder all this open warfare in the family. He found himself saying, 'Were charges brought, sir?'

'What? No. No of course not. I mean it would have been just

too big a scandal for any family to take, let alone ours, which has always been a bit shaky at the best of times. Listen, my wife, Jean, she and my brother dated years ago before we were married. He was in love with her. She was not in love with him. Jean and I fell in love. It was awkward, of course. She was still seeing John when we started. She broke up with him. We waited years before getting married in the hope that the fuss would die down.' Stone went silent and doodled on a clean page with his fountain pen. Neither Coles nor Kennedy spoke and eventually Stone spoke again.

'But it didn't die down, it never could with him. So we all kept well away from each other, and the funeral was the first time we'd all been in the same room in years. Everyone had a few drinks and loosened up a bit, and Jean and John were talking quite a bit and seemed to be getting on, so I left them to it. I was happy that it was all going to end, but sad that it had taken the death of our mother to bring us all together again. I'd had enough of it by that point, and if it hadn't been for our mother's death I could quite happily have spent the rest of my life without seeing him. Anyway, they were last seen heading in the direction of the garden, we'd lots of trees and bushes, and he took her into the bushes, and he raped her and left her crying on the ground. He didn't even have the decency to help her fix her clothes and cover her up. She was found by my aunt. By my mother's sister on the day of her sister's funeral, can you imagine that, finding your nephew's wife lying in the garden crying with her pants and tights around her ankles, having just been raped by another of your nephews.' Stone started to draw larger and larger concentric circles around a point in the centre of the page. Soon the circles filled entire page.

'So you see, if we had called the police there would have been all the ^but weren't you lovers?'' or ^Are you sure you weren't really giving him the come-on signs?'' and ^Come on, you really wanted one more fling with him for old times' sake'', etcetera etcetera. Inspector, I'm being perfectly candid with you now because I want you to know that I have nothing to hide. I am well aware that because of all this I'm bound to be a suspect. I have to tell you that I did not murder my brother. I could admit to you that, at times, I wanted him dead or at least out of our lives. But,I did not, and could not, murder him.'

'Would you have any idea who may have wanted to murder him?' WPC Coles asked.

'Well, you know what, I immediately thought ^Oh shit, it's Brian. He's gone and done it, he's gone and topped that shit and so now, even from beyond the grave he's going to be the ruination of all our lives." '

'How can you be sure it wasn't Brian?' said Coles.

'I just know, that's all. But other suspects? Well, let's see. He dabbled a bit in drugs, but I'm sure you already know a bit about that, and it was only socially so I'm not sure he'd be a target for anyone. From what I've heard John was making a bob or two so I'm sure he could well afford his vices.' Stephen paused for a moment, then said 'Let's see, I've been thinking about this a lot because I knew you'd ask me about it. Maybe a property deal gone wrong? Hey, who knows? Maybe he was caught with someone else's wife or girlfriend, only this time he didn't get off so lucky?'

'Didn't get off at all, sir.' Kennedy added.

'Yes, I see what you mean, but I really don't know. I'm sorry but I have no other direction to point you in. I would like to have because each one would point away from me, so I'm going to help you as much as possible, aren't I?'

'Before all this happened, you know when John B. first started dating Jean, were you all a tight family?' inquired Kennedy, intrigued by this man's apparent honesty.

'Well, our dad died when we were all young and so it was hard for our mum. But we got by, she did us proud, we never lacked for food or clothes or coal on the fire. But no, we were never a Christmas card kind of family. I think you need both parents for that, don't you? A dad to hold it all together and lay down the law and a mum to provide all the love and gentleness. I've never really thought about it before but you need your dad to give the family direction and your mum to bond it all together.'

All three pondered Stephen's final statement and its accidental wisdom.

Chapter Twenty-four

'So what do you think of that, then?' Kennedy asked his WPC. They were in the car heading towards their second interview of the morning, this time with Jean Stone, current wife of Stephen Stone, the brother and chief suspect of murder victim John B. Stone, himself a former lover of Jean Stone.

'I mean to say, can it get any worse than that? Raped by your husband's brother at your mother-in-law's funeral. This John B. Stone must have been a bad piece of work. How could anyone do that?' Coles shivered in disgust.

'Perhaps he felt he'd been wronged in his life. Wronged by a father who'd left him when he was too young, wronged by his mother because she couldn't provide him with all the things, toys, games, sweets, clothes, that his friends had. Wronged by all his relatives who didn't think he was special because he had neither the cuteness of being the youngest nor the wisdom of being the oldest nor the uniqueness of being the only daughter and was consquently the last in line for love and affection. And then ultimately wronged by his brother, who took away the only person he loved, Jean, and whom he felt was the only person in his life who had loved him for himself,' Kennedy answered, trying it out on himself as he went along.

'What?' said Coles, 'So you mean because of losing a father, not being the oldest, not being the youngest, not being the only daughter, and having his first love stolen, this person became a rapist? That but for one simple twist of fate, i.e. his father dying when he was young, he wouldn't have turned out to be a monster?'

'No, not at all. It's hard to say all this because we didn't know the guy and now he's dead and we'll never be able to find out all this stuff. But we have to look into his life and see if we can see things which can lead us to his killer, and this means we have to try and see things from his standpoint. I think he was probably, basically, a bad person. And by bad person I mean he was prepared to live his life without showing consideration to others, he thought mostly about himself and whenever he needed or wanted something he refused to allow any social rules or laws to stand in his way. I think that's the fact, he was a bad person and I think all those other things are mitigating circumstances which possibly he and his social workers, would use as excuses for his actions.'

'I see,' said Coles. 'I'm not altogether sure I agree but I do see what you mean. Oh, we're here.' She had spied an awkward parking spot on the arc of Mornington Crescent, a space violated just thirty seconds before by a Fiat Uno, a pram with an engine. The Uno in turn had taken a space and a half vacated just three minutes since by Mrs Jean Stone's latest visitor, the youngest of the Stone brothers, Brian.

Jean and Stephen Stone had a comfortable apartment on the top two floors of a Victorian house. Jean led them into the well furnished and frequently dusted lounge. Much to Kennedy's satisfaction she gave them them tea and chocolate biscuits.

But Kennedy couldn't help be disappointed in Jean Stone. He had found himself building up a picture of the woman whose attention two brothers had fought over for years. It was a natural, if possibly male, thing to do. But she was ordinary. This wasn't meant as an insult, it was just how she looked. She was tall and slim with cropped blonde hair; she wore a red sweatshirt with GAP written across the front in large letters, black slacks and black slippers. She wore no make-up, and Kennedy felt that this might have been the missing ingredient to turn her into the woman who broke the heart of John B. Stone.

'We have an uncomfortable advantage over you here, Mrs Stone. We know what happened between yourself and John B.'

'It's okay,' she said, 'Stephen rang me just before you arrived and told me about your conversation, all of it.' And she paused to sip some tea. Not great tea mind you; made American fashion where boiling water is not used. More likely the water had been allowed to cool down somewhat from boiling point before it was applied to the tea. This method tends to make the tea sticky and dry and lose some of the revitalising qualities a perfectly brewed cup offers.

'So I'm ready for you, as it were,' she went on. 'I hope it's not going to be too painful. I'm sure, as you both can guess, there are things we'd all rather forget about, but nature has its way of not allowing us to do so, perhaps so we learn from our mistakes. Now with this sad loss of John all these memories will be returning to haunt us again.'

'When did you first meet John B.?' WPC Coles inquired.

'It was ages ago, we were both teenagers, late teens of course, and this girl friend of mine wanted to fix me up with somebody, anybody, just so that we could have intimate conversations about our boys and so that we could go out in foursomes. Anyway, I seem to remember she quite liked John B. herself and if she hadn't been dating the school hunk at the time she probably would have gone out with him.' Jean Stone was surprised at how comfortable she was in this man's company. He was a policeman, yes, but he had kind eyes and gentle hands.

'So we were paired off and we went to this party. But we didn't really click and after an initial chat we parted company and I was chatting to this other guy and at one point, I still remember the incident vividly, I looked across the room and saw John B. laughing and I just had this overwhelming urge to kiss him. So I shipped the chap I was talking to off to get a drink and I went across the room and kissed John B. and, well, we kissed all night. Just kissing, mind you, nothing else, just kissing the first night.

Kennedy and Coles smiled at this part of the confession.

'From then on we were in each other's face and hair for ages; we just seemed to grow together. And then John B., well he seemed to think that being in love with me could be his life and his career. He had no interest in anything else. That was it: he didn't want anything else apart from me and us,' Jean recalled in despair. She was telling them more than she needed to, Kennedy sensed. He also sensed her need to talk about John B., now that he was dead, to people who would listen, as opposed to the inlaws who probably spat fire at the mere mention of his name. Jean Stone hugged her teacup in both hands, resting her elbows on her knees as she leaned towards the detective.

'What do you mean, no other interests, just you? Isn't that meant to be every girl's dream?' Coles inquired.

'No, not really, it made him very boring as a person. I needed him to get a life. He was acting just like a little puppy dog, he was in danger of becoming a wimp. At first the attention was flattering but you know it's like in fairy tales: what happens after "and they all lived happily ever after"? The reality was we weren't going to; nobody does, or if they do they die of boredom. We needed work and money. Food, a house, clothes, a family. I didn't just want to get by. I didn't want to live with him in his bedsitter. I wanted the better life and I wanted someone who shared that dream. Not someone who just gave up when he thought he had found the love of his life. So I was trying to break up with him for ages and we had a few false starts, or stops I suppose really. I confided in Stephen at that point, I'd always liked him. He was older, wiser and sensible. And he was ambitious, at least in those days. He wanted to make something of his life and I found that very attractive.' Jean stopped again, took some tea and, Kennedy assumed, thought once more about the difference in the two brothers.

'Were they really that different?' he inquired.

'Well, as it turned out, no. When John B. set his mind to it he became quite successful, working at the estate agency. He did well from it, although you wouldn't think it to look at him, you'd hardly think he'd two pennies to rub together. But I'm sure he was making a lot more money that Stephen. Where was I? Oh yes, so when I confided in Stephen we started to get quite friendly and then quite close and eventually the inevitable happened, but it had been in one of our fake endings and so I cooled it for awhile with Stephen to try again with John B., but the more it went on the more I realised I wanted to be with Stephen, so we decided, after a lot of heart searching, to come out with it and tell the family and John B. and let them all deal with it.'

'Was there any violence at that point?' Kennedy inquired, finishing off the substandard cup of tea.

'Heavens, no! John B. just went off and listened to Leonard

Cohen and Al Stewart for two years solid and that was it. When he came out of his tunnel of darkness and appeared to be over it, Stephen and I got married. We invited John B. but he didn't show. And that was it,' Jean Stone concluded with a certain air of relief.

'Had he started to date anybody at that point?' Kennedy inquired.

'No. Not at all. I mean I heard he had a couple of one night stands but from what I could gather he preferred not to bother, said he didn't need the grief. Brian once told me that Helen, then his girlfriend and now his wife, tried to get John B. to date one of her friends, one of the girls she worked with. But nothing came of that. He got drunk on the first date and insulted her, said that girls weren't worth the trouble and men could have as much fun doing other things without all the grief a woman brought.'

'And that was it until the funeral?' WPC Coles asked as she too finished her tea.

'The funeral, yes the funeral!' Jean replied, as much to her teacup as to the police duo. 'Yes, we were all there. We had a few drinks; it was the first real conversation I had with John B. in ten years and it was okay, you know? He was telling me about how well he was doing and about how happy he was. He was quizzing me about my life with Stephen; he kept cool about it, he never actually crossed the line of rudeness. Never quite saying, but obviously thinking to himself ^Look at all of us now, you made a big mistake didn't you?" Yes, he was definitely implying that but keeping it fun. Anyway we had a lot of wine and the house was too crowded and too noisy, so he said let's go out to the garden and when we walked out the air hit me hard, I can remember it as if it was yesterday, and I realised how drunk I was.'

Kennedy felt she was close to tears and was about to ask he if she was okay or if she needed to stop for a while; she seemed to read his mind because she forced a brief smile and continued,

'It's okay. I'm okay. I need to get this over with. In a way I feel with John B. dead and me here telling you all this, it's like, it's exorcising it for the first time. So anyway, the air hit me and I felt a bit wobbly. John B. grabbed me to steady me and as he did so he pulled me around to face him and it was like in the movies. The frame froze with both of us just standing there staring at each other, and in another instant he had taken us down to the bushes at the bottom of the garden and we were just staring at each other again, both lost in our memories of each other. But this time we kissed and the kiss took my breath away. And then we were rolling around in the bushes and kissing, and then I realised he was fumbling around in my underwear, trying to remove them and I realised what was happening and I realised I didn't want it to happen, I didn't want this.' Now she was sobbing gently.

'It was my right to say no. Yes, maybe I shouldn't have kissed him. But you know I didn't mean anything else to happen. He forced me, he wouldn't stop. He was too strong. Before I knew it he'd my skirt up and my tights and pants around my ankles and he was in me and he wouldn't stop. He wouldn't stop. He wasn't hurting me or hitting me or anything like that but it was still rape. I told him I didn't want him, I told him NO!'

Chapter Twenty-Five

As Kennedy and WPC Coles were returning, in a somewhat disturbed state, to North Bridge House, ann rea and Daniel Elliot were taking a very slow walk along Climping's sloping pebbled beach.

Kennedy and Coles were discussing how easier it seemed to be getting, in the nineties, for people to reveal their deepest secret thoughts and fears even on first meetings. Anne Coles thought it was an 'an American kind of thing,' While Kennedy, as ever looking for the angle, thought Jean Stone's frankness might have something to do with more than a little prodding from her husband Stephen.

ann rea and her former landlord were discussing the trials and tribulations of growing old. Daniel, far from being morbid, was seeing the funny side of this, even at his current walking pace, which he claimed was something like 'sixty hours a mile.'

'You know,' he said, 'if I had known I was going to get here, you know – reaching the end of my life...' he began as he struggled both to move his feet through the pebbles and to remove his walking stick from deep within the pebbles at each and every minuscule step.

'Oh, shush, would you, you've got ages to go,' ann rea encouraged.

'Perhaps, but I think it's going to take and every minute of them just to get off the beach,' he chuckled, 'No, really, what I meant was, if I had realised I was going to have completed my life before my body has the decency to give up on me I would have planned things differently.'

'How do you mean?' ann rea asked.

'Well let's assume – only for the point of this conversation mind you, I don't want you getting mad at me again – let's assume that the natural end to my life should have come at the same time as Lila passed away. We had a good life together. A full life. A life of loving each other and being there for each other, the same kind of life you could have with that detective fellow of yours if only you'd stop struggling and give in to it.' Daniel stopped in his tracks and turned to face the sea. The old man was protected from the fresh breeze by his well worn brown cords, a vest, the top of which just peered out from the top V of his black striped shirt, itself secured in a heavy green woolly cardigan topped by a brown checked cloth cap.

'It's like swimming, you know. The first time you are out there in the sea and you lose your footing, you panic, you kick, you splash, you splutter and you reach out for an imaginary lifeline while all the time all you should be doing for your own safety is surrendering to the rhythm of the water. Be gentle be calm, go with it, let your body relax and start to float, and then you can move within the sea as you wish; do anything but fight it, ann.' Daniel stared out across the rolling waves to where they melted into the blue of the sky and the white of the fluffy clouds.

'And, Daniel?' ann rea prompted.

'Sorry,' Daniel smiled again as he remembered where the conversation had been heading, 'Yes, so we'd a good life to gether and it would have been nice if our lives had ended at the same time, and what I was trying to say was if I realised I was going to outlive her by this much I wouldn't have led such a healthy life.'

'I'm not so sure you could have controlled it to such a degree,' ann rea offered, enjoying his good humour.

'Well, let's just think about that. Say for instance I had eaten more chips. God, I loved chips. We used to get them in the orphanage every Friday, with our fish, a religious thing. But I loved them and when I joined up, you could get them with everything, chips that is, every single day. But when we moved to London I stopped eating chips altogether for a while, everyone said how bad fat was for your arteries. Same thing with steak; I think a good piece of frying steak is delicious, well done, I love it well done. Lila used to do this meal, my favourite, nothing fancy but I savoured it. Steak, well done, baked beans, a couple of fried eggs and chips. And if no one was around I could have a baked and chip buttie. Oh, the best. Then she'd complete the meal with her own sherry trifle. Forgive me, I'm drooling.'

The memory of Lila Elliot's sherry trifle made ann rea's mouth water as well. 'Oh yes,' she said, 'I remember Lila's trifle. It was exquisite, quite simply the best!'

'Yes, it certainly was, wasn't it?' said Daniel, his deep blue eyes twinkling for the first time since ann rea had come down from London. 'Lila and I, we both had dangerous sweet teeth. So what I'm saying is, wouldn't it have been great to have indulged a bit more. And the Old Bushmills, that certainly brings a flush to your cheeks on a winter's night – maybe I should have finished the bottle on a few more late-night sessions,' he speculated remorsefully.

'So what about cigarettes, would you have smoked more of them?' ann rea asked as they hobbled along the beach.

'God, no. Filthy habit. I'm glad I gave it up when I did. I haven't smoked a fag in over thirty years now. Best thing I ever did. For one thing I was able to taste food for the first time in my life when I quit the ciggys. I never realised what I was missing, just being able to taste, to savour the true taste. But the main thing was losing the smell of that smoke from my clothes and from the house, no more horrible smells. Oh no, a filthy habit. But all those other things I sacrificed for a longer and healthier life, well I'm just saying maybe I shouldn't have,' he concluded as he concentrated on manoeuvering his walking stick through the pebbles.

'Now teeth, there's another thing for instance: we have absolutely no need for perfect teeth. For teeth which are going to last forever. Because we are not going to last forever. Or do we need to feel proud of having the best set of molars in the graveyard? Of course not. So why do we go through all that agony in the dentist's chair? Is that a form of sadomasochism or what?' Daniel was on a roll, and a few steps and quite a time later, he continued with a variation on his theme.

'Another thing I've been thinking about recently. The Lord's Prayer. I worked out the other night that I must have said it over twenty-five thousand times, that's once a day since I was seven, which I think worked out at 23,360, and so I rounded it up to cover all the emergencies when I really needed to say it. You know like when you're scared, like when Lila was ill, like when our daughter was, well you know, like when you're in trouble. When you need a bit of spiritual comfort. Well, what I'd like to suggest to God is maybe I should have cut that down by half. I mean God, the God we pray to, he didn't really protect me when I needed protection, he didn't see our Lila through her illness, did he? She'd quite a few years of good-person credit which should have been taken into account. And my dad, a good man, a great man, when he was dying of cancer and his screams were filling our entire house and I was praying to God that he wouldn't die because I'd have to go to the orphanage: did he help? No! So what was the use of all that praying?' Daniel stole a glance to the heavens as if to make sure he wasn't offending anybody.

'It's like you say, it's comfort for you in your hour of need, it's knowing that there just might be someone there you can talk to when you need to. It might even be yourself that you're praying to,' ann rea offered.

'You might be correct, I certainly don't know. But I just know that my days are a void now. I wake up realising that my life hasn't ended during the night. I accept as I lie there that I have another day to face. I turn on Radio 4. I listen to that until seven-thirty. I get up, read the papers, have a cup of tea. Take a nap. Have a light lunch, maybe go out for a walk, or should I say hobble? Go down the shops, get a few bits and pieces, come home, have tea, watch TV, maybe have a drink. Go to bed at eight-thirty and wake up at five and start all over again.' There was no trace of moaning in Daniel's voice, he was merely stating facts. He continued after turning to look at the sea.

'You know, I've been thinking for the first time about what happens after I'm dead.'

'Daniel, please!'

'No, seriously, I've never thought about all this before but I've been wondering about what will happen in *Coronation Street* after I've gone, what will the new characters be like. How will the Prime Minster do? Who will be the next Prime Minster? What is the future Prime Minster doing at this exact point? Do we know him or her? Will the Tellytubbies be number one in the pop charts next Christmas? Who will live in my houses? What will people say about me? How long will I be remembered? What will happen to my fine leather shoes?' And the old man looked down at his tan shoes, which were shined to Irish Guards standards.

'This will be the first pair of shoes I won't have worn out. In a lifetime this will be the first pair which will wear me out. What will happen to them? Will they be given away? Will someone else wear them? Will they take as good care of them as I have? That one good thing about being in the Irish Guards, you certainly learn how to work up a good shine on your shoes. All that spit and polish and elbow grease, will it all go to waste? I keep thinking, I keep having this vision about what's going to be on the front page of the *Guardian* the day after I die. I've read the paper now for so many years, that's going to be strange, you know.'

'Oh, I imagine it will be about Charles meeting a new princess and getting married.'

'Yes, that's another thing – what's going to happen to them, the royal family? They are all so ill equipped to be living in this century. And then there's the pub, the Black Horse; after I've gone what will it be like in there without me? Who will be the new landlord? Will it be knocked down in a few years to make way for some development when Brighton reaches this far along the coast? You may laugh but it has to happen. How long will beautiful old pubs like that be allowed to stand?' he sighed.

'And money, that's another thing. I get mad now when I think of all the times Lila and myself sacrificed being together just so I could be out earning more money. Now I have more money than I'll ever spend and I don't have Lila. Wouldn't I have been better served by working less, spending more time with Lila and giving less money to the state when I did?'

'Here, you're getting tired,' said ann rea, 'let's head back to the cottage and I'll make you a lovely cup of tea. I've been taught by an expert, you know. Kennedy just loves his tea. Hey, maybe you can even have a drop of Bushmills in the cup,' she suggested and Daniel complied as she steered his elbow back in the direction of the short distance from whence they had come.

'What about Anna? Is that her name? Your daughter Anna,

what about her? Do you ever think about her? About what she's doing now, have you ever heard from her?' ann rea nudged the conversation, like his weary body, to a preplanned destination.

'Not for ages. She was in Birmingham, I think. She felt we let her down. But I didn't know what to do, ann. Lila tried for ages to be close and comforting but she just kept being pushed away. I hope this doesn't sound silly, but it's like she expected me to be there when it happened, and to have protected her from those animals. Is that too strange a thought?'

'No, I don't think so,' ann rea replied sympathetically, 'We depend on our parents for a lot longer that we care to admit. You know you can go and leave home but you do it knowing that you still have a lifeline back to your parents. Kennedy says that every time he's being physically sick he still calls out for his mother.'

'But ann, you can't possibly be there with your children all the time,' Daniel said, his voice starting to crack with emotion.

'I know, Daniel, it's not your fault. Anna didn't have a brother or sister to lean on, you were all she had and on the one occasion she needed you, needed your strength and protection, you weren't there. But if you had been around her all the time, she would have accused you of over-protecting her. Nowadays she'd get counselling and would be taught how to deal with it. To deal with it differently, I'm sure,' ann rea comforted, 'But you know what they say about time; maybe the passing years have healed her pain. Have you ever thought of trying to contact her?'

'Yes, a few times since Lila passed away. But I've never really done anything about it. I wouldn't know where to start to be honest,' Daniel admitted.

'Would you like me to try? To try and find Anna for you?'

'What, use your police connection?' Daniel joked.

'Hey, you,' she playfully squeezed his elbow, 'Don't forget I'm a journalist, I've got contacts of my own.'

Chapter Twenty-Six

Thirty-eight minutes later, following the spiced-up cup of tea, ann rea left Daniel to his nap as she telephoned one of her contacts.

'Kennedy,' she whispered, 'Good to hear you voice. How are you keeping?'

'Fine, yes, fine, ann rea. Why are you whispering?'

'Daniel's upstairs taking a nap and I've got a favour to ask.'

'Yeah?'

'You don't mind, Kennedy?'

'Listen,' he laughed, 'You know Camden CID and how we cherish our relationship with the local media. So let's have it. Pen at the ready.'

'Okay. Daniel and Lila, they had a daughter called Anna and apparently she was raped. It would have been in the seventies. It happened on Primrose Hill. Anyway, Anna blamed Daniel and Lila and disowned them, moved away and never came back. She didn't even contact them again. So I thought I might try and track her down to see if she can make her peace with her father. He hasn't long to live. He doesn't have anyone else in the world and he sounds so lost, Christy. I just thought I'd try.'

'Good, yes. No problem. I'll have Tim Flynn check the files, he's probably the only one who was around then, and see if we can dig up any information for you.'

'Great, Kennedy. I really do appreciate it, I owe you one.'

'What. You're now going to send me back to Lloyds?'

'Ho-bloody-ho, Kennedy. Look, I've got to go. I've also got to see what I can dig up through the *Camden News Journal*. Speak to you later. I'll call you at home tonight,' ann rea whispered.

Kennedy realised his "bye" was heard only by telephonic static and so he replaced the receiver as he wrote the name Anna Elliot on one of his cards.

Chapter Twenty-Seven

Kennedy passed the name card and details to Sgt Flynn. As he was doing so DS Irvine was leaving North Bridge House to go and pick up Hugh Anderson so the villain might help Camden CID further with their inquiries. Kennedy joined him, and on the way they joked about how in the sixties it would have taken at least ten officers to apprehend Hugh Anderson but now he'd probably come with them quiet as a pussycat. Wrong!

They drove a police pool car, a 1995 Ford Granada, still new and shiny blue, to a spot just beyond entrance of Anderson's place of work at the far corner of Belmont Street off Chalk Farm Road. In fact it was nearly opposite the legendary Roundhouse where, in 1967, Paul McCartney had planned a series of comeback concerts for the Beatles. He just (apparently) couldn't persuade John Lennon, or was it (maybe) Yoko Ono.

Though such a historic reunion was the last thing on Kennedy and Irvine's collective mind as they made their way into the building past boxes of leaflets, posters, T-shirts and baseball caps, all unprotected from the weather. They saw a sign marked 'Office' pointing up a rickety set of stairs, and without saying a word both headed in a skyward direction.

Technically they had the evidence (teeth marks in the apple) to be able to arrest Hugh Anderson on suspicion of the murder of John B. Stone, but at this stage they agreed it would be better to just bring him in for questioning.

Anderson looked shocked to see them as they entered the large open plan loft-style office. It was a very seventies-type office, in fact Kennedy was convinced that some of the original seventies dust was still visible around the shelves and windows. Equally it could have become very nineties with a bit of a clean-up, a lick of white paint, a polish of the well trodden floorboards and a highlighting of the rafters hidden by piles of boxes similar to those out in the yard.

'The filth again. What do you want this time?' said Anderson matter-of-factly, a hint of aggression in his voice. He was alone in the office and he made his way to what was obviously his desk which was covered with flyers, well worn telephone directories, a large Wallace and Grommet mug filled to bursting with pens and pencils, a portable TV, a cup of cold (Kennedy was sure) tea, a can of fly spray (probably essential in this sun trap in the summer), a copy of the *Evening Standard* (headline proclaiming 'GLR Seige Ends Peacefully'), a copy of the *Racing News* folded in four, and, over to one side, a small spiral notebook clean page up, a well worn pair of leather gloves and a couple of CDs, the top one the Carpenters, the second one Kennedy couldn't make out. The room smelt of ink from the newly printed posters and shirts, stale milk, and fresh coffee.

'We'd like you to accompany us back to North Bridge House for further questioning,' DS Irvine announced. At this, and for no apparent reason which could be worked out later in discussions with his DI, he went over and grabbed hold of one of Anderson's arms. Bad move. Very bad move.

If you get physical, even a little, with someone like Anderson, they tend to get physical back. In spades.

Anderson's eyes fixed Irvine with a cold stare, 'Naff off, Jock.' and with that he freed his mildly restrained arm, turned away quickly from Irvine, and as he did so he elbowed the DS in the face.

Now, Irvine considered himself to be useful in a scrap, and Kennedy thought the same about his DS, having seen him in action a few times and knowing that he had been the middleweight police boxing champion for a few successive years in the mid-eighties. But though Irvine's pride was damaged he kept his cool.

'That'll be enough of that, laddie,' he said and once more took Anderson's arm, this time more securely.

'Oh will it now?' Anderson shrugged him off like a dead fly and in one movement picked up his gloves, put them on and swung round, very agile for a man of his years. He pulled Irvine towards him using the arm Irvine had taken hold of and bobbed him sharply on the nose with a left jab.

Both men now squared up to each other. Anderson immediately took a boxer's pose and raised both gloved fists to protect himself. Irvine followed suit and both of them shuffled around, their shoes squeaking on the floorboards.

Kennedy tried to interject a bit of lightness, 'Okay, Hugh, enough's enough. You're going to have to come with us, so stop monkeying around.'

'It's okay, sir, leave him to me,' Irvine said somewhat breathily, his pride and and his nose both severely bruised.

Irvine took advantage of Anderson's high guard to pump him with a left, a right and a left again in quick succession just above the waist. Anderson, a fifty-three year old who'd obviously been in the wars more than once, barely batted an eyelid. The daylight from the window above his desk reflected two sharp white dots in the pupils of his eyes, showing how hard his star was fixed on Irvine. He seemed happy to be on the defensive, so the gamely Scot tried a quick one-two to the upper arm, a left and a right to the lower body, but once more he found his usually dependable left hook to be lacking as Anderson kept moving from foot to foot using his fists to spar at the air about Irvine's bloodied face.

Then he landed a deadly right straight through the Irvine guard, which connected to the jaw with a loud crack. The DS shook his head violently to sharpen his focus just as another Anderson right snuck through his guard and connected with a louder crack to Irvine's nose. Kennedy was worried, but he'd seen Irvine before and knew he'd something big in reserve. He'd obviously been holding back with his famous left for fear of hurting the other too much, police brutality and all that. Wrong! Irvine had delivered four of his best lefts and they had had zero effect on the older man. After the last, Kennedy knew the sergeant was in trouble, mainly because the battered Scot grunted 'I'm in trouble.' The trouble came quick. It was all over in ten more seconds.

Anderson jabbed him in the stomach with a quick and painful right. The deep thud of the connection filled the loft and Irvine instinctively dropped his guard to cover his stomach. Anderson hit him twice more, once to the chin with a left, and as this punch was connecting, a right to the side of Irvine's badly bruised face. The DS was already on the way down, pride and tweeds heading for the grubby floor.

'Okay, Mr Anderson. That's enough, you've had your fun, let's go.' Kennedy made to help the winded Irvine to his feet.

'Oh, so you fancy your chances now, Kennedy, do you?' Anderson stepped towards him, fists still up, guard still close to his face, sparring away at him, shoe leather cracking beneath him as he floated on the balls of his feet.

He squared up to Kennedy and from the thug's eyes the detective deducted he was considering which tactics would help him take out a second CID officer. It was all a waste of time. Yes, the villain could probably beat both of them to a pulp, but he'd be apprehended before the night was out.

But Kennedy had a more immediate problem. He could hear the swishing sounds of displaced air as the man's fists jabbed their way in the general direction of his head.

'Come on, Guv, fancy a few rounds?' he crowed, clearly loving every second of this encounter, still fresh as a daisy and eager for more blood.

Kennedy saw blood, Irvine's, as it flowed freely from his nose, over his mouth, over his chin, down his throat and then soaked into his checked shirt and tartan tie.

'Feck this for a game of soldiers,' said Kennedy as he grabbed the fly spray from the desk beside him and sprayed Anderson's face through his guard. As the man doubled up in pain and tried to rub the stinging spray from his eyes, Kennedy took careful aim and kicked him right smack centre in the goolies. He collapsed loudly in a heap, knocking the stuff from his desk and scattering boxes all over the place as he did so. He was screeching at the top of his lungs, the pitch rising all the time. He sounded like a banshee torn between two funerals.

Kennedy quickly secured Anderson's hands behind his back with a set of handcuffs and returned to Irvine, whose wind had returned and who was wiping the bloody nose with a handkerchief while grinning, painfully, from ear to ear.

'Well done, sir. What a bit of style. You can come with me to Glasgow, sir, anytime at all.'

Chapter Twenty-Eight

A Civil Servant's weapon be
A cup of boiling, scalding tea.
One at ten, and one at three
A Civil Servant's life for me.

Much relieved that his features hadn't been seriously rearranged, Kennedy went straight to Superintendent Castle's office on returning to North Bridge House. There was time to kill before interviewing Hugh Anderson; they had to wait until his solicitor arrived. Kennedy liked Anderson's brief, Leslie Russell. Kennedy never judged the brief by the criminals they represented. If Leslie Russell and his colleagues in the legal profession looked after only virtuous clients they'd be as successful as blind driving instructors.

Kennedy had always found Russell to be plain and straight-forward, not scared of advising his clients to face their due on the grounds that as a result of the same they may very well receive more lenient punishment. He was not one for exploiting the many dubious rules in a client's favour.

The Anderson case seemed surprisingly pretty cut-and-dried to Kennedy. Just like Adam and Eve, an apple was about to be responsible for his downfall. It was surprising for Kennedy because it seemed so logical and simple for a murder which on paper had looked so complex. But, as Castle advised him on numerous occasions, don't let yourself be scared off by the simple solutions. In 90 per cent of the cases it will be the simple solution which will also be the correct one. Most people who commit murder are just not that clever, not that devious. It's just the few clever ones who get all the good press. But then we are all used to the telly cops where they have a series to fill and so they have to string it along for a few weeks with complications.

'Anderson's in the nick, sir,' Kennedy announced as he popped his head round the door.

'Good, well done. Come in, Christy, sit down. Let's get some tea, shall we?' Castle suggested in his commanding voice. He had one of those great expressive voices which would work great on radio or in the theatre. It had that rare quality of convincing you of whatever its owner said; merely because of the trouble taken to saying it, was gospel and important, very important. Voices like Castle's could work wonders for their owners' careers. Yes Castle, with his super-fit slim body, distinguishing grey hair and smart uniform proudly displaying his five stars, could always be relied upon to give a good presentation, particularly of himself.

'Yes, don't mind if I do. Thank you, sir,' Kennedy replied, chirpy enough, never one to turn down a good cup of tea, even if it was being served in the lions' den. But then hadn't Androcles gone in to the lion's den? Mind you at least he knew all he had to do was remove the thorn from the lion's foot in order to become his friend for life. But Kennedy knew not what danger he walking in to, and what about being called 'Christy' as well as being offered a cup of tea? He hoped a round of golf was not the poison lurking there on the end of the thorn, because if it was then he was sure the lion was in for a hearty breakfast.

'You know, Christy,' Castle began expansively as he made his way across to his tea-making cupboard. He had taken a (tea) leaf out of Kennedy's book and had recently started to prepare his own brew rather than risk the nail-varnish remover of the canteen or the gnat's piss which was dispensed from the machine (great graphics, shame about the liquid). Castle entertained a lot of visiting top brass in his office, sometimes even local politicians. Whereas Kennedy loved the taste and the refreshing qualities of tea, his Super loved the ritual of preparing it in the company of his guests. He would invariably be the one doing the talking as he opened his teak cupboard, slid out the preparation platform, poured already strained water into the kettle (both containers were silver and highly polished, of course), boiled the water (not personally but with the use of electricity, although it was claimed he could build up enough of a personal head of steam to blow a fuse or two when things weren't exactly going his way), and poured the boiling water into a (matching silver) teapot where the clear bubbling liquid was turned into a reddish brown brew by the waiting teabags (Tetley's circular ones). Then as he waited for the tea to draw, and still rabbitting away ten to the dozen, he would take out his white fine bone china cups and saucers. Castle, like Kennedy, liked the fact that you could see your tea line through these cups. You could always tell how much of your meeting/interview/brief was left, since these were all one-cup affairs. Castle would offer milk and sugar, white with two lumps in Kennedy's case, and have everyone's cup prepared and waiting for the freshly drawn brew to be applied, while all the time addressing his guest(s), rarely entertaining a reply or an opinion.

'You know, Christy, I've enjoyed this case, enjoyed it immensely. I've enjoyed working with you on it. It's exciting when it all happens and comes together so fast. Isn't it?'

Kennedy was about to reply that in his view there was quite a way to go yet, but before he'd a chance to select the correct words to express this in a non-offensive way Castle continued:

'It's really lucky I was at the briefing, wasn't it? I suppose it's is not all about paperwork.' Castle brought the two cups of steaming tea over, floater at the ready to protect Castle's beautiful teak desk, a desk which accompanied him on all his moves. Kennedy considered that at that precise moment Castle looked like the archetypal civil servant.

'This work is all about knowing your patch, knowing your criminal, being in tune with your area,' Castle lectured.

Kennedy felt compelled to nod in agreement. Now that he'd got this far he wanted to at least taste the delights of the tea before leaving.

'I've been thinking, you know, I've enjoyed this so much I might try to take a more active role in seeking out the criminals in our midst,' he declared, proving that the hangman never shakes your hand in friendship.

'We could certainly use you, sir. Use your expertise and knowledge of the area,' Kennedy replied between quick sups of tea. Castle nodded his gratitude as the DI stepped forth into the unknown: 'However, sir, we do need you up here. You know, fighting our politicals battle for us. Don't forget, without you securing our budgets, manpower and generally running North Bridge House, none of the stuff any of us do down below would amount to anything. And the problem is, sir, I'm not sure there's anyone else who could do it as well as you.'

Totally unaware that he was being stroked, Castle lit up in one of those Gary Lineker permanent grins. Kennedy had inadvertently found himself as successful in promoting police politics as Steve McQueen had been with crewneck jumpers.

'Yes, yes perhaps you're right, yes indeed, who would do all of this?' Castle laughed as he surveyed his files, all neatly stacked about his desk. 'Who indeed? Now tell me, Kennedy, about this other matter?'

'Oh?'

'Yes, you know, my dog idea?' Castle prompted.

'Oh, yes.'

'Well? Did you do any more work on it?'

'Yes, sir.' Kennedy nodded.

'And? Did Anderson have a dog?' Castle could barely contain his excitement.

'Yes, sir, in fact he did,' Kennedy replied.

'Great, Gr-ea-t. I just knew it. I just had this feeling. Yes I could feel it in my bones. I knew there had to be a connection between these two murders, Burton and Stone. Just the fact them being found so close together. Never be scared of the simple solution, Kennedy, it's just a matter of putting two and two together.'

'Well, I don't actually think so, sir.' Kennedy dropped his bomb, right on target.

'What don't you think? That there's no connection between these two cases? Oh come on, there must be,' Castle asserted.

'No, sir. I don't think we are going to be able to tie Anderson in to the Burton murder,' Kennedy replied confidently, noticing that Castle's tea was about a quarter of an inch from the bottom of his cup.

'But we must be able to. Can't we get forensic to look at the teeth marks again, or what about the pathologist – can't she get salvia from the dog and compare it to any liquids present in the wounds of the body?' A hint of desperation was creeping into Castle's voice.

'No, sir, I don't think so. You see, Anderson's dog, well sir, in fact it's a poodle, a nice little white poodle, couldn't tear the throat of a butterfly, even if she wanted to.'

'Yes, yes, well I've got… I've got all this paperwork to get stuck into. Erm… keep me posted on the Anderson interview, won't you?' said Castle, coldly finishing off the last dregs of his tea and dismissing the Inspector.

As Kennedy left Castle's office, carefully closing the door and silently hopping from foot to foot like he needed to go to the toilet, he was wearing too large a smile; a smile too large by far.

Chapter Twenty-Nine

As Kennedy entered the interview room he was surprised to see that Hugh Anderson was smiling at him.

He was sitting on one side of the table, again with Leslie Russell, facing WPC Coles and diagonally across from the empty chair awaiting the warmth of Kennedy.

Anderson's smile broke into laughter like popcorn reaching its popping point. 'I've got to hand it to you, Guv, you got me. Totally surprised me. Maybe a bit doubtful about being fair and square, but you got me. As it happens, you know there's not many people who can claim to have beaten me in a fight before.'

'Yes, well, let's get into this shall we?' Leslie Russell nodded in agreement, clean white notepad at the ready, pen hovering eagerly in anticipation. Kennedy turned on the recording machine and announced the time, date and those present.

'At the last interview, Mr Anderson, you told me on tape and in the presence of your solicitor that when you left John B. Stone two evenings ago he headed up Parkway, in the direction of the bridge, and you went in the opposite direction,' Kennedy began to a stony silence from both Anderson and his brief.

'However, evidence has recently come to light which proves that you were, in fact, present at the scene of the crime.'

'Oh, and what evidence might that be?' Russell dutifully inquired.

Kennedy then proceeded to tell them about the apple, and the teeth marks, and Anderson's molars.

'Do you mind if I have a few moments alone with my client?' the solicitor inquired at this juncture in the proceedings.

'By all means,' Kennedy replied, announcing the time of the interview's termination for the benefit of HME (His Master's Ears).

'My client has a statement to make.' This time Leslie Russell started off the proceedings.

'Okay, here's the thing,' said Anderson, 'as it happens I wasn't telling you the truth. I didn't go the opposite way to Stone when we left the Spread Eagle. I took him up Parkway on the pretence of some property which I wanted to sell and told him there was a monkey in it for him if he moved the property quickly. Not to mention the possibility of purchasing his Parkway garage property. He was keen as mustard, Guv, know what I mean?' Kennedy was surprised by the fact that Anderson's voice had been raised an octave, no doubt caused by the re-arrangement of a certain part of his anatomy.

'When we reached the fountain, the one with the washer-woman on top, I put on my leather gloves and smacked him up a bit, hit him on the Vera, but he had a glass jaw, one wallop and he was on his back. I didn't kill him though. When I left him he was still breathing and moaning. Look, Guv, I know what I'm doing when I smack somebody. You just need them to feel pain and the point has been made. It makes them realise they're out of order and hopefully they won't be again. It's a bit like kids, Guv, know what I mean? So I smacked him told him to watch himself, dumped him in the dry fountain and left.'

'Why did you beat him up?' said Kennedy.

'As it happens, I was paid to, wasn't I?'

'Oh come on. What's with all this fiction?' Kennedy could

see a justification running up the road at least a mile off, waving a very large flag declaring 'Not guilty, your Honour, as it happens.'

'No, true, on my honour, Guv. This bird, she contacted me last week. I was up in court on a GBH charge, not proven, case dropped, mistaken identity and all that. Anyways I get a call the next day at the office inquiring if I was the same Hugh Anderson who had appeared in court the previous day. It was a bird, dead posh and all that.'

'Go on, I'm listening.' Kennedy wanted to get this part over, and the sooner they did so the better then they could get down to the nitty gritty and processing the charges. However, it must be said that part of him was intrigued; intrigued with the sort of story professional villian would come up with to justify giving someone a hiding so severe that death was the end result.

'Well, she said she might have some work for me and could we meet for a chat as she didn't want to discuss her business over the phone. So we agreed to meet in the lane by the side of the Danish Church at St Kathleen's Hall. As soon as she sets the phone down I dial 1471 to get her number, and I get the ^the caller has withheld their number" All very cloak and dagger.

'Yeah, I'm sure,' Kennedy added sarcastically.

'So, I've nothing to lose,' Anderson continued unperturbed. 'I meet her as arranged and she's all very Inspector Clouseau kind of stuff. Long black coat, long black hair, I'm sure it was a wig, but it was such an obvious wig I wouldn't be surprised if she really had long black hair, dark glasses and, get this, bleedin' black lipstick. She was quite tall, probably about five-nine. She told me she wanted this guy beaten up, she gave me a photo, it was John Stone as it turns out, and his work address. Apparently he'd been trying to take liberties with Miss Black Lipstick's younger sister and she wanted him warned off. She kept repeating the fact that she didn't want him hurt bad, she just wanted him warned off. She thought that if she overdid it she just might send her sister running into his arms. She didn't want that either, she just wanted it to be a warning.

'Some warning, Hugh,' said Kennedy. 'In his next life John B. will be well scared of you and this Miss Dipstick, but it's too late for this one.' And the DI shifted restlessly and uncomfortably on the hard chair. It's a bit like the movies, Kennedy thought, if it's a great movie you don't notice how uncomfortable the seat is, or how close to your knees the row in front is, or how cold the cinema is or how noisy the sweet unwrapping next to you is. But if it's a not so great movie your back and legs start to ache within ten minutes and cramp sets in within twenty. To Kennedy this movie of Anderson's was terrible; surely the scriptwriters could never have thought anyone, let alone a policeman, would believe such a story. And it continued:

'So I find out this guy drinks at the Spread Eagle, I case him for a couple of nights and on the third night I have someone drop a word in his ear that I'm in the market for a property and I might even have one to sell as well. I had to wait till chucking out time because Miss Black Lipstick wants the deed done by the fountain. Now I have to admit to you here and now that I did find that bit weird. She said that Stone would realise what the warning was about if it happened at the fountain. They don't close the park gates till eleven-thirty so I knew at that time it would certainly be quiet enough for me to get on with my business, they certainly wouldn't be any cars, so no cars, no interfering headlights. You know what, even if someone had stumbled by, it's my experience these days that if people see a bit of a scrap going on they'll cross to the other side of the road double quick and head off in the opposite direction.'

Kennedy wished he could nip out and get an ice cream to distract him but he bided his time and let Anderson continue, hoping that while in freefall, the man just might drop something he later would regret.

'I smacked him about a bit, she told me not to say a word to him, just do the biz and throw him in the fountain. She paid me three hundred lids in advance and another three hundred immediately afterwards. We met in the same place, the lane round by the Danish church, and she was dressed exactly the same as the first time.'

'So what about the baseball bat? Where in the proceedings did you produce and use that?' Kennedy inquired, his right leg throbbing with major cramp.

'What baseball bat? Who said that? Who said I used a baseball bat? What's this all about?' A slight panic appeared to set in as he looked first at Kennedy, and then at Russell.

'Whoever set about John B. Stone used his fists and a baseball bat, or a piece of wood resembling a baseball bat,' Kennedy advised solicitor, client and tape recorder.

'Listen, Guv, you saw me with your DS earlier today, I don't need a baseball bat or a cricket bat for that matter or a piece of wood or iron bars or knuckledusters or whatever. My fists do me fine, thank you very much.'

'Well now, there we have a bit of a dilemma, don't we?' Kennedy said. He'd decided to leave it there. He knew that he would get Anderson, in the presence of his solicitor, to sign a statement. But it would not be a totally satisfying statement. Anderson had admitted taking John B. Stone up to the Fountain of Sorrow. He had equally admitted beating him while there. As a result of the beating Stone had died. The evidence was circumstantial, agreed, but Anderson was guilty, he'd said as much and a good silk would probably get his charged reduced from murder in the first degree to a lesser one of manslaughter.

Chapter Thirty

So that was it, another case solved. Or was it? Kennedy didn't feel entirely comfortable about the whole thing. All this nonsense about Miss Dipstick, or was it Miss Lipstick? What was all that about? The Camden detective was in his office wandering around with his hands in his pockets, as was his habit, lost in such thoughts, when there was a knock on his door.

'Leslie, come on in,' he responded warmly to the solicitor now at his door.

'Thanks. I just wanted to have a chat with you about all this,' the solicitor began.

'Sit down over there, won't you? You'll have some tea with me,' Kennedy stated.

'Yes, yes of course that would be very nice,' Russell smiled. 'Hugh felt that you didn't exactly believe him about his mysterious woman. He wanted me to try to convince you that his claims are in fact true.'

'Do you believe him?'

'Yes, actually I do. I know he's a bit of a rogue and all that but he's never been scared to do his share of porridge. He's just annoyed that now he's going to get all the blame.'

'But come on now, Leslie. He did admit that he beat up Stone.'

'Yes.'

'And as a result of this beating Stone died.'

'Possible, but perhaps not entirely.'

'You're on a sticky one there, Leslie. Sure the mitigating circumstances will get it down to manslaughter, but he's still guilty.'

'Yes I agree, to a certain degree, but surely the fact that this woman, the one with the black lipstick – '

'Miss Dipstick.'

'Yes, if you must, Miss Dipstick,' Russell smiled, 'Anyway

surely the fact that this woman paid Hugh Anderson, before and after the beating, puts her right up there with Anderson on this case. Certainily she must share some of his guilt, be it murder or manslaughter.'

'You're quite right, assuming Miss Dipstick exists,' Kennedy agreed.

'Well I have to tell you that I believe Anderson. I don't see any other motive, do you?'

'No,' Kennedy lied. If someone was going to pay Anderson to murder Stone it could be anyone of the names on his original list of suspects. The brothers, the sister, the sister-in-law, Kevin Burroughs from Northern Properties, William Boatend from Camden Bus Estate Agents, or, person or persons unknown.

Kennedy also knew, however, what Castle would say if a request was made to carry on with this investigation. 'Come on, Kennedy, you've already put it to bed, let's not get too complicated about all this, Anderson did it, I told you he did it, he told you he did it, what more do you need?'

'Has Anderson the slightest idea as to her identity?' Kennedy asked the solicitor.

'No, not really. Not at all in fact. His description to you was exactly the same as the one he gave me. He did say she had a posh voice, though. Maybe a little too posh, as though it was put on,' Russell replied.

'Why meet her in a lane beside the Danish Church?' Kennedy asked himself and the solicitor. 'Could that possibly be a clue? Is she foreign? What happens at the Danish Church anyroads? Does she live near there? Is it handy for her? You see, that's one of the two things I've been thinking about that makes me think there just might be some truth to Anderson's story.'

'Really?'

'Yes. If it was a criminal's tale then why would he have a meeting in a lane by the Danish Church? It's the most unlikely of places. Surely he would have gone for Camden Lock, or by the Roundhouse, or at the tube, the Dublin Castle, the rose garden in Regent's Park... now that would have been the perfect meeting place. Or anywhere really, anywhere except in a lane by the Danish Church.'

'And the other? You said there were two things,' the solicitor prompted.

'Yes, well he just said a very funny out-of-character kind of thing. Your client in his statement said that he felt that Miss Dipstick's wig was so long and so fake-looking that it made him suspect that she really did have long black hair. Now that's been bothering me. Why on earth would he have thought, let alone said anything like that were it not true?'

'True, I hadn't thought about that. What should we do? Could it be… would it be better to try to find her, Miss Dipstick,' Russell couldn't help smiling at the name, 'through John B. Stone. Is there anyone in his past with a motive for murder?'

'Sorry, I can't answer that. Look, we'll do some more digging around to try and tie up the loose ends and if we come up with anything, anything at all, I'll give you a shout,' Kennedy replied, and then added as an afterthought, 'I think, though, it will turn out that your client has helped himself a lot by admitting his involvement so early on.'

'Good, look thanks for the chat. And the tea, your tea is as good as people say it is,' Leslie Russell said gratefully, and within seconds Kennedy was alone again (naturally) in his office.

So, who from his list of suspects would have the bottle to hire Anderson to beat up John B. Stone, or alternately, who would have had wanted to beat up Stone but would not have had the bottle to do it themselves? And if there was a Miss Dipstick, could that eliminate everyone from the suspect list apart from Miss Jean Stone? Perhaps, Kennedy thought, it was time for another chat with the senior Stone brother's wife.

Chapter Thirty-One

A s Kennedy entered Jean Stone's house for the second time that day her found her surprisingly fresh and bright considering how close she'd been to a breakdown on the earlier visit. Perhaps she'd also learned how to master another of our American friends' qualities: a quick recovery.

To Kennedy's trained eye, Jean Stone could be described as slim and would probably peg in at five-foot-nine tall, maybe even a wee bit more. He considered securing a search warrant to see if he could uncover the wig, long black coat and black lipstick, But decided it might be better to have a casual look around and not tip Castle off this early as to what he was up to.

Using the excuse of needing to visit the toilet, Kennedy tried a casual search but couldn't find any make-up, let alone black lipstick. Mrs Stone definitely used make-up. She had effected quite a change since the morning by 'putting on a face'. She'd given her features a lot more character, with eye-shadow, red rouge on her cheeks, false eyelashes, thickened-up eyebrows and a red, redefined set of lips. So perhaps she did her reconstruction business in the bedroom, or maybe even, more likely, her bedroom's ensuite bathroom, if such a hideaway existed. He couldn't really risk wandering around any more, or could he? He heard the voices of WPC Coles and Jean Stone rabbiting away in the living room.

On the spur of the moment he took a left turn up the stairs instead of a right towards the female voices. Kennedy tried to avoid the creaks on the stairs. Now if it's your own house you know where to avoid. But in a strange house every step taken is one step further into a minefield. Kennedy trod close to the edge of the steps figuring there would be less give in the boards where their support was the strongest.

His theory worked, worked that is until the penultimate royal-blue carpeted step before the landing. Luckily it proved to be a short, quiet creak and did not hinder Kennedy's journey into the unknown. He found the second door off the top landing to lead to the master bedroom. He gently opened the door a little further, just enough to let himself in, and found a very feminine room. Lots of light blues, lime greens and cream drapes about the walls, windows and over the bed in a canopy. One entire wall, the one housing the door he had entered by, was covered in mirror. The mirrors were in two-foot-six sections which slid to right and left to reveal a large walk-in wardrobe. Surprisingly it was not packed with clothes but instead was working to about a fifty per cent capacity.

The majority (only just) of the clothes were female. Kennedy found what could be loosely described as a long black coat but he figured it more than slightly too dressy for a potential midnight assassin.

To the left-hand side of the bed was a dressing table with a few books resting on top: Dick Francis, Joanna Trollope, Caroline Graham and a tacky Mills & Boon romance. To the right of the bed was a large easy chair with a reading light suspended over it from the rear on a crane-type stand anchored to the floor with a heavy black base.

To the right and left of the easy chair were two dining chairs, and all three chairs had clothes hung about them. No sign, however, of make-up table or wig stand. To one side of the dressing table, facing the foot of the bed, was another door, painted light blue to match the thick carpet. The thick carpet Kennedy now felt his feet sinking into. He wouldn't mind betting that neither Stephen Stone, nor any other human, would be permitted in this room wearing shoes. He opened the door to be greeted by nothing but darkness. Kennedy fumbled just inside the doorpost with his right hand and found a cord which when tugged threw a surprisingly large bathroom into brightness by way of several small low-voltage bulbs sunk into the ceiling. The bathroom was tiled, floor, walls and ceiling, in lime green. In fact all surfaces, excepting the back of the door and the large mirror above the sink and work top, were covered in the vile tiles. Probably not a pretty sight after fifteen pints of stout!

Three regal wig rests were positioned on guard on the work

top. Two supported wigs, the third would have been at home in Duncan Goodhew's bathroom. Sadly for Kennedy both the wigs on display were blonde, one baby-doll and curly and the other a French bop. But he was pleased to see that at least she did use wigs. For if she did, goodness knows what was going to be found hidden away elsewhere.

Every move he made about the bedroom and bathroom was magnified by the quietness of the rooms. He could still hear, just about, the two female voices from below. His own breath sounded like the wind through the trees on the top of Primrose Hill. He also felt that his heartbeats were vibrating down through his legs to the floor, through the floor to the ceiling of the sitting room where Coles and Mrs Stone were probably wondering what exactly the quiet-spoken detective was up to.

Time was deserting Kennedy as sure as the fact that Cantona had played his last game for Manchester United. But now he was so close, he had to find out if the trademark black lipstick was anywhere to be found.

Then all of a sudden he noticed in the mirror that the bathroom door was slowly being opened. It was ever so gradual but he could positively see the door inch its way inwards. He went through in a split second all his possible excuses. Lost my way. No toilet paper downstairs. I thought I heard a noise upstairs. I was looking for incriminating evidence – no, that wouldn't do. That's too honest, she'd never believe that, but the door was moving towards him slowly, in about seven seconds he was going to be caught. His worst nightmare: CID officer caught prowling in lady's bathroom. Ah, the shame, what would ann rea say? Worse than that, what would Castle say? Searching a property without a search warrant? Oh feck it, he'd go ballistic, so what?

It was all in slow motion. The door kept inching its way towards him and all he could do was stand there and wait to be caught. He decided to wash his hands, at least he'd been seen to be there with the intent of doing something other than prowling. He could work it to his advantage somehow later, hell he'd seen criminals do it often enough, why not use one of the enemy's tricks?

He felt maybe he should go to the door himself, implying that he had nothing to hide. Just at that moment the door stopped moving. What was happening now? Was this a surprise tactic coming up, or what? Then he heard a noise, like breathing but breathing with part of one's nostrils blocked, a bit like purring. In fact a lot like purring. At that precise moment a large moggy strolled in, white as silk, tail arched high as if to say, 'What's going on in here then?'

Kennedy decided there was no time to continue the search. He killed the lights, closed both the doors and glided down the stairs, pausing at the first bathroom to press the flush lever, and walked in on Coles and Mrs Stone, who seemed so wrapped up in their conversation that they hardly missed him. At least neither acknowledged they had and gave him the impression he had easily enough time to seek out the incriminating evidence, if any such evidence ineed existed in this household.

Chapter Thirty-Two

And so it was that Kennedy returned to his office in silence; he felt a little guilty at prying around in the Stone residence uninvited. He was, and most unusually for him, tired. He hadn't slept much last night, nothing to do with the TV, there never was anything worth watching on a Wednesday evening; Mondays, Thursdays and Fridays were the nights he found most use for his video recorder. He caught up with his viewing on Sunday afternoons, usually following a ninety-minute stroll around Regent's Park and Primrose Hill. No matter the weather, his Sunday afternoon stroll was the most sacrosanct event of his week.

It (his fatigue) was probably due to his insomnia, which in turn was probably due to the absence of ann rea. Oh shit, ann rea. He'd just remembered that he'd promised to find out about Daniel Elliot's daughter's case. Oh well, she (ann rea) hadn't rang back, so in a way he was off the hook.

'God, you're a sight for sore eyes,' Kennedy gushed.

'Probably what the apostles said as well, sir,' a battered and bruised James Irvine croaked from just inside the door of Kennedy's office. 'Aye, and I probably look a lot worse than I'm feeling. Mind you I'm not feeling all that great. How's things progressing?' Irvine continued, finding it slightly painful to speak. His copper hair, short-back-and-sides with neat parting, was severely dishevelled and he had a plaster and bandage across the blackness of the bridge of his nose. His usual ruddy complexion was a mess of blues, yellows and blacks, no more a suitable combination for a human face than it was for your granny's patchwork quilt.

'Well, let's see, Jimmy. Anderson claims he was hired by Miss Dipstick.'

'Who?' Irvine asked incredulously.

'A woman who dresses in black. Long black hair, black sunglasses, long black coat and black lipstick. Hence Miss Dipstick,' Kennedy explained. Irvine continued to stare blankly at his superior.

'It was funny at the time. You had to be there. Anyway she found Anderson, paid him to beat up John B. Stone, not kill him, mind you. That's very important. Anderson claims that he was hired just to duff up Stone, just to scare him a bit. He also claims that Stone was breathing when he left him at the Fountain of Sorrow.

'So, do you believe him?' Sean Connery's finest impersonator impersonated.

'Weeeeeell, I do and I don't. I mean I don't particularly believe him, but then again, there is no reason not to. He's going to do porridge either way so he's nothing to gain by inventing this person. And Leslie Russell is convinced he's telling the truth.'

'Yes, sir, but he is Anderson's brief after all.'

'Yes, I hear you. But I like him. He's good, and I do believe him to be honest,' Kennedy stated.

'So any leads, then, on this Miss Dipstick?'

'We went back to see Jean Stone, obviously she had a proba-ble cause and she looks like the right height and build, but I couldn't find any black wig or black lipstick. I'm not sure it's safe to rule her out, though. There's just something too pat going on in the Stone household, she seems too... well, too okay. Let's look at it from her point of view. She dates John B. Stone originally, we have to assume they were in love. She thought he was too in love with her and not ambitious enough. So she tries the older brother, Stephen. He appears to be more ambitious so she leaves John B. and eventually marries Stephen. As it turns out John B. proves to be much more successful. Jean and John B. meet up again at John B.'s mother's funeral.' Kennedy was warming to this theme. He paused to consider how best to further his theory.

'They talk, she susses John B. still has a thing for her, perhaps she also has regrets. You know, regrets about forsaking love for a bank balance only to find she'd lost both. Mrs Jean Stone, the worse for wear on wine, gets involved in a bit of canoodling with John B. Maybe just to see if there was anything still there between them, or maybe just because she was very drunk. But John B. doesn't want to stop at a bit of kissing. He wants to do the wild thing. She refuses, he rapes her. Now she knows he couldn't really care less about her. He was using her to get back at his brother and in a way, his demented way, get his own back on her. She's disgusted, embarrassed and angry. Her disgust and embarrassment vanishes with time but her anger doesn't. It foments into an ugly brew which is destined to boil over eventually. She bides her time. Then dons the famous disguise, complete with black lipstick, and hires Anderson to do the evil deed.'

'Is this not all getting a bit far fetched, sir?'

'That's the thing really, isn't it? It's so far-fetched that no one in their right mind would bother to invent it,' Kennedy surmised.

'I suppose you've got a point there. What about an alibi? Did Jean Stone offer any kind of plausible alibi?' inquired the bloodied and bruised DS.

'She told Coles that on the night in question she and her husband were at home together all evening.'

Irvine gave a sceptical grunt.

'Exactly,' Kennedy concurred.

'So where do we go from here, sir?'

'Well, to be perfectly honest, I feel pretty empty myself. I mean to all intents and purposes we've solved this case. Castle was right all the time, Anderson was our man. Anderson's signed his statement, so in a way it's all done and dusted.' Kennedy looked like he'd said all he wanted to and now began to tidy his desk, but just as Irvine was about to leave he continued, 'It's just like in the movies, you know? The story is resolved, you get ready to leave the cinema. But the lights don't come up, the credits don't roll, the story moves on in a totally different direction and concludes with a final twist.'

'What, like *Taxi Driver*?'

'Exactly like *Taxi Driver*. It's like I'm still sitting in my seat and the lights haven't come up, and the credits haven't started to roll, but...' Kennedy let the 'but' hang in the air because he knew that if the projectionist was a certain chap called Castle then the credits would be rolling soon and rolling fast, followed shortly by the house lights.

'But we don't have any avenues left to pursue, do we?'

Kennedy clenched his teeth, 'Well then I suppose we'll just have to look again. Look at all our original suspects. The basic flaw in all of this is that we are very short of female suspects. It's either Jean Stone or – ' the DI paused, ' – or it's Jean Stone.'

'Or,' Irvine added, massaging the bridge of his nose very gently (it was becoming very itchy and Kennedy's mum would have had one for that: 'it's getting itchy 'cause it's getting better') 'It's person or persons unknown.'

'Ah, Jimmy,' Kennedy sighed, 'If that's the case we're missing something, we're missing something big and we'd better start to dig back into John B. Stone's life again. We've got to find something, someone who wanted to do him harm.'

'And who either has a female accomplice or is female,' Irvine added.

'Okay, take some of the boys and get stuck into it again, Jimmy, we need something, anything. There must be something out there. I can't remember the last death, even of a crook, where no one seemed to give a feck. It's usually, ^Oh you know he was a really nice geezer,'' or ^He was a bit of a shit but he was real good to his kids," or even ^He got into all of this by accident you know, he was forced into it, really he'd a heart of gold," But with John B. Stone not one person, particularly the members of his family seemed to be distressed in the slightest by his demise. I suppose this could work to our disadvantage, because it could mean that perhaps there was more than one person who had a reason to want him dead. Anyway, let's do some digging.'

At this point Sgt Flynn tapped on his open door and Kennedy looked up. 'I dug out that file you wanted,' Flynn announced, 'It seemed pretty urgent, so I brought it straight up.'

'Thanks a million, Tim,' smiled Kennedy, taking the file and putting it straight onto his desk.

'I didn't go through the file much, sir,' Flynn went on, 'but I do kinda remember the case. I'd just started work here when the incident happened, so if you need any further background, just give me a shout and I can go through it later for you,' the ever-helpful desk sergeant offered.

'Thanks. No, I think it should be okay. I just need to dig a bit of info out of it,' Kennedy replied. He was beginning to feel a little uneasy at using police time and resources to help a personal friend, albeit for a good reason. Mind you on the justification side he could remember lots of occasions during his short (fifteen months) relationship with ann rea where her background information had proved invaluable to Camden CID.

'No problem. I'll leave you to it.' And with that Flynn, friendly as ever, nodded and left the room.

No sooner had he closed the door behind him when Kennedy continued on his original line. 'Stone's background, yes, let's dig deeper into that. Let's concentrate, but not exclusively, with the gentler side of the race.'

'I always try, sir,' Irvine smiled.

'Yes, so I've heard. However I think those activities may be somewhat restricted for a while, old chap,' Kennedy grinned as he eyed Irvine's badly mangled face.

'Oh, I don't know, sir. Sometimes the sympathy vote goes a long way,' the Scot replied and attempted to laugh, but this proved to be too painful so he moved the conversation back to business. 'I've just been thinking, sir. If we assume your theory about Jean Stone is correct and we take it a stage further, what if the family know about it, know what she did and are closing ranks and painting the picture that no one cares about John B. so that we'll think, if his own family doesn't care about his death why should we worry. That could also be why Anderson's been implicated. You know, throw a few scraps to the dogs. They could even have planted that half-eaten apple of Anderson's to make sure we'd pick up the trail. We find Anderson, he's been seen in the Spread Eagle with John B. on the night he's beaten to death, we have a piece of evidence which puts him at the scene of the crime, and as you say, we're done and dusted. But you're right, it all is too neat, too pat. Perhaps I should go and see Jean Stone?'

'No, I don't think so. I'm not sure there's much more to be learned from her at this stage. Perhaps the less we bother her the more she'll think she's gotten away with it and the more careless she'll become. No, let's not go and see her. Let's get stuck back in John B. again. Let's find out everything we can about him. I keep feeling if we get to know the more about the man's life this will all fall into place for us,' said Kennedy.

'Okay, we'll start digging into Stone's background immediately and I'll get back to you as soon as we turn up anything of interest,' Irvine said as he left the office. Then, just as Kennedy reached for the recently delivered file, his telephone rang.

It was Castle looking for an update on the case. Well, not so much an update as confirmation that Kennedy now concurred with him, and that now they were in possession of Anderson's statement and the confession (though limited) contained therein, surely the case was concluded.

Kennedy kept the conversation brief, barely mentioning the several loose ends he was tying up. He told only a limited version of the truth because if Castle were to become aware of the full extent of Kennedy's recent instructions to DS Irvine he'd go off on one of his 'You know everything doesn't have to be so complicated, old son' lectures.

Kennedy hoped he would get to the file on Anna Elliot before ann rea rang him, and consequently each time the phone rang, as it did repeatedly for the next eight and a half minutes, he dreaded picking it up. None of the calls were important, however, and thankfully none of them were from ann rea.

Chapter Thirty-Three

When, eventually, Kennedy had a chance to check the file, small though it was (three pages), he had but one word to say: 'JAYSUS!'

Chapter Thirty-Four

So it was at this point, late Thursday afternoon on the third day of the case, which turned out in reality to be the fourth day of the case, when everything went pearshaped, as in totally pearshaped.

Kennedy had now read the file three times and he didn't know whether to ring ann rea – he realised in fact that this was not a possibility   or go and speak with Castle – probably a bad idea since the Super was going to be very disappointed for the second time that day – or regroup with his team immediately and continue with the investigation but in an entirely new direction.

He did none of the above. Instead he reviewed the Anna Elliot files for the fourth time.

Early, about eight a.m. on the morning of the October 20th, 1973, a young girl was discovered by a Regent's Park gatekeeper, a Mr Stanley (Stan) O'Donnell, who was opening the park gates at Gloucester Gate. The gatekeeper thought he saw something move in a pile of autumn leaves which were caught in a wind trap at the back of the washerwoman fountain near the gate.

Stan, the statement revealed, at first couldn't see anything, and had just about convinced himself it was merely the wind rustling through the leaves when he heard moaning. He bent over the fountain's stone and saw a young girl lying amongst the leaves. She was, he stated, sobbing gently.

The gatekeeper helped her out with a lot of coaxing and, on not being able to extract any additional information, helped her the short distance to North Bridge House.

The girl, one seventeen-year-old Anna Elliot, had been reported missing the previous evening by a very distraught Daniel and Lila Elliot. Daniel had rang, the file showed, at 20.50, also at 21.20, and again at 21.47. He visited the station, with his wife, at 22.12 and remained at North Bridge House until 01.20 the following morning.

His daughter had gone out for a walk on Primrose Hill at 18.30 and was due to return at 19.30 to watch her favourite soap. When she failed to return the worried parents had waited a nail-biting one hour and twenty minutes before making the first of their calls to the police station.

Kennedy knew that they would have been reassured with a 'She'd probably gone to see her friends,' or 'She must have met someone on the hill and chatted, forgetting the time as young-sters have a habit of doing.' He also knew that the worried parents would have been asked questions like 'Is she happy at home?', 'Did they have a row?', 'Has she done this before?' and 'Did she have a boyfriend?' The parents would also have been advised that their daughter could not officially be classified as missing until twenty-four hours after her absence had first been reported.

Upon her discovery the following morning her parents were sent for immediately. The file showed the father as being the only parent present. During the interview with WPC Leigh, and in the requested absence of her father, Anna Elliot made a state-ment telling what had happened to her.

She had been abducted by four youths, taken to the bushes near the St Edmunds Terrace entrance to Primrose Hill, and raped by three of the four youths. The file reported that her clothes, although dirty, were not torn.

Anna Elliot had supplied the names of three of her four abductors, who in turn had advised the police of the name of the fourth. All four had concurred that they had not raped the girl but that she willingly had sex with three of them. They all equally concurred that she didn't have sex with the fourth because, they claimed, she wasn't attracted to him.

This was obviously, Kennedy surmised twenty-four years later, going to be the major part of their defence.

Anna Elliot had her medical examination at 09.20 (no marks were found on her body) and left the North Bridge House at 10.12. The final note in the file stated that Daniel Elliot rang the station at 15.47 that afternoon and advised WPC Leigh that they would not be pressing charges against any of the youths.

The file w as marked No Further Action.

Kennedy, saddened as he always was and disappointed by the way humans behave with each other, looked once again at the names of the four youths involved in the incident with Anna Elliot on the evening of October 19th, 1973:

Mr Jerry Clive MacKane, aged 17 years.

Mr John Brendan Stone, aged 17 years.

Mr Rory Nash, aged 16 years.

Mr Neil Robin Burton, aged 15 years.

The detective wasn't as shocked by the second name on the list as he was by the fourth.

Chapter Thirty-Five

Kennedy made his decisions, quickly, efficiently, effortlessly. He summoned Anne Coles, James Irvine and PCs Alloway, Gaul, Shaw and Essex. He advised them of his startling (accidental) discovery.

'Okay, Jerry MacKane was seventeen years old, which would mean he's now forty-one, and Rory Nash was sixteen years old which means he's now forty. Both these people potentially are in danger.' Kennedy paused so that he, as well as those gathered, could take in the enormity of the statement. He made a fist with his left hand and as he lifted it towards his audience he freed his forefinger so that it was pointing heavenward.

'So, we have to trace both of them as soon as possible. We must be diligent and track down every possible lead. Let's go back to all the relations and friends of both Burton and Stone; someone must have a clue as to the whereabouts of their two former friends. You tend to remember your first group of friends.'

'Yes, and your first f-' Essex wisecracked only to be cut dead by Kennedy.

'Yes, PC Essex, you were about to say?' Kennedy found himself being a bit uncharacteristically ratty, but in this case not only did they have to solve the murders and find the murderer, but until such time as they did there was also a chance that two other people's lives were in danger.

'I was about to say,' Essex replied, shrinking at being the focus of unwanted scrutiny, twitching nervously in his seat and running a hand through his prematurely greying hair to divert attention, 'That you never forget your first fling, sir.'

'Yes, well I'm sure you'll tell us all about it when it happens to you,' Kennedy replied briskly before continuing, 'Now, Anna Elliot, she's got to move to the top of our suspect list.'

'You think we've found our Miss Dipstick, sir?' Irvine inquired as he stopped writing in his notebook.

'Yes, I think we can assume that there is a very good chance that Anna Elliot is our lady in black.'

'What about a relation of hers, seeking revenge on her behalf?' Coles posed. Kennedy could tell that she was happy about the way Essex had been dealt with. He knew that she shared his increasing annoyance at the laddish behaviour of some of the younger members of the force. He had hoped there was going to be no room for lager louts and football hooligans in the Met.

'No, none. Well, none capable. ann rea is currently with Anna Elliot's father, who is over seventy and in quite bad health. Her mother died about eighteen months ago and Anna was an only child. The minute I hear from ann rea I'm going to go down and interview the father, Daniel Elliot, myself. ann rea has already spent some time trying to track down Anna. For a totally different reason, mind you. She wants to put father and daughter together again before he dies. So she may have some additional information for us.' And wishing ann rea would hurry up and ring him, Kennedy then dismissed the team, sending them out on the twenty-four year old trail of Jerry MacKane, Rory Nash and Anna Elliot. He asked Irvine to remain behind.

'Listen, Jimmy, could you go over and see Miss Forsythe again?'

'Mrs, sir,' Irvine interrupted.

'What?'

'Mrs, sir. She was married once, a long time ago when she lived in the Midlands. They separated but she kept her married name, although she did go to great pains to point out that she likes to be addressed as Doctor,' Irvine replied carefully so as not to stress his badly bruised jaw.

'Oh. Yes, I see, Mrs, yes, Doctor, of course. I had forgotten you had a date with her. How did it go?' At this stage Kennedy didn't really give a rat's arse about how the date went, but he was too polite not to make some kind of inquiry.

'Well, we had a drink, then another drink, and then we had another drink, and then we sat down and had a few drinks more. And then I was drunk and she still seemed to be sober and she went home and I went home and that was it. But the next day she said she'd had a great time and that we should do it again,' Irvine replied, trying hard to force a smile out of his face. He could feel the dried blood around the bridge of his nose crack a little; he twitched in discomfort and continued,

'But I'm not sure I'm capable of keeping up with her to be honest. Good heavens, I've just thought, sir, is there any chance Anna Elliot could have changed her name to Jean, to Jean – what's Jean Stone's maiden name?'

'To be honest we don't know, but definitely a line worth checking, well worth checking, Jimmy. That would make a lot of sense.'

'Well, maybe some professional interfacing, as our computer experts would put it, will give you a chance for some less stressful and more sociable evenings. So why don't you go and see her and she if she could re-examine Neil Burton: get her to go through all the autopsy notes and find out if there is any way, any way at all, that Burton's injuries could have been caused by… well, I don't know really. How would it be possible to kill someone but do it in such a way that you could persuade a professional, like herself for instance, that a dog was responsible?'

'I see what you mean. It sounds like one for Sherlock Holmes, doesn't it, sir?'

'What?' Kennedy said as his phone rang and he picked up the receiver, then, 'ann rea. Am I glad to hear from you. Hang on, could you excuse me for just a second?' He pressed the mute button and addressed Irvine, 'Okay Jimmy, if you could go and see the Doctor, I'm off to Climping shortly but I'll ring in later for an update.'

Irvine nodded and left the office.

'Listen,' Kennedy said to ann rea, 'you'll never guess what has just happened up here.'

Chapter Thirty-Six

Kennedy was correct. ann rea would not have, even in a month of Sundays, guessed the developments which had taken place up in Camden Town.

The Detective Inspector wasn't used to being surprised on his own cases. Surprised? Shocked would be more apt. Yes, occasionally some one or some thing would throw you a curve, but they were mostly curves whose arcs you could contain and the bearing was rarely as much a shock as a refreshing change of direction.

But this, ann rea's landlord's daughter being involved in a double murder, this was slightly surreal. Not to mention the fact that ann rea was chasing up a few leads as to the current whereabouts of Anna Elliot, leads which could, and hopefully would, prove invaluable to Kennedy's case. However if he was ever to get any closer to solving this case then he was surely in for another bombshell. In the meantime he was composing himself for his meeting with ann rea and the frail Daniel Elliot.

Kennedy caught the 17.22 train from Victoria, arriving in Worthing at 18.40. ann rea was at the shabby station to meet him. The Ulsterman and his lover then cabbed it the seven miles to Climping, where she had booked him a room at the Black Horse, right next door to Daniel Elliot.

The journey from station to pub was quiet, neither wishing to share their news with the talkative taxi driver, 'The Rolling Stones stayed there you know, Climping – at the Bailiffscourt Hotel.'

'Really?' ann rea replied indifferently, and before the driver had a chance to expand she said, 'Kennedy, do you know when you're going to go back?'

'Yes. I'm catching the six fifty-four, it gets me into Victoria at eight sixteen, means I'll be back in North Bridge House at eight forty-five,' Kennedy replied uneasily in the back seat. He wasn't sure whether or not to hold ann rea's hand.

'Remember to book your cab tonight, you'll not be able to get one easily at that time of the morning,' ann rea suggested. She stroked his temple a few times as they travelled the remainder of their journey in silence. The cabbie, not the local expert he claimed to be, took a few wrong turns before pulling up outside the Black Horse.

'Let's have a bite before we go over and see Daniel,' ann rea said as the friendly (very friendly) landlady showed Kennedy to his small but clean room.

'So this is a bit of a case, isn't it?' Kennedy said as he tucked into his cod, peas and chips, passable except for the disappointing soggy fish, washed down with a glass of the house white wine (excellent).

'God, I can't believe it, I really can't. I mean you don't really believe that Daniel's daughter is involved in the murder of these two men?'

'Well, it kinda looks that way, I suppose,' Kennedy replied.

'But I thought you had a confession for the estate agent's murder. And this other guy, wasn't he mauled by a dog?'

'Yes, but here's the thing,' Kennedy replied between bites, 'Hugh Anderson, the guy who beat up John B. Stone, claimed he was paid by a woman, dressed all in black, black wig, long black coat and black lipstick, to do it. He further claims that he left Stone alive. Burton's death, the autopsy revealed, was caused by a savage attack from a dog. Now, if we are to believe that Anna Elliot did this in revenge for the rape then it's possible she hired a thug to beat up Stone; perhaps she hired another one with a dog for Burton. Irvine is checking it with Dr Forsythe to see if there is any way Burton's death could have been caused by someone trying to make the death appear to be a mauling.'

Kennedy washed down the last of his food with the remainder of the wine.

'So,' he continued as he wiped his mouth and chin with his paper napkin, 'What progress have you been making in tracking Anna down?'

'Good, really. I mean I haven't found her yet but a mate at the *Camden News Journal* knew Anna's best friend at the time of the rape. There wasn't too much information on the incident except for, surprisingly, or so they all thought at the time, she wasn't bruised or marked or anything, and none of her clothes were torn,' said ann rea.

'So what are they all saying? She wasn't raped, just because she wasn't beaten up?' Kennedy replied in disbelief.

'No. No, not at all. I mean, I think not at all. I think that was offered as some kind of explanation as to why no charges were ever brought: too hard a case to prove, too traumatic for Anna to have to go through a court case with four people swearing that she asked for it, she wanted it. But for the short time she remained in London after the incident she was a changed person. Withdrawn, very quiet, wouldn't go out and mix with her friends any more. Then she moved to Wolverhampton to continue her education.'

Kennedy thought for a moment. Here he was sitting with ann rea, the woman of his dreams, and certainly since her absence very much present in his dreams, and all they were talking was business. He could hardly believe it.

'Look, we'd better go over and see Daniel, I told him you were coming down to see me. I also told him that you are going to help me find Anna. I did not tell him about your suspicions. Honestly Christy, it could be the final straw. He's barely got the will to live as it is.' ann rea checked her watch. 'It's nearly eight o'clock, we'll stay with him till about nine, he usually goes to bed about then. Then you and I can go for a walk along the beach, it's only five minutes away, and by the look of your furrowed brow a bit of a distraction just might be exactly what the doctor ordered. I'll go and buy Daniel his nightly pint and we'll be off.'

Christy Kennedy and Daniel Elliot had never meet before, although Kennedy had heard a lot about Daniel from ann rea. Kennedy was shocked at how fragile the once-proud Irish Guard looked. His eyes were soulless and disinterested. Kennedy wasn't even sure he had either energy or enthusiasm, or cared enough to help track down his own daughter.

Daniel, did however, show some enthusiasm for his nightly pint and after his first, generous gulp he apologised to Kennedy. 'I've heard so much about you,' he said, 'I'm sorry not to be in better health to greet you.'

'Oh, don't you worry about that, Mr Elliot,' Kennedy replied but Daniel continued as though he hadn't heard the detective.

'She's a great lass you know. Me and the Mrs, we were always very fond of ann. We knew her before she lost her capitals,' the old man joked. 'She could never do enough to help us, so unusual for the younger generation.' Daniel took another sip of his beer. Kennedy used this break as an excuse to move the conversation in the direction of Anna.

'You'll get no arguments from me on that one, sir,' Kennedy began, his green eyes smiling their magic smile. 'Your daughter, Anna, I was wondering if there was anyone around who might have known her.'

'Oh, I've been through all this with ann rea. Has she put you up to this in case I've forgotten something? No, after the trouble, I mean Anna's trouble...' Daniel stared until Kennedy nodded to show he was aware of her trouble, '...she just literally became a different person, wouldn't go out, wouldn't talk, even to the Mrs and me, wouldn't see her friends, she just stopped living, really. A friend of mine from Dublin had moved to Wolverhampton and he suggested taking her in for awhile, he thought a new environment where no one knew her and knew of the...trouble, might encourage her to start living again. He thought it just might kickstart her life again.' Daniel stopped for another sip of beer; neither ann rea nor Kennedy filled the gap.

'She went willingly. In fact we were quite hopeful because she seemed to get back some of her buzz, and then I remember when she left she wouldn't kiss or hug her mother or me. I mean I could understand her not wanting to kiss me, a male and all that, but Lila... I can tell you it broke Lila's heart, broke her heart right in two. Anyway, off she went to Wolverhampton, we rang her every night at first. She just wouldn't talk to us. But Peter, my friend from Dublin, he said she was okay, coming out of herself a bit, forming new relationships and that, but he couldn't get her to talk to us.' The old man stopped and Kennedy could see great tears rolling freely down his cheeks.

ann rea went to Daniel and wiped his face with her handkerchief. She sat by him on the arm of his chair where she remained with her arm around his shoulders, petting gently, saying, 'There, there.' After some time Daniel got his breath back and said,

'You know what, Christy? We never spoke with her again. We got a call after six weeks from Peter saying Anna had moved out, moved to Birmingham. She promised to keep in touch but of course she didn't and that was that. I don't know, I've been thinking a lot about it recently and I've been trying to think what we did wrong. I keep feeling that Lila and I were treated as though we had done something wrong. Can you tell me what we did wrong?'

'Well,' said Kennedy, 'you can't apply normal logic to a situation like that. Here she was, probably thinking exactly the same as you were thinking: 'What did I do wrong? I didn't do anything to deserve, or encourage, this.' She probably thought she was dirty, spoiled, no longer your special daughter. She probably never wanted a man, any man, near her again in her life and she took it out on the only people she could, her mother and father,' he said very quietly.

'But why so? Why her family?' Daniel pleaded with the pain and agony of someone who just had through it all yesterday and not twenty-four years ago.

'Because you are her family and she felt that as her family you would protect her in her life, protect her against such evils.' Kennedy was trying to temper honesty with gentleness.

Daniel looked at Kennedy with shock, hurt and anger in his eyes. ann rea's eyes were screaming at Kennedy, 'Enough of this!'

'I'm not saying it's true, Daniel. I am saying that there was a good chance that your daughter felt it to be true. So she found it impossible to forgive you, because when she needed you you weren't there, and what are parents for if not to protect their offspring? But in a way it wasn't you and your wife she hated, she hated the fact that there was no way to make all her dark thoughts go away; and who else is there to take all that anger out on? She was trying to hurt someone, someone she loved, as much as she had been hurt. You and your wife were the obvious targets and as such you were the most vulnerable and therefore you were allowing her hatred to be effective,' Kennedy concluded.

Daniel Elliot was silent. ann rea was silent. Silent but still staring daggers at Kennedy. Slowly Daniel started to nod his head in acceptance.

'Well, you know what, young lady,' he said, 'this is a good man of yours. His explanation makes sense to me, painful but true. I just wish he'd been around before to talk to Lila to let her know what all this was about. Because we both blamed ourselves all these years and maybe if we'd had a better understanding of of all of this we could even have done something to help her. You know we never tried to track her down, there was no point, what were we going to do? What were we going to say? Sorry? We knew sorry certainly wasn't enough. It's hardly enough when it *is* your fault. Because you're right, we parents do have a responsibility to look after our children. They don't ask to come into the world, you bring them into it and so they must be your responsibility. But what are you meant to do? Wrap them up in cotton wool, lock them away, never let them out of your sight? You know how badly children are going to react to that.'

'That's the thing Daniel isn't it, you can't,' said ann rea. 'You're right, because if you did, if you had said to her, ^Listen Anna, you're not going out for a walk on the hill by yourself tonight, you might get raped, I'll come with you,'' what would she have said, ^Oh, please daddy, don't be silly, of course I won't, everyone will make fun of me, out for a walk on Primrose Hill protected by my father, I could never hold my head up with my friends again,''? There's evil and badness in the world and evil always finds its victims. We can't change that, nobody can. We just have to get on with our lives the best way we know how and hope that somehow the love which surrounds us will protect us,' she consoled as she continued to pat Daniel gently on the shoulder.

'Look you two, I'm off to bed,' he said as he rose, kissed ann rea on the cheek and shakily made his way to Kennedy to shake his hand. He shook it more firmly than Kennedy had expected for a frail man. Perhaps he put all his energy into the handshake so that Kennedy would be aware how much his words had been appreciated.

ann rea helped Daniel to take off his blazer which proudly displayed the Irish Guards' emblem on a crest covering the entire breast pocket. Kennedy couldn't help but feel that this is when you see how old an old man really is. The blazer or jacket always conceals the wasting, thinning arms and torso.

The moon illuminated (thankfully, for there was no other form of light) the pebble beach where ann rea and Kennedy found themselves ten thoughtful minutes later.

Chapter Thirty-Seven

It so happens as Kennedy and ann rea were about to start the 'date' part of the evening DS Irvine and Dr Bella Forsythe were about to embark on the second date of their short relationship, if indeed you could count it as a relationship. Irvine had rang the doctor, as directed by his boss, to see if Burton's wounds could have been caused by something other than a dog.

Dr Forsythe had been friendly, but busy. She suggested they discuss it further over dinner, promising, unsolicited, to abstain from the whisky which had so wrecked Irvine on their first date.

She had picked Irvine up at North Bridge House at nine-fifteen (fifteen minutes late) and they had walked the short distance down Parkway to Trattoria Lucca to be greeted by the owner, Frank. His greeting was as warm and generous as those which various members of his family had been bestowing on the patrons of Camden's finest Italian resturant since it first opened (in half its current space) in 1955.

'So, your DI still thinks Neil Burton could have been killed by something other than dog's teeth?' Forsythe began as she thirstily drank her (still) mineral water.

'Yep,' Irvine replied in his finest (and 100% natural)

Connery as he toyed with his glass of lager. He was itching for a thirst-quenching swig but he didn't want to repeat the alcoholic charge of their first date. Hell, he liked the taste of the barley as much as the next man, but to his mind (and the rest of the diners that evening) Bella Forsythe was a beautiful woman, a stunning woman, and he had other hungers he wanted to satisfy. He could always buy a case of lager or a crate of wine, but how many chances would he have to be out with a woman who was so well preserved he couldn't believe that she was only (just) entering her forty-first year.

'And what do you think?'

Irvine was cagey. 'Kennedy, he's not your usual cop you know. Sure he sometimes gets hunches which are way off base. Even then he's usually onto something which though it may not ultimately provide the solution, will help us arrive at the solution which we probably wouldn't have found were it not for the elaborate journey. So I'm kinda happy to follow his hunches.'

'I think he may be way off base on this one, James,' she smiled. He liked the precise way she always pronounced his first name. 'No human could have left those marks. Unless of course it was a full moon and someone swapped their bloody Mary for some fresh blood,' she laughed. Irvine joined in. He supposed she was right. The body, in the opinion of this expert, had died not at the hands of a fellow human, but at the teeth of a dog and a crazy dog at that. Mind you, Irvine thought to himself, how come there had been no similar attacks reported?

'Look,' Forsythe began, switching line as their starters arrived, hers hot asparagus with melting butter and his a green salad, 'I'm sorry about the other night. I don't know what came over me. But… I'm shocked, maybe I was nervous but I never usually drink. If I'm honest I rarely drink at all but the first whisky felt so warm and exciting as it went down and we were having a great laugh and the next thing I realised I was completely blotto, and next morning I'd couldn't even remember how I got home.'

'I dropped you off by taxi,' Irvine reminded her, 'you seemed totally in control of your senses. I, on the other hand, was distinctly feeling the worse for the wear so we said goodnight at your door. The taxi driver and myself watched you let yourself in and then I went home to suffer. All night. And most of the following morning.'

'Thanks, I knew I'd be in safe hands,' she smiled sincerely.

'Where I come from, I'm not sure that's exactly a compliment.'

'Well from me it certainly is,' she cut in very firmly, 'But the following morning I woke up feeling great and it was a case of 'Wow, where's the big hangover everyone keeps talking about?'

'Maybe I was suffering enough for both of us,' Irvine offered as she ordered another glass of mineral water to accompany her main course. She had the vegetarian lasagne and Irvine had ordered Kennedy's pasta.

'I was intrigued by your order, I couldn't wait to see what it was,' she said as she prepared to eat, fork at the ready, waiting for an ample spray of ground pepper but refusing the cheese.

'Yes,' said Irvine, 'The DI always has this, it's not on the menu, they make it specially for him, it's just spaghetti with the most amazing pesto sauce you will ever taste, and some peas.' The way he, and most of his fellow Scots, pronounced the word amazing made you believe that the very least it could be was amazing.

'Your DI, you like him a lot, don't you? In fact all his team really like him, don't they?'

'He has his moments, but he does look after us and that's not always the case, is it?'

'No. Not from what I hear. And Dr Taylor swears by Kennedy as well.'

'How is the old soul?'

'Fine, he's back on Monday,' she said, taking a digestive pause and a sip of water.

'Really? I didn't think he was coming back so soon.'

'No, he's fine again, and besides he'd better be. I'm off on my holiday at the weekend.'

'What?' Irvine didn't conceal his disappointment. 'How long for?'

'Aren't you meant to ask where, first?' she smiled. 'Five

weeks actually, if you must know.'

'Five weeks?'

'Yes, James. Five weeks, I've saved up a full year's worth of leave to take it all at once, and I'm going to travel around for a bit, just go with the flow. I've been dying to do it for years.'

'Where? Italy? Spain?'

'No, silly. England. You won't get anywhere better than England, God's own country.'

'I'm not sure, ancestrally speaking, that I'm allowed to agree with you,' Irvine replied, regaining his composure after the initial shock. 'You'll have fun, I'm sure. Will I get a chance to see you before you leave?'

'Sorry, sadly no. It won't be possible, I'm leaving first thing Saturday morning and I'm working late tomorrow night to get all the lab reports up to date for Leonard, and then I've got to pack. But I like it that you want to see me; will you miss me?' she teased.

'Oh, I'd like to,' Irvine replied dolloping on a shovel (too much) of bravado, 'But Kennedy will have us all running ragged on this case. We've got three people to track down now.'

'Three people?' she quizzed, and stopped eating for a few seconds before breaking into a smile again. 'How come three people? Surely Kennedy doesn't think there are three people other than Anderson involved?'

'Yes,' Irvine said immediately, but then paused as he wondered how much he should be telling her. Although they were both on the same side he thought better of it and back-tracked, 'Yes, there are three more people the DI wants to track down to help us with our inquiries.' The moment he uttered these words he felt a right prat. Here he was talking to a colleague, working on the same case as him for goodness sake, and he was uttering things like 'to help us with our inquiries.'

'If there is a connection between Stone and Burton then the Boss thinks that two other people may be in danger,' he said quietly and conspiratorially.

'Oh, for heaven's sake, James,' and Bella laughed so loud that some of their fellow diners and Frank the owner turned to stare, 'there's no connection. One was killed by a dog and the other by a thug. I think this must be one of the DI's tangents you were telling me about. He may be so far off the curve on this one that you'll need to check he doesn't stray off on to another case entirely.' The Doctor continued to laugh so loudly that after a few seconds the dapper DS in his finest tweeds joined in.

It was lucky he did, for he was to have no more fun on that particular evening as it ended twenty-eight minutes later with a long, but soulless kiss.

Chapter Thirty-Eight

Meanwhile, back on the beach, Kennedy was faring better, professionally, romantically and sexually. In fact, if the truth be known, and there seems no reason to hide it, he and ann rea went a lot further on the beach, so to speak, than either of them expected.

Neither, it has to be mentioned, was disappointed. No aimless groping, no fumbling with catches, hooks, buttons, zips or undergarments. No, none of this; in fact it started with a kiss. But then doesn't it always? It was more of a 'missed you' kiss than the lifeless 'tell me when you've finished with my lips, mouth and tongue,' that DS Irvine was experiencing eighty-five miles away.

The 'missed you' kiss' grew into a kiss of hunger, though neither Kennedy nor ann rea, if pressed as to when the kiss changed from one to the other would be able to pinpoint the exact moment of change. Did one lead to the other, or did one kiss just naturally develop out of the other, or did it just grow of its own accord? With these two particular lovers it was never a foregone conclusion that once they started kissing it would lead on to the main event. No, Kennedy loved kissing too much to be part of that deck of cards.

Anyway, it might have been the beach, might have been the lapping of the water, might have been the moonlight, might even have had something to do with the fact that they hadn't been with each other for four days. Or, you know what, it could even be, in a perverse way, that they both had taken a look at Daniel Elliot, alone, old, ill and without his woman and decided (unconsciously, subconsciously or whatever) that they need not waste any more of their special time. Not that Kennedy was one for wasting time in that recreational area. ann rea also, 'God bless her cotton socks,' thought Kennedy, 'particularly her white cotton socks,' was not backwards at coming forwards.

So our lovers are on the beach and they kiss, passionately. They touch, they feel, they move to a more secluded part of the beach where there is a canopy of trees. The moonlight is broken into hundreds of rays by their many leaves and branches. Neither asks 'shall we?' 'can we?' 'could I?' or 'would you?' They are leaning against a tree, Kennedy's back to it. ann rea presses harder against him. Their kiss grows in hunger. Kennedy feels himself involuntarily pushing back against ann rea's pressure. ann rea in turn responds.

Kennedy has no thoughts of North Bridge House, Miss Dipstick, Castle, Taylor, Irvine, Coles, Stone, Burton, Jean Stone, the Fountain of Sorrow, Primrose Hill twenty-four years ago, estate agents, Anderson or wild dogs. Neither is he conscious of the tree digging into his back. He can hear the wind rustling through the leaves all around him. When he occasionally opens his eyes he can make out parts of ann rea's face in the moonlight.

Blood is being dispatched by Kennedy's brain to every outpost of his body, he is aware of how loud he is as he inhales gulps of air through his nostrils. He knows he should have his eyes closed during these intimate moments but he can't help stealing glimpses of ann rea. She looks so soulful, so beautiful, her almond-shaped eyes, her white skinned face which beams in the moonlight. Kennedy can just make out the beginnings of a flush on her cheeks. Her short Beatle-bobbed hair is dishevelled but not messy. He fondles her perfect body (perfect for him and does anyone else matter?), every part of her perfect body. Her clothes just seem to make way effortlessly to accommodate his wandering hands. She likes Kennedy's hands, she has told him so many times. She likes his hands because she loves what they do to her and she trusts them completely as they do their will.

Again Kennedy steals another glance at ann rea, and at that precise moment he loves her, her hands, feet, heart, bottom, eyes, ears, nose, soul, intrigues, sense of humour, darkness... yes, he loves her darkness, it's the one thing, the only thing which prevents him from taking her for granted, prevents him from thinking 'this is it, we are happy ever after,' her darkness forbids this, he loves her laugh, he loves her tears, he loves her hair now so messed up in a French kind of way, he loves every single thing about her, except maybe... and that's just a maybe.

At that split second the thing he loves the most about her is the fact that she is turned on. She is turned on by him and this in return is the single biggest turn on for him and very soon they are as one, protected, and they move and breathe and kiss and groan and laugh and cry and push and pull and sway and cling and wait, as one.

They wait until they know they are ready, ready to love together, and they do so on that lonely beautiful beach at Climping between the trees, under the leaves and close to the lapping water. But it's not really a lonely beach because at that moment, the moment which they have managed to capture forever, the beach is the entire universe and they shudder and convulse against each other in ever-less powerful and less frequent waves.

And the world is complete and perfect, so perfect Kennedy feels like they've drifted into the sea. He can feel the breeze now about his legs and it feels wet, they must be in the sea, but they can't be. And then they hear 'Buddy, Buddy where are you?'

Kennedy realises that the wet sea breeze is a rather large Labrador licking about his neither regions. He quickly tries to shoo it away as the Yorkshire accent gets closer and closer: 'Buddy, aye where are you? Buddy, here boy!'

ann rea catches a fit of the giggles. Kennedy moves to regarment himself, ann rea pulls him closer and refuses to let him go, 'No. Please stay like this, stay as you are. Like this, with me. Hold me,' she whispers.

Kennedy clings on to her for dear life and buries his face in the nape of her neck. They are both still breathing faster than normal. Not as fast as they were breathing a short time ago and not as fast as they will be breathing if Buddy's owner, the silly sod who thinks that dogs not only can understand but also answer human questions, finds them.

Buddy, however, unlike his owner, does have a bit of sense. He realises that his two new friends are going to be no fun. They have eyes, and arms and legs, and other bits, only for each other. So Buddy beats a hasty retreat in the direction of the fine old Yorkshire accent.

Chapter Thirty-Nine

'God, they're all on our bloody doorstep!' DS Irvine declared on hearing the information from the WPC (at the same time as Kennedy) that Rory Nash had his offices literally a stone's throw, well, more like a Steve Batley super javelin throw, from North Bridge House.

The WPC was noticeably, and naturally, disappointed when Kennedy invited Irvine and not herself to accompany him on the interview with Mr Rory Nash.

'Look,' Kennedy offered in a roundabout compliment, 'We need you to stay here and track down the fourth guy, Jerry MacKane. You're obviously very good at locating missing persons.'

If Kennedy had looked closely, as in too close, at the WPC's face he would have noticed that her chiselled good looks had started to blush, just ever so slightly mind you, and she turned in her chair to attack the phones, hopeful of avoiding further embarrassment.

The offices of Concoction Management Company were cool, as in very cool. When Kennedy and Irvine reported at reception they were showed to pink sofas located on a island created on the white marble floor by a matching pink carpet. And this was just reception. The DI and DS sat on opposite sofas separated by a large smoked-glass coffee table. Kennedy's eye was caught by the flash headline of one of the music mags lying there: 'Pauley Valentine signs to Camden Town Records'. Kennedy was about to read the article to find out how much Camden Town Records had paid for the privilege when a stunning middle-aged woman appeared and introduced herself as Esther, Rory Nash's PA.

'He can see you right away, if you'd just like to follow me.'

Kennedy knew that Irvine was about to reply 'Anywhere,' so he replied simply and quickly 'Good,' and the three of them climbed the two flights of glass-encased stairs in silence.

As they reached the second floor Esther said, with a smile large enough to forgive the Spurs another home defeat, 'We're through here.' Body language-wise she was dealing mostly with Kennedy, probably because he was the one doing the least leching. 'Would you like a drink of any kind?'

'Yes, thanks, that would be great, I'll have a tea, white, two sugars,' Kennedy began, 'and my DS here would like…' And he left a gap for Irvine to fall into. But Irvine had fallen into another gap, one of lust, so Kennedy filled in the narrative himself: 'And my DS would just like to suck his thumb.'

The lovely Esther was obviously used to people staring at her so, because Kennedy could almost swear she winked at him as she replied, 'Oh don't worry about him, he'll get over it, perhaps some mineral water will help cool him down?'

'That would be great, yes great, yes indeed, that would be fine,' Irvine's babbling was broken by an arrival from the inner office, which was just off Esther's reception area. The arrival was an incredibly well dressed man who immediately extended his hand in the general direction of the two policemen. 'Hi, I'm Rory Nash,' he said, or rather proclaimed, with a warm, confident smile.

'Hello, I'm Inspector Christy Kennedy and this is Sergeant James Irvine,' Kennedy replied as they performed a superb bit of synchronised hands-in-inside-pocket, remove-wallet, one-handedly-open-wallet, flash-warrant-card-and-Met-badge, close-wallet-and-return-to-inside-pocket. Unsynchronised, they both shook Nash's hand.

Nash was solid. If he wasn't so subtly dressed you'd say he was heavy, stocky, well built, but never fat. However, the fact that his waist had all but disappeared was carefully (unsuccessfully) hidden by a beautiful loose-fitting blue silk shirt hanging over black Armani slacks, perfectly pressed. Rory was aware that his slacks were perfectly pressed because as he sat down in his conference area, inviting the two officers to join him, he carefully caught the crease just above the knee and tugged it a few times to allow the material to flow freely before crossing his legs and doing the same with the other crease.

His office was large, pretty much this entire floor save for Esther's little area, and one end, the entire front of the building, was glass from floor to ceiling. Kennedy found this a little unusual. Mainly because the view through the transparent wall wouldn't exactly inspire you the way the view from the top of Primrose Hill might. Not to mention the fact that the heat in the height of summer must be pretty much near unbearable. Nash had three large plants, more like small trees actually, along the glass wall. The floor was covered in a plush royal blue carpet and the office was divided, not physically, but decoratively, into three sections.

The far end was the casual end, where two small windows lit a comfy space of three expensive multicoloured sofas around three sides of a large wooden coffeetable, the fourth side protected by a large swivel chair, seat height positioned a few inches above that of the sofa. This would not only give physical advantage but an even greater, negotiating advantage to the occupant.

Centre table was a large bowl of fruit and lots of mags, including another copy of the one with the Valentini story, which was, as luck would have it, positioned directly in front of Kennedy. Camden Town Records had paid out £250,000 for the privilege of Mr Valentini's signature. The article further claimed that the company's executives would have paid more should the hijacker have been available for promotion. However, Kennedy thought, the only reason that Valentini would have been available for promotion would have been due to the fact that he had not hijacked the radio station. Now taken to its logical conclusion, should he not have hijacked the radio station in the first place then the likes of Camden Town Records would certainly not be paying out a quarter of a million pounds for a career which at best had easily passed its sell-by date.

Kennedy also knew for a fact it would be several long years, not to mention many career durations, before Pauley Valentini was going to be able to perform in public again.

The next section of the room was the official office, with a long maghony desk complete with computer terminal and telephone switchboard. In the middle was a large leather bound notebook (closed) and a couple of floaters (for tea or coffee cups). On the user side of the desk was a large leather swivel chair and on the visitors' side were two high-backed wooden chairs with a magnificent Native American pattern cut into the back. Yes, Kennedy thought, these chairs would have looked perfect positioned around the campfire.

The final section of the room was the conference area with a large simple oak table surrounded by eight farmhouse-style chairs. The one at the head of the table again appeared to be a couple of inches higher than the others, but maybe it was just his imagination.

The walls, unusually for music biz walls, were a gold-disc-free zone. Behind Nash's desk was a painting. Kennedy couldn't make out what it was meant to be of but it looked expensive and the paint had been lashed on quite liberally giving an impression of depth, particularly between the colours. Kennedy had never been able to work out why people would seemingly pay a lot of money for a painting for their office and then position it behind their head where they would rarely be able to experience its delights, if any.

The conference area walls were decorated with photographs. Some of Nash with a woman who made up what she lacked in looks with a beaming smile, some of Nash's artists (Kennedy assumed) some of Nash with some of these assumed artists and some of Nash with local politicians. But pride of place was given to a large black and white print of Marc Bolan.

The walls of the den (sofa area) were covered by glass

shelves containing what looked like thousands of models. Before last weekend both Kennedy and Irvine would have referred to them as toys, maybe even 'Bleedin' Dinky Toys' but now the newly inducted experts recognised them as Corgi Classics. 'A multicoloured display for a lost or longed for childhood,' was how Irvine had chosen to describe them.

Nash was slow and controlled in all of his movements. Extremely graceful, but an acquired grace nonetheless. All his body movements were planned and well orchestrated. Nash reminded Kennedy of that great photograph of David Bowie, the one which had proved the be the blueprint for a thousand poseur bands of the seventies. Bowie's left hand is caressing a Shure Hammerhead mike. His right hand is dangling by his side, a lit ciggy between his fingers from whence the coiling of the rising smoke provides the only movement in the photograph. Kennedy realised this pose was great, only for an instant, but that Bowie would probably have spent the entire concert as that statue breathing his air of cool, were it not for the flesh burning capability of the cigarette.

'Well, gentlemen,' Nash said very quietly, 'What can I do for you?'

As he finished his request he put his hand in his trouser pocket and retrieved a tube from which he sprayed some liquid into his mouth.

'We believe you may be in danger, sir,' Kennedy said, deciding that if they were to get anywhere with this particular gentleman his cool would have to crumble.

'Interesting,' was Nash's only reply, veneer still intact as he gently and precisely palmed his right hand over his closely cropped head, 'And who, pray, wishes to do me harm?'

'We don't know exactly. But we do have reason to believe that a Miss Anna Elliot may have something to do with it. She may be employing someone to do her evil for her,' Kennedy replied.

When Nash didn't show any sign of responding Irvine asked, 'Are you aware of this woman, sir?'

'No, I don't think I am. There is, however, something strangely familiar about it though. Did I used to manage her?'

The professional personal manager inquired as he uncrossed his legs, recrossing them in the opposite direction and repeating his creasing procedure as he did so.

'Well, sir we have reason to believe that you and three of your friends, a Mr Neil Burton, a Mr John B. Stone and a Mr Jerry MacKane were accused of raping Miss Anna Elliot when she was a young girl, about twenty-four years ago,' DS Irvine replied, checking his notebook to make sure all the names were correct as he dropped his bombshell.

Rory Nash turned from his usual red flush to a whiter shade of pale. But there was not one iota of change in the tone of his voice.

'Ah yes, that. Oh come on, gentlemen, I'm sure that you have already seen from the reports that no charges were ever brought. It was just a case of a few boys and girls having a bit of fun.'

'Girl,' corrected Kennedy. 'We see from our report that it was four boys and just one girl. Just one, a sixteen-year-old Miss Anna Elliot, and it doesn't seem to me as if it was fun at all.'

'As I said, it was just a bit of fun. We, including the girl, were exploring our sexuality and she later regretted it. I suppose having sex with three boys isn't exactly great for one's reputation. But as I said, no charges were brought against us quite simply because there were none to be brought. Nothing was forced on this girl that she didn't invite or encourage, and from my memory, blurred though it may be all these years later, she was a willing, eager and inventive participant.' Rory Nash once more removed the tube from his pocket and sprayed his mouth before continuing.

'Quite frankly, officers, I have to tell you that if you are planning to leak any of this to the press, I mean we all know about the press and their policy of print-now-check-your-facts-later, I and my legal people will take any action necessary to claim compensation for any damage done to my reputation. I should also warn you that it is my long-term intention to go into politics and I advise you of this so that you many realise and comprehend the extent of damages and compensation I am talking about.'

'I have to ask you, sir,' Kennedy began clearing his throat in annoyance, 'Do you have any idea where this Anna Elliot may be now?'

Chapter Forty

As Kennedy and Irvine were concluding a very unproductive interview with Rory Nash, WPC Coles, on the other hand, was making progress on the case back at North Bridge House.

She was worried about this case. Generally speaking you find a body and then you (hopefully) go off and find the person who committed ther murder. Simple? Well not really simple, but the basic procedure is quite straightforward.

However, on this case they already had two bodies and there was a good possibility two more were about to be murdered. This fact alone put the team under quite a bit of pressure. Pressure to find the two people in question, namely Rory Nash and Jerry MacKane, before the murderer, (allegedly) Anna Elliot, caught up with them.

The Camden Town bush telegraph (actually an ex-girl-friend) reported that Jerry MacKane had moved to Birmingham about four years previously. Apparently this girlfriend was quite happy to see the back of him and had no further communications with him. She did not know the whereabouts of any of MacKanes's relatives, she just kept repeating the fact that her life had taken a major turn for the better upon MacKane's departure.

Jerry MacKane, in his girlfriend's words, 'was a slob,' and the only regular work listed on his CV was that of 'electrician' but he tended to get fired from most of his jobs due to the lightness of his fingers.

As she continued to buzz the phone lines, WPC Coles was happy that Kennedy and Irvine were taking so long over the

Nash interview. She currently had two leads on MacKane – police files for the thieving and electrical firms for places of employment. She decided to start with Birmingham CID and see what they might have on MacKane.

The rolling drawl at the other end of the line accessed a computer listings, and surprise surprise, not Cilla but Jerry MacKane with a list of crimes (all thieving) as long as your arm. Coles had been expecting this had merely said 'Yes, and?' with each item, until the shock of the final entry.

'Oh, look at this!' PC Henry Burke continued in his best Kevin Turvey accent. Coles thought she might if she was looking over his shoulder, but rather than say 'read it out to me you dimwit', she very charmingly said, 'Something of importance you think?'

'I'd say so.' Henry Burke replied, milking the situation.

'Yes?' Coles inquired, raising her voice a little.

'Well, it just that your Jerry MacKane is deceased, he is no more.'

Coles prayed that the Brummie wouldn't be so tasteless to use the rest of the Monty Python line. He was.

'He's a stiff!'

'Really?' WPC Coles wanted to get beyond these short exchanges, but she was cautious, perhaps these stories about the brain capacity of the Midland's finest were true.

'Yes, and it looks like he came to a very, very sticky end, more like a bloody end, actually,' Burke continued as he read from the file.

'Was he murdered then?' Coles was now fearing the worst, that Anna Elliot had beaten them to it again.

'No,' came the telephonic reply.

Coles breathed a huge sigh of relief. She felt for ann rea's friend Daniel Elliot, and didn't want to see him falling under the spotlight any more than he was already. Not that the pressure of being the father of a woman who had murdered twice was much less than being the father of a woman who had murdered three times. He'd still get pointed to and stared at in the street and in the supermarket. He'd still get shite tabloid journalists hunting him, and then just when he felt it had all have died down they'd come up with the pretence of some anniversary and they'd all be back camping on the doorstep.

'No, our friend Jerry MacKane was savaged by a wild dog, a little over two years ago.'

So PC Burke could string a full sentence together after all, and when he did, boy what a full sentence.

'Holy shit!' Coles exploded into the mouthpiece, 'Do you have the autopsy report there as well?'

PC Burke didn't hear her question because he was still holding the phone away from his ear waiting for the ringing to die down. When he got back to her and she repeated her question, 'No,' he said, 'that would be in a different file. If you want I can dig it out for you if you just want to hold on for a few minutes.'

'No – look, could you possibly fax it to me as soon as you can, it's Camden CID. There is someone who needs this information ASAP,' Coles replied excitedly.

'Okay, fine. Faxing should prove easier on my eardrums,' said Burke.

Chapter Forty-One

The interview of Rory Nash by Irvine and Kennedy was interrupted by a gentle tap on the door. Esther popped her head around the door and said 'I'm awfully sorry to interrupt, Inspector Kennedy, it's North Bridge House on the phone for you, and they say it's urgent.'

'May I?' Kennedy inquired of Nash.

'Yes, please, use the one on the desk.'

'Hello. Yes. Really?' is all Irvine and Nash hear before 'Okay we'll be back in about ten minutes.'

Kennedy walked back purposefully to his seat, his fingers twitching, and sat down. 'That was WPC Coles, a colleague of ours,' he announced. 'She's just had a word with Birmingham CID and, well, Mr Nash, I have to tell you that Jerry MacKane has also been murdered. About eighteen months ago. He too was savaged by a dog, just like Flute Burton.' He paused, then said solemnly, 'I'd like to take you into protective custody immediately, sir.'

Nash though for awhile before spraying his mouth again. When he had completed this ritual he said, 'I thank you for your concern, Inspector, but I assure you it's not really necessary. I mean apart from anything else it's going to look bad, isn't it? What happens if you have to keep me in for a few days, maybe even a week? Tongues are going to wag, and, as I explained to you before, I can't really afford that.' Nash rose from his chair and went across to his Corgi Classic collection. He seemed to lose himself in the models. Kennedy thought that he looked and acted like someone who was being intrigued by this world of models for the first time rather than being an old hand. Nash lifted a bus from the shelf like a pigeon fancier with a prize bird.

'You see this? This is a Bedford OB Coach,' he said. This particular model, the Southdown coach, was the sixth one Corgi made in this series, hence its serial number C949/6. They have made sixty-one Bedford OB Coaches in total but for some reason this one which was made in 1987 is the most popular and consequently the most sought after and therefore the most expensive. It's worth about four hundred pounds. Now for some reason, unlike the earlier OBs in the series, Corgi made only 4,400 of this Southdown and to me it's not as beautiful as say the MacBaynes or the Pearce & Crump, or even the Grey-Green of George Ewer, but for whatever reason this one caught people's imagination, perhaps it sparked off memories of childhood journeys to the seaside, and the entire run sold out very quickly. And now they're near impossible to get for love or money.'

Kennedy was interested, to a degree, but he felt better for any interruptions and felt that Nash might just be dealing in his own way with the devastating news which the detective had just relayed to him. The collector took what looked like a large make-up brush, one with very flexible bristles, from a lower shelf and proudly dusted his Southdown Bedford OB coach. He turned to the detectives, model in one hand, brush in the other, and continued the shop talk.

'To a non-collector this probably looks like just another £5 to £10 toy, but, as I've said it's actually worth about £400 if it's in as good as condition as this one and the box and packaging are mint. My point, Inspector, is that looks can be deceptive. Should I accept your protective custody then it wouldn't matter how much I were to protest my innocence, or how much you were to back me up in my claims, a certain fraction of the media would say there's no smoke without fire and other such rubbish.' He returned the Southdown neatly into its pride-of-place position on the well dusted shelf and Kennedy guessed that Nash had each and every one of the sixty or so Corgi Classic Bedford OB coaches if not the entire Corgi Classic range. His body language, clasping his hands as if in prayer, advised the detectives that the Nash address was not yet over.

'You know, this is all great,' and he unclasped his hands and used one to draw an arc over the room in particular, but the building in general. 'We've got a fabulously successful company. Malan are a good band. I don't believe for one second they're a great band in the way our generation had the great ones, the Beatles, the Kinks, the Stones, the Small Faces, the Spencer Davies Group, Them… they were all great in the true sense of the word. So coming from that background I can't really take any of these new groups seriously can I? As I said Malan are a fine band, but I'm sure you've noticed that every single one of their eleven hits have been rewrites of Marc Bolan and T Rex songs.'

'Now you come to mention it,' said Irvine, 'I did think that 'Sailing on White Wings' was dangerously close to 'Ride a White Swan'.

'Yes, you're right but we still had a big hit with it and half the publishing on someone's else's song if you know what I mean. But you don't know the half of it – another time, perhaps. Anyway, the buzz is fading for me you now. You know the buzz of having your first chart hit? That is such a great feeling, you'll never know. You get your midweek chart prediction on Thursday and, say, if it's 39 you spend every second wishing and hoping that by the time it comes to the chart announcement at seven p.m. Sunday evening that you haven't slipped to 41 and out of the public view. And then again, when you start off at 30 and the midweek is 23 but by the Sunday night it drops to 28 and you're totally devastated even though your net chart is three places better. And the other feeling of elation is when your single is rising and it looks like it stands a chance of going to number one and it does, it's like winning the lottery, the Cup Final, the Masters, the British Grand Prix, having sex for the first time, your first child being born, buying your first house, all rolled into one. But do you know what the problem you have then is?'

Neither Kennedy nor Irvine knew or were prepared to hazard a guess, so Nash did the gentlemanly thing and told them, because he had been there and done that.

'The problem is that after reaching number one in the charts there is nowhere else to go. And that is the biggest come down there is. But once you've been there a few times it's like you're repeating yourself trying to relive that initial virginal excitement. There was also a time when it used to be great, a great feeling to know that somewhere, even tonight, an act is going to go on stage in some dark corner of this country and that I am (maybe was) one of the six managers who could take this act and could turn them into world beaters. Pop managers are the new wise men of the 21st century, they know everything about everything. We have to, we're dealing on a worldwide stage: Hell.' Nash paused for effect. 'People don't realise how important an ingredient the manager is,' he concluded.

'Oh, I don't know, I think that someone like the Beatles could have been managed by anyone and would have been just as successful simply because they were brilliant,' Kennedy challenged.

'Brian Epstein is all I have to say to you, sir, Brian Epstein.'

'Well now, there is a very good point. He couldn't even get them a record deal in the early days. And then signing them to the lowest of the low, a record label for comedy artistes. And even that couldn't get in the way of the band. And wasn't he famous for doing bad deals, publishing, movies, merchandising, records... wasn't all of that supposed to be a mess?'

Kennedy inquired.

'But gentlemen, he had a vision, he believed in his band, he believed they were as great as they were to become. And who's to say that his unconditional belief didn't give them a little bit of the freedom needed for them to be as creative as they were to be? When he was doing those deals he was sailing unchartered seas, he was making it all up as he went along. But hear this, a lot of the artistic favours which we all now insist are in our clients' contracts are only there because men like Brian Epstein paved the way for us. And you know, he took the Fabs to the top, you can't do much better than that, can you?' Nash smiled and continued before either could answer, 'But my point is that I can do all that, make an act a worldbeater, it's not a challenge to me anymore. However, politics does hold a challenge to me. To someday to be able to serve as a member of parliament, to perhaps spearhead Britain's foreign policy. You see, with my worldwide knowledge I'd be very good at that, and I will be, just wait and see. And that is why I can't come with you,' he concluded.

Irvine merely shrugged his shoulders.

'Look, sir,' said Kennedy, choosing his words carefully, 'I can't stress enough to you how much your life is in danger. The facts are all there plain as daylight. Of the four people involved in this incident, you are the only survivor. If we believe, as we do, that Anna Elliot is behind this, then you are next. Simple as that.'

'Yes, I take your point, but don't worry about me. I've got some private security people who will watch me around the clock and I assure you I'll be okay. If you want me to I'll sign something stating that you advised me of the danger, offered me custody and of my own free will I chose not to avail myself of your kind offer,' Nash replied, enjoying his heroics.

'No, it's okay. No need for that. You know where we are if you need us.' And with that Kennedy and Irvine were up and out of the building and just short of running back to North Bridge House. Irvine was convinced that Kennedy was about to break into a trot at any second and was trying (very hard) to keep abreast.

'I just hope,' Irvine began breathlessly, 'that if, and when, Rory Nash comes face to Anna Elliot and her wild dog, that he's got his brown trousers on.'

Chapter Forty-Two

It was six o'clock Friday evening and all of the team, including Superintendent Castle, were in Kennedy's comfortable office. It has to be said though, that at this point in the proceedings Kennedy was feeling anything but comfortable and, rather than Castle, he was the one asking the questions.

'What are we missing here?'

No one replied.

'Okay, let's go through it all once again and see what we have,' he began, turning to his crowded notice board. 'Neil ^Flute" Burton and now Jerry MacKane have both been butchered by a ^mad" dog, nearly two years and exactly 110 miles apart. John B. Stone is beaten to a pulp by Hugh Anderson, who claims he was paid to carry out the evil deed, and that when he left Stone was still alive.'

No comments nor observations from the floor, but Kennedy paused and wandered back to his desk to take another sip of his tea before continuing.

'Anderson advised us of the mysterious Miss Dipstick, who is so unbelievable that she is either a figment of his vivid imagination or someone trying so hard to be unnoticeable in a noticeable way.' Castle looked decidedly confused at Kennedy's last statement, so the DI explained, 'She got herself up in a way which was so noticeable that the character stuck in your (Anderson's) mind – but gave no clue to the actress playing the part.'

Castle nodded in agreement.

'Now, subsequently, we find out that John B. Stone, Jerry MacKane and Flute Burton, along with a colleague of theirs,

Rory Nash, were accused, twenty-four years ago, of raping Anna Elliot. The charges were dropped, but we have to believe that Anna Elliot and Miss Dipstick are one and the same and she is out seeking revenge. It would seem to me that there are two basic points here. One, we have to find Anna Elliot, and two, until such time as we do we have to assume that Rory Nash's life is in danger.'

'But he doesn't want police protection.' Irvine complained. He was keen to get the briefing over with; he still held a faint hope that Dr Forsythe was going to ring him and he was going to have a last chance of seeing her before she departed on her holiday.

'Yes, I know. But if he's not going to come to us then it's still our duty to go to him, I want us to at the very least have a visible presence so that if our assassin does get close, she will realise she'd get caught and scarper. It would appear that our Miss Anna 'Dipstick' Elliot has a mad dog. So if she is planning such an end for Nash perhaps we can ensure, as our friends from America would say, we don't present her with a window of opportunity to carry out her evil deed. I've spoken to Anderson again and Miss Dipstick never mentioned requiring his services again in the future.'

'Maybe she felt it would take away from the credibility of her story, sir. You know, using Anderson twice?' Coles offered.

'True,' Kennedy replied, 'But how about if we are discussing two different investigations?'

Castle grunted 'What?' Irvine said, 'I beg your pardon?' and Coles cried, 'Pardon?' all at once.

'Well, let's look closer at this. Let's assume for argument's sake that John B. Stone was murdered by Miss Dipstick and Anderson. Let's assume further that Miss Dipstick is in fact Jean Stone seeking revenge. We know Jean Stone is not an alias for Anna Elliot. Stone has never lived outside of London in her life; Elliot has spent a lot of time in the Midlands. Stone uses Anderson, Elliot uses a mad dog. It's a coincidence that John B. was involved with Burton and MacKane in the orginal rape. That's why Anderson's only involved in the one case. Jean Stone doesn't have an alibi for the night of John B.'s murder, apart from spending it at home with her husband, that is. Miss Dipstick didn't ask Anderson to murder Burton because she wasn't involved.'

'How about if Jean Stone and Anna Elliot were mates and now Stone is seeking revenge on all of the people who raped Anna, including one, John B., who also raped her?' Coles suggested.

'Look, Kennedy, aren't we straying too far from the pathway now?' Castle put in, 'This thing with Anderson, I'm still not entirely comfortable with it. Are we saying here that we don't believe that he ultimately murdered John B. Stone? That he just duffed him up a bit? And if so, then who finally did kill him? It's all a bit far-fetched to me.'

At that precise moment (Friday, 18.17) a vital part of the case fell into place for Detective Inspector Kennedy. A bit of the puzzle which had been floating around in his head finally decided to come down and take its place in the ever growing picture this case was turning into.

'An alibi, sir,' he said, 'an alibi of sorts. What if, for argument's sake, our Miss Dipstick did hire Hugh Anderson to do the business on John B. Stone? At the exact time Anderson is concluding his handiwork, Miss Dipstick is elsewhere giving herself the perfect watertight alibi. Okay, Anderson duffs him up a bit, dumps the body, as requested, behind the Fountain of Sorrow. But later Miss Dipstick returns with a baseball bat and finishes off the job.'

'But then her alibi would be totally blown, wouldn't it? She'd have no one to vouch for her at the actual time of death,' Irvine suggested, adding 'Sir,' as an afterthought.

'True, true. However, I imagine when we find this Miss Dipstick, we'll find she has a black and white kind of alibi, which is probably why we have to rule out Jean Stone. Someone, maybe even several people, at a party or at the theatre or whatever, who will vouch for her company. There will be some grey areas, but as she will have been covered for a major part of the time we would have to rule her out,' Kennedy replied. 'I would also bet that the apple was planted there by her to draw attention to Anderson. He's got form.' Kennedy smiled at the Super. 'It's obvious we were going to suspect him. Miss Dipstick would want the clue to lead us straight, via the Spread Eagle, to Anderson, which is in fact what happened, and we would think that we had our man. Case solved, end of story, no further action required.'

'But what about the mad dog murders, how is she going to be able to account for that?' inquired Castle, ever the doubter.

'It's simple: what had we first assumed with Neil Burton, the first case up by the bridge?' said Kennedy.

'We'd assumed he'd been killed by a mad dog,' said Coles.

'Absolutely, and I bet our friends up in the Midlands did exactly the same. Oh, by the way, have we got the autopsy report down from them yet? I want to give it straight to Dr Forsythe so that she can compare them with her own report on Burton.'

'No, sir,' said Coles, 'I'll ring them again. Henry Burke, the PC I spoke to first time, had gone off duty and WPC Davies promised to send it when she had a moment, apparently the locals start drinking early in Birmingham on a Friday and the station was packed with offenders already. Anyway she said she'd dig it out and fax it down to us.'

'I'm afraid you've missed Dr Forsythe, sir,' said Irvine. 'She's... well, today was her last day before her holiday.'

Kennedy looked at his pocket watch, an antique gold guardsman's watch with a matching gold chain attached to one of the buttonholes in his waistcoat. It had a plain white face, no roman numerals or ticks for him, just plain classic numbers. It showed twenty-five past six.

'Give her a ring from here please, DS. See if you can get her before she goes, I'd really love her to check this report for us before she does. She's up to speed with the Burton one and she'll be able to spot any similarities immediately,' Kennedy instructed his DS as he returned his prized watch to its pocket.

'I'll try,' said Irvine and went to Kennedy's phone and dialled Forsythe's number, surprising himself that he had already committed her seven digits to memory. 'Dr Forsythe, please.' Pause. 'When did she leave?' Pause. 'At lunchtime? But I thought –' Pause. 'Oh, okay. Thank you very much.' Irvine put the phone down looking surprised. It was a few seconds before he spoke.

'Apparently she rang in this morning, said she wasn't feeling too well and that she was going to take an extra day's leave, and go off on holiday immediately. And before I'd a chance to ask,' Irvine continued before Kennedy had a chance to ask him, 'They said that they didn't know where she had gone. I believe she was going to be doing quite a bit of travelling around.'

'Oh well, I'm sure it won't take too long for the good Dr Taylor to get up to speed. I'll ring him later when we get the Birmingham report in and take both that and the Burton report over to him tonight, hopefully.' Kennedy made a mental note to ring Taylor at the end of this briefing.

He drank the remainder of his tea in one gulp; it wasn't yet cold, but soon would be and he hated anything other than hot tea. It was Coles who spoke next.

'I've just been thinking, sir. You said that only three of the four accused raped Anna Elliot. Do we know who was the one who didn't rape her? It's possible that if this were Rory Nash, then she has already completed her revenge and the case could be over.'

'Interesting point, but sadly I have to tell you that Jerry MacKane was the one who didn't, and he was the first one to be killed. I wonder if there is anything in that for us?'

No one had any theories to put forward, so Kennedy started to sum up.

'So,' he began, 'DS Irvine, could you liaise with Esther, Nash's PA, about his movements over the weekend and put two PCs on to him. Maybe have one of the marked cars pass his house regularly tonight; let's keep up as much of a visible presence as possible.'

'What about this – what's her name – Anna Elliot,' Castle inquired, 'how are we getting on with tracking her down? Do we have any pictures or anything?'

'No, sir,' replied Kennedy, 'She hasn't been seen by her father since shortly after the rape and so the only photograph he has is about twenty-five years old. I have one of the visuals experts enhancing it, ageing the picture, as we speak. I hope to get the results later on this evening. Miss ann rea, a friend of Anna Elliot's father Daniel, has managed to trace her last known address – it's in the Birmingham area but apparently she left there about two years ago.'

'Probably shortly after she and her mad dog did away with… oh what's his name?' Castle fumbled in a vain attempt to do what he'd never been able to do, remember people's names. He still had, in his top left-hand drawer, the full names of everyone in the station and their job description, which he frequently used as a prompt. He was one of those high-ranking officers who had been very grateful when name tags were first introduced for their numerous police conferences.

'Jerry MacKane, sir,' said the ever-helpful WPC Coles.

'Thank you.' Castle gave her a warm personalised smile, as in 'This one's just for you!' 'Yes,' he said, 'she probably would have left shortly after the MacKane death. Mind you I'm not so sure anyone would want to hang around that city for too long anyway.' He attempted to ingratiate himself with his troops by this attempt at a joke.

'Quite,' said Kennedy. 'I'll speak to Miss rea later and see if she's made any progress. We'll also supply the name and early photo to Birmingham CID, who are being extremely helpful but didn't, unfortunately, have Anna Elliot anywhere in their files.' Kennedy was not sure if Castle was aware of his year-plus relationship with ann rea. He and Castle were not exactly matey, so Kennedy had never seen the point of discussing personal relationships with his Super, or anyone else on the force for that matter. Which was probably why he enjoyed the dark horse reputation he currently basked in.

'I find it incredible,' said Castle, 'that in 1998, someone can just disappear from the face of the earth. I mean we've got computers coming out of our earholes and they spew out about a forest's worth of paperwork per week with facts, figures and information, but can we pinpoint where one middle-aged, and dangerous, woman is? No!' Castle exclaimed as he rose from his comfy chair, one of the few exceedingly comfy chairs in Kennedy's office.

'If someone wants to disappear, sir,' replied Kennedy,

'they'll disappear. Even if you could tag the entire population, people would still find a way to be untraceable. The other important thing we have to remember is that Anna Elliot has been planning her tactics for twenty-four years now, so I imagine she probably started to melt back into the woodwork quite some time ago. She probably created a whole new set of misleading tracks for us as well as a few new personae, including the Miss Dipstick one, for herself. The main thing to remember here is that in her mind she doesn't think she is doing wrong. In her mind, she is the one who was wronged and she is seeking vengeance against those who did her that wrong, on the four men who ruined her life.' Kennedy was voicing his thoughts but appeared distracted by his own words.

'So?' the Super prodded as he reached the door.

'So,' Kennedy replied and sighed, 'We have to assume that she will stop at nothing, absolutely nothing, until she tracks down and kills Rory Nash, our self-confessed wise man of the twenty-first century. We have to assume that she is out there, somewhere, and at this very moment stalking Nash,' he said, losing his original train of thought.

'You might well be right Inspector, but the important thing we also have to remember is that in this area we are the professionals and she is the amateur, and because of this we will find her and bring her to justice, because that is our job, and hopefully the fact that we do it well will be a deterrent to other would-be criminals,' said the Super, and without missing a beat continued, 'Well, I must leave you all to your art of detection. Mrs Castle and myself are going up west tonight to the theatre, something with that chap John Thaw in it; she's got a bit of a thing about him you know, dammed fine actor too, and I'll get a terrible earfull if I'm not home in time to get ready.'

With that he was gone and Kennedy and his efficient team got down to their art of detection. But Kennedy wasn't sure that Superintendent Castle was accurate in calling Anna Elliot an amateur. So far she was responsible, Kennedy was pretty sure, for the deaths of John B. Stone, Neil Burton and Jerry MacKane. Not something to be particularly proud off, but then again not too bad for an amateur. Furthermore, Kennedy was forced to believe that she was currently closing in on Rory Nash, and whereas the professionals were trying very hard to get up to speed on the case, she'd been planning all her moves for twenty-four years.

Chapter Forty-Three

K ennedy worked until very late that Friday evening. At one point in the proceedings, the point where he stopped working long enough to make himself a cup of tea, he couldn't help thinking (with a certain amount of disbelief) that less than twenty-four hours earlier he was on a beach with ann rea getting as close as it was possible for two humans to get. Close as in physically and spiritually if love is involved, as had certainly been the case on the beach in Climping.

Yes, love had certainly been involved. Sometimes Kennedy wasn't as sure about ann rea's love for him. She sometimes seemed to feel more than her fair share of guilt in that area. He had the impression that ann rea was fighting the 'He loves me more than I love him,' line of thought.

An ugly thought this may be, but, Kennedy figured, better to exorcise your demons rather than let them eventually destroy your relationship. His only worry was whether his knowledge, the knowledge that perhaps ann rea didn't love him (well, didn't love him as much as he loved her) could, and would, eventually eat away and destroy the love he felt for her. Where there is no love put love and you will find love, was all fine and dandy to be sure but on the other hand where there is no food, you will find only hungry people.

Also, when was all this shit about who loved whom the most, or the least, or whatever, going to end? Were they ever going to get on with it, get on with living their lives together, or not? He couldn't help feeling that if they could only get beyond this point, the worrying about love and the intensity of the same, and spend an equal amount of energy just living and dealing with each other in moving forwards, then – then just how fulfilling would their life together become? Or not?

If 'or not' was the case then that was fine too as far as Kennedy was concerned. He was a big boy, he'd get over it. But he just wanted to be in a position where he could get on with his life, his personal life that is. His professional life was going exactly the way he wanted it: pace, direction, contents, everything was fine.

But this personal stuff, God, sometimes you just wanted to scream. Kennedy realised now why he had been prepared to put his personal life on hold for such a long time following the break-up of the relationship previous to ann rea.

Even now he couldn't help do that male kind of thing, you know, 'Do I really love ann rea as much as I loved Linda?' Linda Longreen, that is. Each time his 'self' would hit him right between the eyes with a 'Don't be stupid.' Well, maybe not quite as short and sharp as that, more like 'Of course you love ann rea, you love her like you have loved no other and like you will probably never love another in your life, so you'd better get your shit together, get out of all these mind games and pathetic thoughts and do exactly that, love the woman, forget all the rest, just love the woman.'

If only. If only it were all that easy. Kennedy wandered back to his desk and dialled Daniel Elliot's number to speak to ann rea.

'Christy, it's yourself.'

Something's up, Kennedy thought, she rarely called him Christy and then only in tender moments.

'Hi. How's it going down there today?' he began tentatively.

'I was just thinking about the beach last night,' she replied.

'Aha.' A more positive response from Kennedy, realising where the 'Christy' had come from. 'Our walk, you mean?'

'Well, no, not actually the walk, Kennedy,' she answered moving out of her floating mood. 'But anyway, enough of that, how are you? How has today been?'

Kennedy brought her up to date with all the recent developments in his usual precise and concise manner.

'Daniel's been having a really bad day,' ann rea began hesitantly, 'He's blaming himself for all of this. He's now saying that if he and Lila had known what to do, how to support their daughter, then she would have been okay and none of this would have happened. He also now thinks he remembers a second, a split second, when he gave her an ^Are you really sure you didn't ask for this?" look. He may have doubted her by thinking ^Did these four young lads from good families really force you into this?" '

'It's a funny thing, ann rea, a lot of people think exactly that. They think that children of good and honest parents are incapable of doing wrong. Sadly, it's rarely the case. People are innocent, not because they are children from good families, but simply because they don't commit the crime,' Kennedy offered in support.

'He says he keeps examining his thoughts and motives to see if that could possibly be true – did he display some disbelief to Anna? He can't think of any other possible reason why she would have run away and failed to contact them again,' ann rea continued.

'Has he said anything about before the incident, before she was raped? Were he and his wife close to Anna or had there been any problems?' Kennedy inquired as he began to experience the early stages of tea-leaf deprivation.

'Yes, he has been talking about that actually. Quite a bit today in fact. He feels that, perhaps as an only child, Anna might have been too dependent on both of them. Anna was a difficult birth for Lila and the doctors advised them both against trying again. Daniel said they were very concerned that they would try again and do permanent harm to Lila. He said that Lila was prepared to risk it but that he hadn't been. Anyway, as an only child, Anna was spoilt and that maybe they needed and wanted too much from their only child, but mostly all his memories are fond ones. During one of his stories he referred to her as Annabella and said that Lila was the only one who always used her full name, which was in itself a major source of irritation to Anna.' ann rea paused to collect her thoughts before continuing.

'Anna was incredibly bright, did extremely well at school and college, they were always very proud of her. Daniel knew she was bound for university, and knew she was going to do well. He felt that she would submerge herself completely in her studies to block out the rape and use her academic life to replace her family life.' ann rea could sense Kennedy forming a question down the telephone line.

'In case you were about to ask, Kennedy, I've traced her to Aston University and I've been on to them and they've promised me that by Monday they'll have her file, but apart from that I'm afraid I still don't have any other leads on her whereabouts. How can someone just disappear like that, Kennedy? I mean just completely drop out of the system? And here's me subscribing to the big brother is watching you theory. But it would appear not.'

'Maybe they don't disappear, maybe they just become someone else,' Kennedy replied absent mindedly. 'Do you know when you're coming back?'

'No I don't,' she replied quite firmly, 'I can't really leave him when he's like this, can I?'

'No, I agree, I didn't mean you should.'

'I know, Kennedy, I'm sorry if I was short with you, I don't mean to be. It's just that, if I'm very honest, I'd been hoping, well, hoping that I'd be able to use some of my time to sort things out, you know? But it's just not been possible. I haven't read anything. I haven't done any walking, apart from last night, I haven't done any work on the project I brought with me. I've done nothing but talk and I feel absolutely drained, completely exhausted.'

At this distance Kennedy felt unable to do, or say, anything other than, 'Look ann rea, just take it easy.' He felt completely stupid when he said it but now he'd started he'd have to take it somewhere. 'He needs you. Daniel needs you. You told me that you wanted to be down there for him because of all the times he and his wife had been there for you and so you need to keep your energy up, for him and for yourself. We don't know how long all this could last, but it could be some time.'

'You're right, and you know what, I probably wouldn't react

to anyone other than yourself this way, and I'm sorry for dumping on you. You always allow me to do that, you're always there for me. But you know what, Kennedy? You never dump on me. You always seem to keep it on the rails, keep it all together. How do you do that? Where do you get all your strength from, Kennedy?'

'Spinach, it works great for me, and for Popeye,' he replied, trying hard to derail her current dark mood which could only end up in the predictable 'I don't seem to be able to be there for you, ever, so maybe it's not love' siding.

Equally, Kennedy felt that his simple theory might not be so well received in ann rea's current state of anguish. His engine was stoked with the philosophy of, 'You know what, all this stuff really doesn't matter because come what may at the end of each and every day you are going to go to bed and go to sleep and then it will another day, and if it's not, if this is to be the night, the one you don't make it through, then it's all over and done with anyway, so who cares? The whole thing will go on with or without you.' Definitely not worked out by a rocket scientist but equally, absolutely one to get you through the night.

'Shit, does that mean I'm Olive Oyl? Ah, come on, Kennedy, that's definitely not fair,' said ann rea, forcing a laugh. She knew from experience that this was positively one area Kennedy was not prepared to follow her into.

'Well, I'd have to say, it's close,' Kennedy lied, 'But I still think it's you by a… well, at least a couple of beautiful breasts.'

'Kennedy! Is that you bordering on the sexist or are you just thinking about our time on the beach again?' she teased.

Kennedy was indeed thinking about the beach again, but he knew it was not something he should dwell on this weekend. He immediately snapped himself out of it and concluded the conversation with, 'Well, I better chase up Dr Taylor, ann rea. I need him to come in tomorrow, we're expecting the Jerry MacKane report and Dr Forsythe has broken James Irvine's heart and gone on holiday for a few weeks, so I need to see what Dr Taylor will make of all of this. I'll talk to you later. Bye.'

He just about heard a very small, and dejected, 'Bye' in reply.

Chapter Forty-Four

On the fifth day, also known as Saturday, things fell into place. Normally this would have been a major relief to everyone involved.

Kennedy and the theatrical Dr Leonard Taylor were sitting in the latter's office. It was packed, literally, to overflowing but Taylor had the well justified reputation for knowing exactly where everything was, and could put his hand on a required file at a moment's notice.

There were files on the floor, files on the sofa, files on every chair, files on his desk, files by the sink, even files precariously close to a two-bar electric fire. The entire office looked like it was about to sink under a sea of files. And today the space was even more packed than normal on account of his recent absence. Everyone seemed to have used his absence as an excuse to dump their unwanted files in Taylor's office, which was on the third floor of St Pancras All Saints Hospital, on the borders of Camden Town and King's Cross.

Taylor and Kennedy had worked quite a lot together over the years and had a mutual respect; and on that Saturday morning the doctor was only too happy to delay his round of golf to meet with Kennedy. Kennedy had said that it was important, and that was good enough for Taylor.

Kennedy was amused at seeing Taylor, already at his desk, dressed in his golf attire of green plus-fours, white rollneck jumper under a pink v-neck jumper, and pink socks, all magnificently set off with a pair of brown and cream brogues. The detective felt positively underdressed in his black crewneck sweater, black casual slacks, green pumps and dark green windbreaker.

Taylor made some tea. When I say some tea, I mean great tea. He wasn't by any stretch of the imagination a tea fanatic but he had the knack of consistently making a great cup of brew, much to Kennedy's delight. Today's brew was no exception.

There were the initial greetings and inquiries about each other's health: 'I've been told to slow down,' said Taylor, 'and when you've seen as many insides as I have you know exactly what your doctor is on about. I have no excuses. It's just, you know me, old chap, I absolutely love good food, good wine and great brandy. How's your health, Christy?'

'No, complaints, touch wood,' Kennedy replied.

Kennedy had brought the recently received Birmingham file and autopsy report on Jerry MacKane. Taylor, for his part, had dug out Dr Forsythe's autopsy reports on Neil Burton and John B. Stone.

The DI also had a large amount of paperwork with him. He intended to use the time Taylor was studying the reports to catch up on some of his more boring duties such as approving rotas, going through the recently emptied contents of his in-tray, filling out the monthly man- (and woman) hour reports, filling in the monthly crime stat. sheets and on and on in the never-ending distraction to the art of detection.

One of Taylor's options was to re-examine the body of Neil Burton if he were not 100% confident of Forsythe's report. He had extended an invitation to Kennedy to stick around should this be necessary. Kennedy expressed a hope, for the sake a) of Dr Taylor's golf, and b) his own stomach, that such additional examination would not be deemed necessary.

They both proceeded with their work, occasionally grunting (Taylor) and mmming (Kennedy) and making notes (both). Then about twenty minutes into the research, revision and form-filling, both Kennedy and Taylor let out a shout at exactly the same moment.

'Good Lord! Unbelievable! I don't believe it!' was Taylor's exclamatiom, while Kennedy's was equally religious.

'Holy shit!'

'You go first, old chap,' said Taylor in a high state of anxiety.

'No, this will wait. What's yours?' Kennedy invited.

'Well, it's just this, my dear friend. Have you had a chance yet to check the Birmingham autopsy report on MacKane?'

'No,' Kennedy replied, willing the Doctor to cut to the quick, 'It was in my in-tray this morning, along with a lot of this other stuff I've been ploughing through just now.'

'Well,' Taylor began as he raised his large frame from behind the desk and waddled around to Kennedy's side, swerving to avoid various piles of files. 'Look at the name of the doctor who carried out the autopsy on MacKane.'

Taylor placed the report, relevant page to the fore, on top of Kennedy's reading material, and his plump forefinger kept jumping up and down under the signature and typed name of one Dr Bella Forsythe.

The words 'Holy shit!' escaped Kennedy's lips for the second time in as many minutes. 'Coincidence? Coincidence that she would be responsible for carrying out an autopsy on two people in two cities both apparently attacked by a wild dog, and both these people were involved with each other twenty-four years ago on a rape charge. Coincidence?'

'Possible, I suppose, but not probable. But then again, they're called coincidences because they are strange things which happen together which aren't meant to happen, but do so nonetheless. Could that be the case here? Could it?'

'I don't think so, Doctor,' Kennedy replied with a triumphant smile, 'Look at my discovery.'

Kennedy handed Taylor an identifit picture.

'Yes!' Taylor said without hesitation, 'Quite like Dr Forsythe.' Then the penny dropped, at least part of the way. 'What? You don't surely mean to say that someone saw her at the scene of the crime and gave you this description?'

'No, not like that at all. This is the girl who was raped. Abducted by Neil Burton, currently lying in your morgue; John B. Stone, also in your morgue; Jerry MacKane, the Birmingham mad dog victim you've just been reading about; and Rory Nash, as of yesterday alive and well and living in Camden Town. The girl whom three of four of these gentlemen allegedly raped was called Anna Elliot. The only photograph we had of this person was taken shortly before the rape twenty-four years ago when she was sixteen. So I had the computer boffins in forensic age the photograph to predict what she might look like today, and this is what they've come up with.'

'Dr Bella Forsythe,' both said in unison.

'Dr Bella Forsythe, aka Dr Annabella Forsythe, aka Miss Anna Elliot, aka Miss Dipstick,' Kennedy solo'd.

'What?'

'It's a long story, and with no real punchline to justify wasting your time with the full explanation.'

But there was more.

When Dr Taylor examined (for the record) the body of Neil 'Flute' Burton he stated for the record, being recorded by an overhead suspended microphone,

'This is certainly not the work of a wild dog, a dog of any kind for that matter. These intrusions are too neat and tidy. If these injuries had been caused by the teeth of a dog this would all have been ripped apart more crudely. These cuts, in my opinion, were most certainly made by a knife, possibly even a scalpel. The cuts are all clean and precise. Again, I repeat, if they were made by a dog's teeth this tissue would all be shredded and uneven. It's easy to see how all the blood was lost.' Taylor invited Kennedy to have a look.

Kennedy's stomach felt like a car engine trying to turn over on a cold morning without the assistance of the choke. He looked over Taylor's arched back and closed his eyes just as the area referred to by Taylor was about to come into view. He was more than happy to take the doctor's word for it.

❐

'Okay,' Kennedy announced twenty-seven minutes later back at North Bridge House. The entire team, thankfully minus Castle, had reassembled and there was a certain amount of joviality in the air. Overtime, after all, was overtime. 'Okay, let's get out and about around Camden immediately with these pictures. We really do need to look under each and every stone. Don't forget this is the most recent photograph Dr Taylor could find for us of Dr Bella, sorry, Dr Annabella Forsythe. It is also worth remembering that although she's not a master of disguise, she's been known to try out a few fancy dress party-pieces, i.e. her Royal Blackness, Miss Dipstick. Today we haven't a clue as to how she'll be trying to conceal her identity.

Through her contacts with us she'll certainly know we're on her trail, but hopefully she'll be unaware of this morning's developments.'

The joviality subsided as one by one each member of the team realised that they recognised the name, and the likeness, as not only someone they all thought they knew but also as someone who had been working with them on this very case.

Indeed, amongst their number was a gentleman of Scottish extraction who had allowed himself to grow quite fond of the doctor. His voice was the next to be heard.

'Are we absolutely sure about this, sir?' The Connery sparkle was missing this time.

'Alas, I'm afraid so, DS Irvine, and I think it's very important for all of us to remember how dangerous she is. For certain she's now killed three times that we know of.' Kennedy held up three fingers to emphasise the point.

'Neil Burton, throat and innards slashed with a scalpel to make it look like the work of a dog. The exact same for Jerry MacKane. And John B. Stone, bludgeoned to death.'

'But I thought we had Anderson banged away to rights on that one, sir?' a Welsh voice at the back chipped in.

'Anderson has claimed all along that after his beating Stone was still alive. Now I'm prepared to believe him and believe that Forsythe returned to the scene of the crime to finish off Stone herself.'

'Ingenious!' WPC Coles admitted.

'Yes, but before we get too far into blind adulation let's remember that she is now after Rory Nash. Only this time she's even more dangerous because she's nothing to lose, nothing at all. They can't give her more than a life sentence whether it's for three or for four murders. Now Nash, the eejit won't come in to our custody to protect himself, so you, WPC Coles, and you, PC Alloway, I want you both stuck to him like glue. I want you to be as close to him as Coe was to Ovett, all day and night, until Forsythe is apprehended.'

'What if – ' Coles began.

'No what-if's,' Kennedy rejoined, 'He doesn't have a choice, 'Go, and go now. Please. We weren't able to help the first three poor sods and we may not be able to force Nash into our custody but let's do our dammedest to keep him alive.'

Before Kennedy had finished WPC Coles, with PC Alloway in tow, was off. Off to protect a future politician.

'Okay, DS Irvine, here's Dr Forsythe's address, or at least the last known one Dr Taylor had in his files for her. I've requested warrants for her arrest and to search her property to be issued urgently. Tim Flynn should have a copies for you by the time you leave the station. Go round there and take whoever you feel you will need. No doubt Forsythe will not be there, but find me something, Jimmy, anything. We need some kind of lead. A clue about what she intends to do, or her whereabouts, or possibly clues as to what disguises she may be using, or even what she's been doing for the last twenty-four years. Photos of friends, I don't really know what. Just look and look and look and then look once more,' the DI instructed as Irvine nodded compliance with the order.

The DS's war wounds were now healing quite well, well as could be expected, so Kennedy thought that Irvine should not be feeling as bad as he looked. Everyone in the conference room that morning had seen better looking corpses. Irvine made eye contact with one WPC and two PCs and nodded them to follow him.

Kennedy was half-tempted to visit the Forsythe apartment in person. He had a yen to see the home of the person who had without any apparent remorse murdered three people, all males and all, at least on paper, stronger than her. He wanted to walk in to her living space and sense and savour his first impressions. However, he resisted the temptation, feeling the case would be better served should he remain at North Bridge House and be on hand to assess any and all developments.

He managed a quick call to ann rea advising her of the breakthrough. She remained perfectly calm and advised Kennedy that she and Daniel Elliot would catch the next train back to London and come straight to North Bridge House.

Kennedy despatched the few remaining members of the team to Nash's office at 12 Oval Road, to keep watch in case Forsythe happened to show up there. He wasn't entirely sure about this, as Esther had convinced him that the building was never in use at the weekend. That was the time the cleaners came in.

Even the cleaners knew something was up at 12 Oval Road on that sunny Saturday morning. Not only were there lots of police officers loitering with intent, but the cleaners' usually stingey bosses at OfficeKlean had laid on an extra pair of hands. Mind you none of them complained at the new, identically dressed pair of hands because she knew her way around the offices and seemed more than prepared to pull her weight.

Kennedy assumed that Forsythe would be well aware that Nash would not be in his office on the Saturday and would be making her plans accordingly. She was hardly one for the rash attack. Anyone who had spent twenty-four years planning to murder four people would make herself well aware of her prey's each and every move. Kennedy realised that if he didn't pull his finger out quickly Nash's movements were going to become very restricted, as in stopped, if one Annabella Forsythe had anything to do about it.

No sooner had he dispatched the team to Oval Road when, back in the peace and quiet of his office, he took a call from WPC Coles.

'Er, there's a bit of a problem, sir.'

'Yes?'

'Well, we're at Nash's house and his partner tells us he's not here, sir,'

'Yes, and does sh- does the partner know where Nash is?'

'Well, you see, that's the problem, isn't it?'

'Yes? Is it?'

'Well, apparently when Nash is in London at the weekend he likes to spend Saturday mornings wandering around Camden Market.

'For how long?'

'The partner tells us that he doesn't usually come back till about two o'clock,' Coles replied.

'Can you find out where he goes – the Stables, Camden Lock, Dingwall's, Chalk Farm Road, Camden High Street. I know, some Saturdays the Electric Ballroom down by the tube station is used for a record fair; check if he ever goes there and if one is on today.' Kennedy could sense the panic in his voice and hoped it wasn't evident. If Rory Nash made a weekly pilgrimage to Camden Market then you could bet, as sure as you could bet on Eddie Irvine never being allowed to overtake Michael Schumacher as long as they both drove for Ferrari, that Annabella Forsythe would be equally aware of this fact and be aware of it long before Kennedy had been. She'd equally be aware that it would be nigh impossible to protect someone totally in such an environment.

Kennedy remembered the case of the Bulgarian diplomat who had been openly assassinated on the streets of London; his attacker had simply injected him with poison from the tip of his umbrella. The diplomat collapsed to his death on the busy London streets within seconds. Frightfully un-British to use one's brolly thus, but damned effective. From this maze of visions Kennedy kept hearing Coles' voice saying, 'Well, that's just it sir, apparently he loves the street buzz at the market and just wanders aimlessly around the entire area.'

'Okay,' Kennedy replied, jumping to his feet and pulling his green windbreaker over his arms as he alternately held the handset in opposite hands, 'I'll meet you at the optician's on the corner of Chalk Farm Road and Castlehaven Road, across the road from Dingwall's.

Kennedy threw the phone back at the rest, hoping it would reach its destination, but he didn't really care because at that point he was on the way out of the door. He stopped briefly at the desk to order Sgt Flynn to get as many people as possible down to Camden Market to meet up with himself and Coles. He further instructed Flynn to pull everybody, except Irvine and his team, off everything else and get them down to the market.

'God bless Sgt Flynn,' Kennedy thought as he ran down Oval Road, took the first right into the arc of Gloucester Crescent, first right into Inverness Street, first left along Arlington Road, first right down Jamestown Road, first left into a packed Camden High Street, over the canal bridge and under the railway bridge to the start of Chalk Farm Road at Castlehaven Road.

Once he reached the High Street, Kennedy's running was hampered, as everyone seemed to be walking against him and the pavements were packed with punters and traders selling everything from pirate cassettes to leather jackets, shoes and boots (lots of boot stores but none selling Wellingtons; Kennedy had checked once unsuccessfully on his way to Glastonbury).

By the time he reached the optician's he was covered in a fine film of sweat, but on the positive side Coles was already there waiting for him with several other officers, obviously those already on duty on the busy streets of Camden Town.

'Okay,' Kennedy began, surprised at himself by not being at all breathless (tell that to his heart, which was doing a Keith Moon set of paradiddles inside his chest). 'We're looking for Rory Nash and we're looking for Annabella Forsythe looking for Rory Nash. Now, here's the important bit: we have to find Rory Nash before Annabella Forsythe does.'

With that he divided them up as best he could and sent off twenty-three fine officers to locate two people in a crowd of about twenty-five thousand. Most of the police knew Forsythe as a colleague, and Nash as a local minor celeb. The photo of the Elliot helped a bit but it was still a pretty formidable task. The phrase 'needle in a haystack' came to a number of minds.

Chapter Forty-Five

'So, how's he dressed?' Kennedy asked Coles.
'Black tracksuit, black baseball cap, no markings, and white running shoes. According to him indoors he always dressed the same, it's his healthy Saturday morning dress,' she replied.

'What, you mean he's jogging through all of this?' Kennedy indicated the thronging masses threatening to knock him off his feet even as he spoke to the WPC.

'No, not at all, he just goes for a wander; we should check out the record stall, and no, there is no fair this morning at the Electric Ballroom but he is apparently a bit of a vinyl junky, sir, and occasionally returns with some rare sixties albums.'

'Okay. Let's get on with this search,' Kennedy instructed. He had decided that there wasn't much sense in running about or hurrying. No, that would create a greater chance of missing Nash. He would walk slowly, taking everything in. He crossed the zebra crossing dividing Camden High Street and Chalk Farm Road and melted immediately into the market by Dingwall's dancehall.

The first thing which caught his attention was a stall absolutely laden with doughnuts. Every possible kind of doughnut one could imagine, even a few which no human could. On another morning he would have stopped, helped himself to a couple (at a pound each) and happily munched his way around the rest of the stalls. Not today.

Forty-five minutes later Kennedy's eyes were tiring from punks, spikey hair, leather shirts, micro skirts, miniskirts, long skirts (and that's just for the boys); beer bellies, fat bellies, pregnant bellies, nose piercing, ear piercing, eyebrow piercing, lip, tongue and even cheek piercing; large people, little people, little people appearing to look large in high platform shoes, English people, Irish people, Scottish people, Indian people, Japanese people, lots of Japanese people, French people, London people, hippies, dippies, new romantics, old romantics, butchers, bakers and candlestick makers, yes, really, even candlestick makers. Every bleeding type that you could think of, excepting that is, an overdressed, overweight and overcool bleedin' pop group manager.

Kennedy suddenly remembered a old party trick of his. When he went to parties, and it was rare of him to do so, rarer still these days, instead of wandering around he would position himself in one comfy spot (near food, drink, tea making facilities, toilets, clean air, not too many people, an acceptable distance from the music and in close proximity of a relaxing easy chair) and by the end of the evening he invariably found that the entire party had passed by his hangout point. This gave him an idea.

Camden Market was a party. A magical, colourful Saturday-and-Sunday fifty-two-weekends-a-year party, so why not position his team in key strategic spots and let the masses pass them all by? Surely they would have a greater chance of spotting Rory Nash using this technique? Kennedy's logic being that if they all moved around, the laws of coincidence meant the chances of their paths crossing diminished.

As for Dr Bella Forsythe, well he had to assume that she knew the police were on her trail and so, equally they had to assume she'd be in one of her master (mistress?) disguises, but definitely not the Miss Dipstick one.

Kennedy radioed through to Sgt Flynn, described his idea, and had him work out a location system and radio through to the team the new plan and the part (where) the various members of Camden CID were to play in it.

Kennedy himself took up residence at the main gate to the Stables where he could observe people come in from the Chalk Farm Road entrance, see them come down through the Stables from the Safeway entrance, or see them come in from behind him, through the side entrances which led to the Lock.

After about ten minutes he spotted some regular activity going on behind one of the stalls on the way through to the Lock. Dealers (drug) at work. He watched them work the patch and worked out their system. They would politely approach potential clients with all the charm of a cobra luring its prey. A deal would be nodded through to one of their fellow charmers behind the stall. This fellow would act as the mule, to ensure the dealer was never actually caught with any drugs about his person, and even if the mule was caught he would only have enough of whatever the vice was 'for personal use'. The dealer and mule would meet up with the client, the client would pay the dealer. When the dealer had the money in his hot sweaty hands he would quickly vanish. Only then would the mule pass the consignment over to the client. The dealer would reappear behind the stall, depositing the money with the banker and starting the entire process over again. Kennedy realised he need not take any immediate action; they'd be there for the rest of the day, and he'd tip off the drug squad on his return to North Bridge House.

A scuffle broke out at the main gate. A middle-aged lady caught a young ginger-haired boy trying to pick her pockets, actually trying to nick her purse out of her hand. However, the woman was a match the boy, she grabbed him violently by his Hendrix-styled hair and swung him around, screaming at him. Within seconds the Stables security and three of the closest stall workers were over and rescuing her, or rather the boy, shortly before he was about to have no ginger hair at all.

It was very important for the stall owners that no such criminals worked their patch. Hence the extreme politeness of the dealer and his team. Tourists had to feel safe, and news of pickpockets or interference from drunks or gangs of any sort travelled fast. So they duffed the ginger-haired boy up a bit, nothing too violent, Kennedy noted, just enough to frighten him off and a sign to other potential tea-leaves. Talking of tea, Kennedy would loved to have had a cup right now. Being around the crowded market with it's major dust movement was thirsty work.

The other thing to consider was all the various aromas floating around the market. Fresh bread, crêpes, delicious crêpes with their various hot or cold, sweet or sour, healthy or enjoyable fillings. Fried bacon, sausages, falafal with salad in pitta bread, fish and chips, doughnuts (the doughnut stall was about twenty yards from Kennedy but he could still smell the toppings: chocolate, caramel, honey, fresh strawberry jam, cinnamon, Smarties, – yes, doughnuts covered with Smarties ginger, cream and on and on, all hitting his taste buds. And all a lot more appetising than the taste of dust. The thought of a fresh cup of tea to wash it all down made the craving irresistible.

The other smells circulating were less enticing but equally aromatic. Blankets and carpets which had been sitting in the stalls a little too long, clothes, smelling of sleep, sweat and cannabis (not necessarily in that order) and beer (there was invariably the odd empty beer can lying around but the stall owners made sure no alcoholics made the market their patch for boozing or begging, again very bad for business).

At that precise moment a beautiful young woman passed Kennedy giving off a symphony of other rich and enticing aromas, smelling absolutely body beautiful with a slight hint of coconut, believe it or not, and freshly washed skin and hair. She looked clean, as in very clean, apart, that is, from a smear of chocolate around her mouth from a fresh-filled crepe which was slowly disappearing, enticingly, into her exquisite mouth. Kennedy found himself gawking at her and he tried to convince himself his gawking was at the gorgeous crêpe and not at the delicious lady.

Kennedy could resist it no longer and so he made his way to the crêpe stall, eye still clocking the gate and the entrance from the lock. He was now closer to the Safeway entrance and so he could observe this more easily from the stall at least. He placed his order. A crêpe filled with banana, nuts, raspberries and honey plus a cup of tea, white with two sugars. Kennedy hadn't considered how he was going to manage to negotiate eating, drinking and watching all at once.

Just as he was reaching across the counter to claim his prize he felt a solid thud on his shoulder.

'Inspector Kennedy, what an unusual place to find you.'

Kennedy immediately recognised the voice, with its affected diction, and turned to face the man in black (black apart from the white pumps of course), Rory Nash.

Kennedy looked to the heavens with a wry smile. The sky

was blue, a stunning ice-blue, and was filled with lots of little fluffy clouds, a bit like cotton wool on an ambient music CD cover.

'Mr Nash, we've got the entire Camden police force out looking for you. Am I glad to see you,' Kennedy said, unzipping his windbreaker.

'I've rarely received such an effusive greeting in this market,' said Nash, 'I'm happy to have made your day.' He sighed and smiled and turned to catch the stall owner's attention, 'Two crepes please, one with chocolate, vanilla, nuts and apples and one banana, strawberries, chocolate and lemon – oh, and a mineral water too, please.' The last part of the order was emphased, as if he believed the sugar-free value of the mineral water was going to compensate for the high fat content of the double crêpe.

Kennedy now had his treat in hand and started to munch and sip. Out of the corner of his eye he noticed a woman running at great speed in their direction. She had long flowing grey locks and a full-length loose red dress which flapped in the wind and waved around violently behind her as she made her way fiercely towards them. She had a Mike Tyson look fixed in her hazel eyes, the look you have just before you're about to bite into someone's ear.

Kennedy chucked his tea and crêpe swiftly to the ground. The crêpe hid the ground with a sad, dull thud but the tea splashed up from the cup and exploded in several directions, each one leading to Kennedy and Nash's legs.

Nash shouted, annoyed and very London, 'What the eff are you doing, mate?'

Kennedy pushed Nash forcefully towards the other end of the stall, hoping to get him out of harm's way. But the man wouldn't move. He stood staring at Kennedy in belligerent disbelief. It was all happening in slow motion. Kennedy could still see the red-dressed witch baring down on them at a great rate of knots out of the (trusted) corner of his eye.

The detective didn't have any time remaining to argue with Nash, so he charged full-on into him, taking the pair of them in the direction Kennedy required. Nash lost his balance and both of them fell to the ground in a heap which included the rubbish from the bin they had toppled over in the process.

As they were gathering their wits about them, Nash still in shock, Kennedy jumped to his feet and turned to tackle the witch. He was just in time to see her run spiritedly past him shouting, 'Nigel!'

Kennedy looked to his right and saw Nigel running towards her shouting, 'Audrey!'

They reached each other with arms and jackets and red skirts making a great theatrical to-do for the benefit of anyone caring to watch. Most not caring to watch were looking instead at the man in black still lying in the rubbish and the man with the green windbreaker trying to find a hole in the ground big enough to climb in to. Nigel and Audrey both kissed the air beside their cheeks and went away arm-in-arm to view the futons, or some such. Kennedy was left to pick up the pieces, or Mr Rory Nash, future politician of the parish.

Luckily Nash saw the funny side of it. For this Kennedy was grateful. Castle would have been most upset if he (Kennedy) had made an enemy out of a future (potential) politician. On the positive side, at least Nash was still alive, dirty and bruised with ruffled feather and pride, but still alive and still with his tea and crêpes. Which was more than Kennedy could claim.

Chapter Forty-Six

'She rang, sir.'

'Who has rung, Jimmy?' Kennedy replied, immediately recognising the spirited Scottish tones.

'Dr Forsythe, sir. She rang me just a couple of minutes ago.'

It was early evening on the Saturday. Kennedy and his team were relaxing a little. Rory Nash was under police supervision. Not at North Bridge House, as Kennedy had hoped, but safely in a top floor suite at the Marriot Hotel at Swiss Cottage. Camden CID would only have sprung for the regular single-room rate and Nash, clearly a man who liked his home (and away) comforts insisted he pay the bill himself. Kennedy had agreed, feeling good about protecting both Castle's budget and Nash's life in the one deal, and so Nash had booked the Marriot's best suite with an interconnecting room. And there he was safely holed up for the foreseeable future with three police officers.

One, PC Terence Shaw, was in the hall. Luckily the suite and ajoining room were the only rooms down the corridor to the right as you came out of the lift, so there was no reason for anyone to be there unless authorised. The other two, PC Tony Essex and WPC Doreen West shared the interconnecting room, doors open. Kennedy had given specific instructions to give Nash as much space as possible. He'd heard from ann rea that music business types like to have as much 'space' as possible. So Kennedy told his constables to maintain a discreet presence but to keep the interconnecting door open at all times.

'And?'

'She said she wanted to see me, but only me, sir.'

'What are her other conditions, Jimmy?' Kennedy replied into the phone, the phone in his house near the foot of Primrose Hill.

'She said she just wanted to talk. She knew we'd picked up Nash in Camden Market.'

'All of bleedin' Camden Town knows that,' Kennedy declared, his face reddening at the memory.

'Yes. And she said that it was all over now but she'd like to meet to talk before she gave herself up. She said for it all to work she had to give herself up, but before that she said she wanted to spend some time with me and for us to talk. She said after that she'd allow me to bring her in to North Bridge House. I'd like to do it, sir.' Irvine could not conceal the emotion in his voice.

'Jimmy, please don't forget that this woman has now killed three times, three times that we know of. She could be wanting you for a hostage; perhaps she sees you as a way of doing a trade for Rory Nash, or something along those lines. Don't forget she doesn't think the way you and I think.'

'She seems resigned to the fact that it's all over, sir.'

'Jimmy, you're not asking me to go along with this are you? Because you know that I can't, you know that you can't. Now where did you agree to meet?'

'Euston, sir. Euston Station at seven-thirty. She told me to walk around in front of the arrivals and departures board and said that she would contact me but if she saw any sign of police she'd be off and we'd never find her. Surely it's worth the risk, sir?'

'No, Jimmy. I don't know what has gone down between you and this woman and I don't want to know. But here's what we are going to do.' And he explained his recently formed plan.

So, at precisely seven twenty-five a very nervous DS James Irvine walked back and forth across the concourse at Euston Station. Being a Saturday, Euston was packed. People with a free Sunday making their way to the Midlands or Manchester, or people returning to London from the Midlands and Manchester for work on Sunday, or people returning North, or coming from the North for the purpose of viewing twenty-two men and a wee man dressed in black with a whistle chasing a leather ball about a large field. Or people simply coming down for a Saturday night of fun in the west end.

'The train now standing on platform three...' the estuary-accented voice began to announce over the PA.

'...should get off the bleedin' platform and back on the rails,'

Irvine said to no one in particular in his best English accent. He went and bought himself a cup of tea – polystyrene cup, tea brewed to death and longlife milk, the most consistent spoiler of a good cup of tea known to humankind. He took one swig and dumped it, from mouth and cup, into the nearest rubbish bin.

Just as he released the cup from his fingers and was watching it fall, in slow motion, in with the rest of the rubbish, he felt a hand gently squeeze his elbow.

'Sir, would you give some money to help a London child?'

'No,' Irvine thought, 'I'd kill a social worker.' At the same time he said, 'Not today, sorry. Thank you.'

Then he recognised Annabella Forsythe *née* Elliot and with that he gave the prearranged signal of tipping his newspaper into the same rubbish bin. In seven seconds flat, a very long seven seconds for Irvine, they were surrounded by three officers, two (including Kennedy) dressed as Railtrack staff and one (Alloway) dressed as a commuter (lots of mystery, no substance). Kennedy and Alloway each grabbed one of Forsythe's arms, gently, for it has to be said she offered no resistance, none whatsoever.

Irvine felt about three inches tall though, because Dr Forsythe, the woman he'd grown quite fond of, even though he'd never actually managed to get close to her, showed nothing, nothing save the look of disappointment in her eyes. Disappointment (total) in Irvine. He tried to speak to her several times but found it impossible to complete a sentence.

'I'm sorry... look, I... I couldn't really have.. you have to realise... we have to face... I'm really sorry.'

With that Kennedy and Alloway led Forsythe away to the awaiting police car. They took her back to North Bridge House where Sgt Flynn attended to the paperwork on Annabella (Forsythe) Elliot for the second time in his career. This time he was offering her less sympathy, a lot less, as in none. The abovementioned doctor would not say a word, not a simple word to anybody during the interview, so at nine twenty-four Kennedy discontinued the proceedings, advising Elliot that they would resume at nine on the Monday morning.

Chapter Forty-Seven

Saturday night was blown for Kennedy, and ann rea, who by this time had dropped Daniel Elliot off at his house, the house they used to share, the house that a young Anna Elliot had also shared, which is how ann rea had managed to get stuck in the middle of this whole episode in the first place. In a way it was lucky for Kennedy, and Camden CID, that she had. Because without ann rea's involvement it would have taken Kennedy and his team a hell of a lot longer to get a handle on this complex and confusing case, let alone solve it.

Kennedy had personally rung Nash and told him that Forsythe was now in custody. Nash immediately decided throw throw a party – 'Why waste the suite?' – and duly invited Kennedy 'and your partner.' Kennedy declined. ann rea never did find out about the invitation.

The conversation between ann rea and Kennedy turned to their relationship. It took this somewhat predictable turn about halfway through the first glass of wine (St Venan).

'I've been think a lot about us since yesterday, Kennedy.'

'Aha?'

'To be honest I couldn't not think about us really, what with all this death and talk of death and seeing how much Lila and Daniel had meant to each other and also seeing, Christy, how much you want us to be together.'

'You mean, as in I want it too much?'

'Well frankly, probably, yes,' she replied, solemnly taking another sip of wine.

'I don't think this is about who loves who the most, you know,' Kennedy said shakily, feeling things begining to spiral recklessly out of control.

'But Christy, I don't think I'd ever be able to love you the way you love me and I feel that's exactly what it's about. I do love being with you, I love hanging out with you. I love making love with you. It's absolutely great when we have a laugh together. But surely there has to be more? In fact there does seem to be more for you.'

Kennedy just shrugged as if to say, 'So?'

ann rea read his body language easily.

'Two things actually, Christy.'

This is bad, she keeps referring to me by my first name.

'One, I don't want your love to eventually turn to hate just because you think it's not been returned; and two, and I'll admit this one is selfish, I want more of what you are feeling and I don't want to leave it too long. Time is slipping by and I might want to have children.'

'Children?' Kennedy thought, 'She's never discussed having children with me. Christ, this is serious. I've fecked it up, big time.' But he said nothing. They just sat there, physically close but emotionally miles apart, on the sofa.

'So what? So what are you saying exactly? Are you saying you want to end this?' Kennedy could hear himself say the words but he couldn't believe that he was saying them. What would happen if she said 'Yes'?

ann rea didn't reply. She tried, in vain, to smile.

'This is weird,' he said, 'Recently I've been thinking that you are not really in love and you've been trying to find a way to break up without hurting me. I'm a big boy, ann, I'll get over this. This is what happens to people. I can deal with it, you know. As you get older you learn two things, you learn how to keep secrets and how to get over a failed relationship.'

'Well, yes, Kennedy, sometimes I do feel I don't love you, but not all the time. Most of the time I was feeling that it was great. And, shit, it is great, and you're the nicest… and the best thing which has ever happened to me,' ann rea declared, draining the last of her wine. Kennedy rose from the sofa, went to the kitchen and retrieved the bottle from the fridge. He freshened both their drinks and said very quietly, 'But it just isn't enough, is it?'

'Well, maybe it is. Maybe this is all that there is, all that I should be expecting. But, in this permanent state of doubt, we'll never – sorry, I mean I'll never – find out, and I do need to try.'

'Hey, look ann rea, as I said I'm a grown man, do you really realise this? Sometimes I don't think that you do. Sometimes I think you think I'm an innocent, a kid. Well, I'm not and I do need to get on with my life as well. Believe me, I can deal with this. But you know now that I think the important thing, more than anything, is that I just want to get on with my life, and if this is not going to work then so be it and let's deal with it, for heaven's sake.' He spoke firmly, but he wasn't sure where his words were coming from. Here he was inviting the person he'd loved most of all in his life to dump him. He took a large gulp of wine, finishing off his newly filled glass. He rose from the sofa again, topped up her glass and refilled his own. He stood alone by the fireplace, barely looking at her.

'But you know,' he said, 'I can't abide all this shit about ^let's try to split up for a while and see how it works," It's always, always a recipe for a disaster. The writing is on the wall at that point. If you take something apart to see how it works or how good it really is, you're never able to put it back together again the way it was.'

'Okay.' was the one-word reply from a voice barely able to speak it.

'Okay?'

'Yes, okay!'

'Yes okay we spilt up, or yes okay we don't?' Kennedy felt his anger rising.

'We should split up. It's not right like this. Christy, I want to love you, I really do. It's just that I don't seem...' ann rea struggled for words.

'It's okay, ann rea, it is really,' Kennedy said as he went back to the sofa. ann rea rose to meet him. They held each other tightly, gently swaying, Kennedy patting her on her back, saying, 'It's okay.'

'But I don't want to lose you as a friend.' ann rea was now sobbing unashamedly.

'Let's just deal with this part first, once we manage to get over this I'm sure we'll be friends, it'll just take time,' Kennedy replied, himself now close to tears.

They stood there in his living room hugging each other, letting the beginning of the healing time pass.

Kennedy spoke first some time later when ann rea's sobbing had subsided.

'You should go now.'

'Could I not stay tonight?'

'I don't think that would be right. You should go.'

'But I don't want to leave you, Christy.' ann rea was now crying uncontrollably.

'We need to start the ending, ann rea, it's wrong delaying it, it's only going to make it harder,' Kennedy said, mustering all the resolve he could. He felt himself a single split second away from saying, 'Okay then, let's just go to bed and we'll deal with it tomorrow,' but he knew the tomorrow would become a couple of months of hurt, and not just for him.

'Oh Jesus, Kennedy, look at me, I'm a mess.' She kissed him, sealing her resolve. It was a goodbye kiss, a long, passionate kiss but a goodbye kiss all the same. It was a kiss where they both tried to convey what they had meant to each other, and they broke it off in a mellower mood.

They spoke no further. ann rea gathered together her things and made to leave. She turned to face him in the hall and was about to speak but then quickly turned away and let herself out, closing the strong, protective door behind her.

On Saturday night at ten forty-five precisely, Detective Inspector Christy Kennedy lost the love of his life. While on the other side of the door, anyone witnessing ann rea's gentle consistent sobbing would not have believed that she would ever love anyone in her life more than she loved Kennedy at that point.

Chapter Forty-Eight

On the seventh day of this case, Kennedy walked to his office via Primrose Hill, he didn't feel so bad, at least not as bad as he thought he should. He'd slept okay, thought about ann rea a bit, not as much as he thought he was going to. But then again he figured the gap which she was now making in his life was not yet evident since it was only a matter of ten hours, seven of which he had been asleep, since they split up.

But then, he thought, how could anyone feel bad while walking over Primrose Hill on a morning such as this. It was truly a magical place and, to make matters even better, he had spied two magpies as he entered the park. He recited the 'one for sorrow, two for joy' rhyme and said, quietly to himself, 'Well you know, maybe this is what I needed, to get this thing with ann rea finally resolved, and if it's not going to be her, and after last night that is certainly the case, at least that part of my life is over and resolved, and now it's time to get on with the next part. And I'll take two magpies anytime to start anew.'

One good thing you could say about Kennedy: he was great company for himself and he had over the years grown very used to his own company and, in fact quite liked it. Liked it to a degree that at that point, early on the Monday morning, he didn't feel as much the loss of ann rea as he felt of having escaped from a situation which, on paper, was never going to work. He knew not why: old baggage, he was a romantic she wasn't, lots of things. But he knew that accepting it wasn't going to work and that it was over, and having the will to get on with things, was turning out to be a bit of a major relief.

He knew for a fact that soon in his lone moments his memories of the times with ann rea would come flooding back. He'd hear the fun things she had said, or would picture them together in an intimate moment; and then he would definitely feel the loss, and a great a loss it would be, too.

But not today; today was for drinking the many pleasures of Primrose Hill. Primrose Hill was unique in that it had all the soul you needed when you walked over it and equally it had all the fun and colour you needed when you were lost in it with your lover. But today it was for crossing, recharging one's batteries and getting to North Bridge House and tying up the many loose ends on the Forsythe triple murder.

Chapter Forty-Nine

At North Bridge House there were few signs that Camden CID were detaining a triple murderer in their basic, but clean and freshly painted cells. Kennedy was immediately visited in his office by DS Irvine, looking less haggard than on Saturday evening. Irvine explained that he had been able to spend some time with Forsythe in the cells making his peace with her. He had successfully explained to her that there really wasn't much else that he could have done other than help set the trap which had eventually snared her.

Apparently, according to Irvine, she was now over it and accepted that, as Irvine now reported to Kennedy trying to raise a smile, 'A man's got to do what a man's got to do.'

But the good news was that she was ready, willing and able to talk with Kennedy and was foregoing her right to have a solicitor present.

Kennedy elected to have Anne Coles present with him on the interview. He began with the now-traditional intro for the benefit of the ever-present third eye, the tape recorder. He announced those present, PC Gaul, standing by the door, WPC Coles and himself on one side of the barren table and Dr Annabella Forsythe alone, as requested, on the other.

Forsythe looked as happy as someone on Prozac. She appeared stress-free, laid back and willing them to throw any and all questions at her.

'Could we start with Neil Burton?' Kennedy began.

'Yes,' Forsythe replied quietly, ever so quietly, barely competing with the ticking of the clock, 'Although he wasn't the first, I'm sure you know that by now. Jerry MacKane was first, but that was up in Birmingham, and both of them were the same, they held a leg each, you see.'

'How did you meet up with Burton again?' Coles inquired.

'Oh, it was easy. The lowlifers of Camden Town all have their locals. I found out which pub he hung out at, it didn't take long really, and I went and checked him out a few times first. Then I dolled myself up and went back and allowed him to chat me up. It's so easy with you men,' said Forsythe, 'You make eye contact with a man and he thinks he's pulled. He puffs up his chest and steps in for the kill. They think that they are doing you a favour. I got him drunk, whispered in his ear that I was up for a bit of outdoor activity, wanted to have some fun with him in Regent's Park. He nearly fell off his chair. At one point I was convinced he was coming in his pants, he couldn't believe his luck.'

'So you…' WPC Coles prompted.

'So I took him up Parkway, whispering in his ear about how great it was going to be under the moon, and when we got to Gloucester Gate Bridge I suggested we sit up on the bridge for a while. We were at this end on the left. I got the idea when I used to wander around this area a lot, just before I left. At this side of the bridge, I don't know if you've ever seen it or not but there's a plaque showing a wild dog attacking a hapless traveller, and that's when I first started to think about ridding the world of the four of them. I knew this would not be easy, though, because they were all stronger than me.'

'So you saw the dog and you…' Coles again prompted Forsythe gently.

'First off I thought about getting a dog, you know, and setting it on them, killing all of them. Then I realised that was pretty impracticable, it might have even attacked me.' Forsythe broke into nervous laughter. Kennedy stared at her, trying to fathom how this frail woman, dressed in cream slacks, belt removed, white baggy blouse and simple white slip-on shoes, had taken the lives of three fellow humans. He found no clues being offered in her demeanour.

'Anyway, we were sitting on the bridge, he readied himself for his pleasure, and when he was least expecting it I elbowed him directly in the throat as hard as I could. Luckily I caught him off balance and he toppled backwards off the bridge. I jumped down after him. He'd landed on that large pile of stones and that knocked the wind out of him. That's what I was counting on. I allowed him to regain just enough consciousness to be aware of what was happening to him and I tore into him with my scalpel. You should have seen the look of fear in his eyes as I cut him for the first time,' Forsythe reported proudly.

'Jerry MacKane was the same?' Kennedy inquired.

'Pretty much,' she sighed, 'Different location, Birmingham, same come-on, use of alcohol, although MacKane had more front than Sainsbury's. He really did think he was God's gift and I…' She tailed off, perhaps deciding what not to say.

Kennedy and Coles let the silence fill the room; the clicking of the clock overhead seemed to grow louder and louder.

'You know,' said Forsythe after thirty ticks of the second hand and resumed her narrative. 'The thing which surprised me the most is how easy it is to kill someone. I was quite prepared for the episode to be so horrible and upsetting that I wouldn't have what it takes to do it again and I'd let the other three off. But when I saw that look of fear in his eyes when he realised what was about to happen to him, same with Burton, I felt fully vindicated. It was so exhilarating, and I couldn't wait to get to the next one, Burton.'

Coles was shocked at the (now former) pathologist's candour.

'And the other great thing,' Forsythe laughed, leaning over the desk, uncrossing her legs and clasping her hands together in front of her, 'was that I got to carry out the autopsy. That was a great touch, wasn't it? Mauled by a mad dog, I loved all that. I loved it so much I did it twice. And you all looked to me in my professional capacity to tell you, and none of you doubted me. You might have pondered other reasons for the injuries, but you never for one second doubted the soundness of the information I was giving you.

'Why did you change your approach for John B. Stone?' Kennedy quizzed.

'Well,' she said, 'I was tempted to repeat the mad dog trick but I felt I might be getting a bit too careless. I didn't mind being caught, you know, I just needed to cover up my tracks enough to be able to get the job done. And the name thing, Elliot versus Forsythe and Bella versus Anna, could only work for so long. I also knew if the mad dog attacked twice you'd be looking even closer at the victims to find a connection. And I knew at some point the Primrose Hill rape thing would come up and you'd connect all the names, so I had to make sure I kept my distance.'

Kennedy leaned back in his chair, fingers interlocked behind his head. 'So you hired Hugh Anderson?'

'Again, I was surprised at how easy it was, I was shocked at how simple it is to commit a crime. I got the idea for the perfect alibi when I was examining bodies. I kept thinking about how the murderer nearly always left some clue to their identity. And I went from that to thinking, how about leaving the wrong clues? Clues which would lead you to Anderson and not me. You know, set it up so that a) I had a perfect alibi, I knew what time the stooge was going to start proceedings so I made sure I was in company; and b) I planted enough evidence to lead the police back to the stooge. It's so obvious I'm surprised no one has ever used it before.'

She smiled to herself and sat back in her chair again. 'I checked with the *Camden News Journal* and discovered that he'd been done for GBH. They gave out his address just like that, they just didn't care. I couldn't believe it. That's the thing, though – on the phone you make yourself sound official, there's no worry about giving your telephone number, no one ever checks, and you can get whatever you need. I contacted Hugh Anderson, a professional villain, good manners, no sexual overtones at all, agreed the fee, and he went away and did his business as ordered. I made sure that at the time the crime was about to commence I was up to my neck in an alibi. And since I was doing the autopsy I was able to register the time of death as the time Anderson was doing the thumping, the exact time that I was dining in a restaurant with a friend. I also dropped the apple on the scene. Our Mr Anderson likes his fruit, doesn't he? He's got to that stage in life where he thinks a daily diet of apples and pears will cancel out all the years he's been abusing his body. I've seen inside those bodies and my advice to the Andersons of the world is forget the poxy fruit, smoke yourself happily to your inevitable death. Anyway the apple, just like it betrayed Eve, put Anderson at the scene of the crime, and I had every confidence that you, Inspector, with your great reputation, would do the rest. I met up with Anderson later that evening, paid him his due and went back to the fountain by the bridge where I had told him to dump Stone's body. I'd found a baseball bat in Regent's Park a few days before. I'd hidden it up in the lane by the Danish Church. I brought it with me after Anderson had left with his money, then I went back to the fountain and beat Stone to death.'

Kennedy was struck by the apparent ease with which Forsythe recalled the incidents, and he noticed that Coles seemed disturbed at the way this woman was relating her story. The WPC was shifting in her seat and fidgeting with her blouse cuffs. He thought that Coles' body language might be off-putting to the other woman, but Forsythe was now fully into her stride and nothing was going to slow her down.

'That's also where I went after they attacked me – the fountain. After they raped me I went and hid in the fountain, I felt that the washerwoman would protect me in a way that my parents had not. That's where I was found. So that's where I felt John Boy should be found. They were very clever, you know, no bruises, no torn clothes, no beating. I could even hear them saying to the police, there in the station, ^What rape? No, no, she wanted it, she kept leading us on.'' And it was so embarrassing because I could see the police, and even my father, looking at me and thinking, ^Well she doesn't look like she's been raped, maybe she did ask for it.'' '

This thought could still make Annabella Forsythe Elliot shudder violently all these twenty-four years later, and as she did so now there came a distant deep thud, as if someone was aggressively slamming a far-off door. So aggressively Kennedy could have sworn that the walls of North Bridge House were shaking. Castle in a bad mood, perhaps?

Forsythe sank further back in her chair. Kennedy wasn't entirely sure but he thought he saw a brief smirk creep over her face.

'And Nash? What had you planned for Nash?' he asked as the interview wound down.

'Ah!' she replied, sitting up in her chair again and engaging him with one of her coquettish looks, 'You'll see, soon enough!'

Chapter Fifty

Nash had returned to his office a happy man. Gone was the one worry, the one taint on an otherwise unblemished past. A past fit for a future member of the cabinet, and hell, maybe even a past fit for a prime minster. Well, why not?

Anyone can do anything, was Nash's motto. It was all down to putting yourself in the proper position and then having enough energy and knowledge to motivate your people. Now wasn't that the same as running a pop group? Well, very nearly.

He wandered around his office happy to have this free time. Most people in the music industry reach their office at the crack of lunchtime. That was more the old school really. Nash's generation, apart from being positively more ruthless than those before, knew that a major part of any success in the music biz had to do with putting in the hours. It was all to do with putting in the hours. The early bird gets the worm and the late bird gets the west coast (of America) as it rises.

Due to the trauma of the weekend Esther would shield him for the first part of the day, field his calls and allow him to gradually work his way back into things. Rory Nash felt like he'd been away on holiday for a month and that this was his first day back. It reminded him of his first days back at school, new smells, new crisp clean exercise books, new clothes, new haircut, newly shorn finger (and toe) nails. He could smell the fresh polish on the floor. His office was looking spick and span, the weekend cleaners had done a great job.

He went over to his Corgi Classics collection. He felt at peace with the world and at peace with himself. He loved the sight of his multicoloured display, supposedly one of the best collections of Corgi Classics in existence.

Corgi Classics had started in 1985, before the the famous 007 Aston Martin and Beatles' Yellow Submarine and so on, which were now referred to as Corgi Obsoletes. Nash had a few of these but not many, he didn't really collect them. No, he collected Corgi Classics and had mint copies with matching boxes of nearly all the thousand (or so) models Corgi had produced since 1985.

Collectors tend to place their collections in an easy-to-talk-up sequence and Nash's was no exception. All the Chipperfield Circus set was together, all the US of A buses, all the Showman Fairground set, all the Morris Minors, all the VW vans, all the Bedford CA vans, all the Bedford Pantechnicon vans and so on were displayed in their complete sets. Nash's sequence began with the police collection, and pride of place in that set was given to the Inspector Morse Maroon Mark II Jaguar. He had three of these worth about £150 each, not bad for a model which had come on the market four years ago at £9.99.

He lifted some models from the shelves as he moved along dusting them gently with a flexi-bristled make-up brush, very effective for this task.

Eventually he worked his way to the centre of his collection, his favourite section. His complete set of sixty-one Bedford OB buses. They looked so cute in their vibrant colours. From the greens of the Maltese model to the two shades of blue on the Premier Travel (Cambridge) model. And there in the centre, dead centre, of the entire thousand-plus collection was the famous green Southdown coach shining beautifully in the sunlight. The model looked so lifelike. Nash often wondered how grown men could enjoy so many hours of satisfaction from just standing and staring at model buses and cars and lorries. What was it about them? What was their attraction? For Nash it had to be their cuteness. The fact that some of them were so hard to find because the numbers produced fell way short of demand, and the rarer they are the more attention you paid once you'd tracked one down. And the chase itself, that in itself was something very exciting. Locating a rare model at some collectors' shop, bartering with the owner on the phone to try and have them reserve it for you until you'd a chance to go and view your prize. Then travelling to some far-flung outpost and discovering that the model was either damaged or its packaging was in poor condition so you would have to return home dejected. Equally there was the chance your rare model and its box, once you had found the shop, would be in mint condition. Then you try not to appear to be too excited about it just in case the price went through the roof in search of your initial smile. Collectors' fairs, such as the one just over a week ago in the Electric Ballroom, were the perfect place to track these specials down. The only problem was that you were usually racing three or four people after the same model. The bartering would be less civilised, and louder, than on the telephone but that was okay too, that was a different kind of excitment. But all of this chasing and haggling made the enjoyment of your collection, particulary the rarer classics, so much greater.

The collector gently picked up his favourite Corgi Classic, the Bedford OB Southdown coach, to lovingly dust it. As he lifted it from its pride-of-place position with its very own mini spotlights built into the shelf above, he felt a slight resistance to his pull. As he lifted it further the resistance gave way and there was a loud click from within the model, and in its wake a short length of nylon thread which was pinned to the shelf.

Nash heard the further clicks of a mechanism hidden within his beloved Bedford OB Southdown coach. For some reason he founding himself counting the clicks.

One: He felt his body drenched in sweat from the top of his well shaven head to the tip of his toes.

Two: Rory Nash felt nausea in the pit of his stomach. He felt his bowels try to activate, and he resisted this with severe butt clenching. At that precise moment he saw in his mind's eye Primrose Hill. He saw Flute Burton, John Boy Stone, Jerry MacKane and Anna Elliot along with himself. They were all in the bushes and they, all the boys, were laughing and joking and all being mates, having fun together.

Three: He wanted to drop the Corgi Bedford OB Southdown coach. His instincts told him to drop it and run for the door but he was magnetised to the floor. His legs were as heavy as lead they would not move at his command. The Southdown coach stuck to his fingers the way frozen metal does. He felt the only way he could remove it would be to tear the very skin from his fingers. He did manage to drop the brush and tried to use his free hand to pull the model from the other. The brush hand in turn became stuck to the Southdown coach.

Four: He wanted to shout, he wanted to scream. Then his mind flipped back to the Primrose Hill scene, where this time Burton and MacKane were holding Anna Elliot's legs apart and Stone was holding her hands above her head. He saw himself above Anna and he heard his voice, a voice still young in years, tell Anna not to scream, not to struggle. He saw tears make their way down her face in spite of her brave attempts to hold them back. He saw her mouth the word, 'NO!' He saw himself move closer to her, ready to engage her.

Five: Before forty-one year-old Rory Nash's brain had a chance to translate the sounds of the explosion and the stench of the mess around his feet, he had ceased to be.

And in the end, the love you take
Is equal to the love you make.

John Lennon & Paul McCartney.

And finally, the John Lennon and Paul McCartney quote used
on page 230 is from 'The End' (*Abbey Road*)

New titles from The Do-Not Press:

Ken Bruen: A WHITE ARREST Bloodlines
1 899344 41 1 – B-format paperback original, £6.50

Galway-born Ken Bruen's most accomplished and darkest crime noir novel to date is a police-procedural, but this is no well-ordered 57th Precinct romp. Centred around the corrupt and seedy worlds of Detective Sergeant Brandt and Chief Inspector Roberts, A White Arrest concerns itself with the search for The Umpire, a cricket-obsessed serial killer that is wiping out the England team. And to add insult to injury a group of vigilantes appear to to doing the police's job for them by stringing up drug-dealers... and the police like it even less than the victims. This first novel in an original and thought provoking new series from the author of whom Books in Ireland said: "If Martin Amis was writing crime novels, this is what he would hope to write."

Mark Sanderson: AUDACIOUS PERVERSION Bloodlines
1 899344 32 2 – B-format paperback original, £6.50

Martin Rudrum, good-looking, young media-mover, has a massive chip on his shoulder. A chip so large it leads him to commit a series of murders in which the medium very much becomes the message. A fast-moving and intelligent thriller, described by one leading Channel 4 TV producer as "Barbara Pym meets Bret Easton Ellis".

Jerry Sykes (ed): MEAN TIME Bloodlines
1 899344 40 3 – B-format paperback original, £6.50

Sixteen original and thought-provoking stories for the Millennium from some of the finest crime writers from USA and Britain, including **Ian Rankin** (current holder of the Crime Writers' Association Gold Dagger for Best Novel) **Ed Gorman, John Harvey, Lauren Henderson, Colin Bateman, Nicholas Blincoe, Paul Charles, Dennis Lehane, Maxim Jakubowski** and **John Foster**.

Ray Lowry: INK
1 899344 21 7 – Metric demy-quarto paperback original, £9

A unique collection of strips, single frame cartoons and word-play from well-known rock 'n' roll cartoonist Lowry, drawn from a career spanning 30 years of contributions to periodicals as diverse as Oz, The Observer, Punch, The Guardian, The Big Issue, The Times, The Face and NME. Each section is introduced by the author, recognised as one of Britain's most original, trenchant and uncompromising satirists, and many contributions are original and unpublished.

Maxim Jakubowski: THE STATE OF MONTANA
1 899344 43 8 half-C-format paperback original £5

Despite the title, as the novels opening line proclaims: 'Montana had never been to Montana". An unusual and erotic portrait of a woman from the "King of the erotic thriller" (Crime Time magazine).

New titles from The Do-Not Press:

Miles Gibson: KINGDOM SWANN
1 899344 34 9 – B-format paperback, £6.50

Kingdom Swann, Victorian master of the epic nude painting turns to photography and finds himself recording the erotic fantasies of a generation through the eye of the camera. A disgraceful tale of murky morals and unbridled matrons in a world of Suffragettes, flying machines and the shadow of war.

"Gibson has few equals among his contemporaries" –Time Out

"Gibson writes with a nervous versatility that is often very funny and never lacks a life of its own, speaking the language of our times as convincingly as aerosol graffiti" –The Guardian

Miles Gibson: VINEGAR SOUP
1 899344 33 0 – B-format paperback, £6.50

Gilbert Firestone, fat and fifty, works in the kitchen of the Hercules Café and dreams of travel and adventure. When his wife drowns in a pan of soup he abandons the kitchen and takes his family to start a new life in a jungle hotel in Africa. But rain, pygmies and crazy chickens start to turn his dreams into nightmares. And then the enormous Charlotte arrives with her brothel on wheels. An epic romance of true love, travel and food…

"I was tremendously cheered to find a book as original and refreshing as this one. Required reading…" –The Literary Review

Geno Washington: THE BLOOD BROTHERS
ISBN 1 899344 44 6 – B-format paperback original, £6.50

Set in the recent past, this début adventure novel from celebrated '60s-soul superstar Geno Washington launches a Vietnam Vet into a series of dangerous dering-dos, that propel him from the jungles of South East Asia to the deserts of Mauritania. Told in fast-paced Afro-American LA street style, The Blood Brothers is a swaggering non-stop wham-bam of blood, guts, lust, love, lost friendships and betrayals.

Jenny Fabian: A CHEMICAL ROMANCE
1 899344 42 X – B-format paperback original, £6.50

Jenny Fabian's first book, Groupie first appeared in 1969 and was republished last year to international acclaim ("Truly great late-20th century art. Buy it." –NME; "A brilliant period document" –Sunday Times). A roman à clef from 1971, A Chemical Romance concerns itself with the infamous celebrity status Groupie bestowed on Fabian. Expected to maintain the sex and drugs lifestyle she had proclaimed 'cool', she flits from bed to mattress to bed, travelling from London to Munich, New York, LA and finally to the hippy enclave of Ibiza, in an attempt to find some kind of meaning to her life. As Time Out said at the time: "Fabian's portraits are lightning silhouettes cut by a master with a very sharp pair of scissors." This is the novel of an exciting and currently much in-vogue era.

BLOODLINES the cutting-edge crime and mystery imprint...

PAUL CHARLES

LAST BOAT TO CAMDEN TOWN by Paul Charles

Hardback: ISBN 1 899344 29 2 — C-format original, £15
Paperback: ISBN 1 899344 30 6 — C-format paperback, £7

The second enthralling Detective Inspector Christy Kennedy mystery. The body of Dr Edmund Godfrey Berry is discovered at the bottom of the Regent's Canal, in the heart of Kennedy's "patch" of Camden Town, north London. But the question is, Did he jump, or was he pushed? Last Boat to Camden Town combines Whodunnit? Howdunnit? and love story with Paul Charles' trademark unique-method-of-murder to produce one of the best detective stories of the year.

"If you enjoy Morse, you'll enjoy Kennedy" — Talking Music, BBC Radio 2

I Love The Sound of Breaking Glass by Paul Charles

ISBN 1 899344 16 0 — C-format paperback original, £7

First outing for Irish-born Detective Inspector Christy Kennedy whose beat is Camden Town, north London. Peter O'Browne, managing director of Camden Town Records, is missing. Is his disappearance connected with a mysterious fire that ravages his north London home? And just who was using his credit card in darkest Dorset?

Although up to his neck in other cases, Detective Inspector Christy Kennedy and his team investigate, plumbing the hidden depths of London's music industry, turning up murder, chart-rigging scams, blackmail and worse. I Love The Sound of Breaking Glass is a detective story with a difference. Part whodunnit, part howdunnit and part love story, it features a unique method of murder, a plot with more twists and turns than the road from Kingsmarkham to St Mary Mead. Paul Charles is one of Europe's best known music promoters and agents. In this, his stunning début, he reveals himself as master of the crime novel.

JOHN B SPENCER

Tooth & Nail by John B Spencer

ISBN 1 899344 31 4 — C-format paperback original, £7

The long-awaited new noir thriller from the author of Perhaps She'll Die. A dark, Rackmanesque tale of avarice and malice-aforethought from one of Britain's most exciting and accomplished writers. "Spencer offers yet another demonstration that our crime writers can hold their own with the best of their American counterparts when it comes to snappy dialogue and criminal energy. Recommended." — Time Out

Perhaps She'll Die! by John B Spencer

ISBN 1 899344 14 4 — C-format paperback original, £5.99

Giles could never say 'no' to a woman... any woman. But when he tangled with Celeste, he made a mistake... A bad mistake.

Celeste was married to Harry, and Harry walked a dark side of the street that Giles — with his comfortable lifestyle and fashionable media job — could only imagine in his worst nightmares. And when Harry got involved in nightmares, people had a habit of getting hurt. Set against the boom and gloom of eighties Britain, Perhaps She'll Die! is classic noir with a centre as hard as toughened diamond.

Quake City by John B Spencer

ISBN 1 899344 02 0 — C-format paperback original, £5.99

The third novel to feature Charley Case, the hard-boiled investigator of a future that follows the 'Big One of Ninety-Seven' — the quake that literally rips California apart and makes LA an Island. "Classic Chandleresque private eye tale, jazzed up by being set in the future... but some things never change — PI Charley Case still has trouble with women and a trusty bottle of bourbon is always at hand. An entertaining addition to the private eye canon." — Mail on Sunday

BLOODLINES the cutting-edge crime and mystery imprint...

Hellbent on Homicide by Gary Lovisi
ISBN 1 899344 18 7 — C-format paperback original, £7
"This isn't a first novel, this is a book written by a craftsman who learned his business from the masters, and in HELLBENT ON HOMICIDE, that education rings loud and long." —Eugene Izzi
1962, a sweet, innocent time in America... after McCarthy, before Vietnam. A time of peace and trust, when girls hitch-hiked without a care. But for an ice-hearted killer, a time of easy pickings. "A wonderful throwback to the glory days of hardboiled American crime fiction. In my considered literary judgement, if you pass up HELLBENT ON HOMICIDE, you're a stone chump." —Andrew Vachss
Brooklyn-based Gary Lovisi's powerhouse début novel is a major contribution to the hardboiled school, a roller-coaster of sex, violence and suspense, evocative of past masters like Jim Thompson, Carroll John Daly and Ross Macdonald.

Fresh Blood II edited by Mike Ripley & Maxim Jakubowski
ISBN 1 899 344 20 9 — C-format paperback original, £8.
Follow-up to the highly-acclaimed original volume (see below), featuring short stories from John Baker, Christopher Brookmyre, Ken Bruen, Carol Anne Davis, Christine Green, Lauren Henderson, Charles Higson, Maxim Jakubowski, Phil Lovesey, Mike Ripley, Iain Sinclair, John Tilsley, John Williams, and RD Wingfield (Inspector Frost)

Fresh Blood edited by Mike Ripley & Maxim Jakubowski
ISBN 1 899344 03 9 — C-format paperback original, £6.99
Featuring the cream of the British New Wave of crime writers including John Harvey, Mark Timlin, Chaz Brenchley, Russell James, Stella Duffy, Ian Rankin, Nicholas Blincoe, Joe Canzius, Denise Danks, John B Spencer, Graeme Gordon, and a previously unpublished extract from the late Derek Raymond. Includes an introduction from each author explaining their views on crime fiction in the '90s and a comprehensive foreword on the genre from Angel-creator, Mike Ripley.

Shrouded by Carol Anne Davis
ISBN 1 899344 17 9 — C-format paperback original, £7
Douglas likes women — quiet women; the kind he deals with at the mortuary where he works. Douglas meets Marjorie, unemployed, gaining weight and losing confidence. She talks and laughs a lot to cover up her shyness, but what Douglas really needs is a lover who'll stay still — deadly still. Driven by lust and fear, Douglas finds a way to make girls remain excitingly silent and inert. But then he is forced to blank out the details of their unplanned deaths.
Perhaps only Marjorie can fulfil his growing sexual hunger. If he could just get her into a state of limbo. Douglas studies his textbooks to find a way...

BLOODLINES the cutting-edge crime and mystery imprint...

The Hackman Blues by Ken Bruen
ISBN 1899344 22 5 — C-format paperback original, £7
"If Martin Amis was writing crime novels, this is what he would hope to write."
— Books in Ireland
"...I haven't taken my medication for the past week. If I couldn't go a few days without the lithium, I was in deep shit. I'd gotten the job ten days earlier and it entailed a whack of pub-crawling. Booze and medication is the worst of songs. Sing that!
A job of pure simplicity. Find a white girl in Brixton. Piece of cake. What I should have done is doubled my medication and lit a candle to St Jude — maybe a lot of candles."
Add to the mixture a lethal ex-con, an Irish builder obsessed with Gene Hackman, the biggest funeral Brixton has ever seen, and what you get is the Blues like they've never been sung before. Ken Bruen's powerful second novel is a gritty and grainy mix of crime noir and Urban Blues that greets you like a mugger stays with you like a razor-scar.
GQ described his début novel as:
"The most startling and original crime novel of the decade."
The Hackman Blues is Ken Bruen's best novel yet.

Smalltime by Jerry Raine
ISBN 1 899344 13 6 — C-format paperback original, £5.99
Smalltime is a taut, psychological crime thriller, set among the seedy world of petty criminals and no-hopers. In this remarkable début, Jerry Raine shows just how easily curiosity can turn into fear amid the horrors, despair and despondency of life lived a little too near the edge.
"Jerry Raine's Smalltime carries the authentic whiff of sleazy nineties Britain. He vividly captures the world of stunted ambitions and their evil consequences." — Simon Brett
"The first British contemporary crime novel featuring an underclass which no one wants. Absolutely authentic and quite possibly important."— Philip Oakes, Literary Review.

That Angel Look by Mike Ripley
"The outrageous, rip-roarious Mr Ripley is an abiding delight..." — Colin Dexter
1 899344 23 3 — C-format paperback original, £8
A chance encounter (in a pub, of course) lands street-wise, cab-driving Angel the ideal job as an all-purpose assistant to a trio of young and very sexy fashion designers.
But things are nowhere near as straightforward as they should be and it soon becomes apparent that no-one is telling the truth — least of all Angel!

It's Not A Runner Bean by Mark Steel

ISBN 1 899344 12 8 — C-format paperback original, £5.99

'I've never liked Mark Steel and I thoroughly resent the high quality of this book.' — Jack Dee

The life of a Slightly Successful Comedian can include a night spent on bare floorboards next to a pyromaniac squatter in Newcastle, followed by a day in Chichester with someone so aristocratic, they speak without ever moving their lips.

From his standpoint behind the microphone, Mark Steel is in the perfect position to view all human existence. Which is why this book — like his act, broadcasts and series' — is opinionated, passionate, and extremely funny. It even gets around to explaining the line (screamed at him by an Eighties yuppy): 'It's not a runner bean...' — which is another story.

'Hugely funny...' — Time Out

'A terrific book. I have never read any other book about comedy written by someone with a sense of humour.' — Jeremy Hardy, Socialist Review.

Elvis – The Novel by Robert Graham, Keith Baty

ISBN 1 899344 19 5 — C-format paperback original, £7

'Quite simply, the greatest music book ever written' — Mick Mercer, Melody Maker

The everyday tale of an imaginary superstar eccentric. The Presley neither his fans nor anyone else knew. First-born of triplets, he came from the backwoods of Tennessee. Driven by a burning ambition to sing opera, Fate sidetracked him into creating Rock 'n' roll.

His classic movie, Driving A Sportscar Down To A Beach In Hawaii didn't win the Oscar he yearned for, but The Beatles revived his flagging spirits, and he stunned the world with a guest appearance in Batman.

Further shockingly momentous events have led him to the peaceful, contented lifestyle he enjoys today.

'Books like this are few and far between.' — Charles Shaar Murray, NME

The Users by Brian Case

ISBN 1 899344 05 5 — C-format paperback, £5.99

The welcome return of Brian Case's brilliantly original '60s cult classic.

'A remarkable debut' — Anthony Burgess

'Why Case's spiky first novel from 1968 should have languished for nearly thirty years without a reprint must be one of the enigmas of modern publishing. Mercilessly funny and swaggeringly self-conscious, it could almost be a template for an early Martin Amis.' — Sunday Times.

Also available from The Do-Not Press

Charlie's Choice: The First Charlie Muffin Omnibus by Brian Freemantle – Charlie Muffin; Clap Hands, Here Comes Charlie; The Inscrutable Charlie Muffin
ISBN 1 899344 26 8, C-format paperback, £9
Charlie Muffin is not everybody's idea of the ideal espionage agent. Dishevelled, cantankerous and disrespectful, he refuses to play by the Establishment's rules. Charlie's axiom is to screw anyone from anywhere to avoid it happening to him. But it's not long before he finds himself offered up as an unwilling sacrifice by a disgraced Department, desperate to win points in a ruthless Cold War. Now for the first time, the first three Charlie Muffin books are collected together in one volume. 'Charlie is a marvellous creation' – Daily Mail

Song of the Suburbs by Simon Skinner
ISBN 1 899 344 37 3 – B-format paperback original, £5
Born in a suburban English New Town and with a family constantly on the move (Essex to Kent to New York to the South of France to Surrey), who can wonder that Slim Manti feels rootless with a burning desire to take fun where he can find it? His solution is to keep on moving. And move he does: from girl to girl, town to town and country to country. He criss-crosses Europe looking for inspiration, circumnavigates America searching for a girl and drives to Tintagel for Arthur's Stone... Sometimes brutal, often hilarious, Song of the Suburbs is a Road Novel with a difference.

Head Injuries by Conrad Williams
ISBN 1 899 344 36 5 – B-format paperback original, £5
It's winter and the English seaside town of Morecambe is dead. David knows exactly how it feels. Empty for as long as he can remember, he depends too much on a past filled with the excitements of drink, drugs and cold sex. The friends that sustained him then – Helen and Seamus – are here now and together they aim to pinpoint the source of the violence that has suddenly exploded into their lives. Soon to be a major film.

The Long Snake Tattoo by Frank Downes
ISBN 1 899 344 35 7 – B-format paperback original, £5
Ted Hamilton's new job as night porter at the down-at-heel Eagle Hotel propels him into a world of seedy nocturnal goings-on and bizarre characters. These range from the pompous and near-efficient Mr Butterthwaite to bigoted old soldier Harry, via Claudia the harassed chambermaid and Alf Speed, a removals man with a penchant for uninvited naps in strange beds.
But then Ted begins to notice that something sinister is lurking beneath the surface

The Do-Not Press
Fiercely Independent Publishing

Keep in touch with what's happening at the cutting edge of independent British publishing.

Join The Do-Not Press Information Service and receive advance information of all our new titles, as well as news of events and launches in your area, and the occasional free gift and special offer.

Simply send your name and address to:
The Do-Not Press (Dept. FS)
PO Box 4215
London
SE23 2QD
or email us: thedonotpress@zoo.co.uk

There is no obligation to purchase and no salesman will call.

Visit our regularly-updated web site:
http://www.thedonotpress.co.uk

Mail Order

All our titles are available from good bookshops, or (in case of difficulty) direct from The Do-Not Press at the address above. There is no charge for post and packing.
(NB: A postman may call.)